The Matchmaker's Rogue

REGINA SCOTT

To Edward, my own rogue, and to the Lord,
who also has a special place in His heart for rogues.

CHAPTER ONE

Dorset, England, May 1804

THERE WAS SOMETHING TO BE said for routine and order. Most days.

One of the reasons Jesslyn Chance loved the village of Grace-by-the-Sea is that it rarely changed. The same hot mineral water had been bubbling out of the limestone cliffs since before the Romans had landed in the little horse-shoe-shaped cove below. The same families fished from the cove, farmed the chalk Downs above, worked at the spa, married at St. Andrew's Church, and had babies who grew up to marry and have more babies.

For the last hundred years, the same sorts of people, from young misses nervously awaiting their come out to vener-able military gentlemen nursing war injuries, had come to drink the spa waters and bathe in the sea. The village had grown up to cater to the needs of its guests, boasting shops and conveniences few of its size ever managed. It was all very civilized.

Until you introduced a rogue.

She didn't notice him when he first strolled into the Grand Pump Room. The columned space, which served as the social center of the spa, was already crowded. She could

only catch glimpses of the light blue walls and bronze wall clock across from her.

And she had been busy welcoming the other arrivals—a pair of spinster sisters, hair pulled back from their wrinkled cheeks; a weathered-faced general who'd served in India; and a mother and daughter fresh from London, their pale muslin gowns proclaiming the latest fashion. She guided the general to Lord Wesley Featherstone for conversation and pointed out an eligible bachelor to the mother and daughter, who promptly inveigled an invitation.

She thought perhaps the elderly sisters might enjoy her aunt Maudlyn's company, as her aunt had yet to take up her place at the harpsichord in the southwest corner of the Pump Room. But her tiny aunt positively vibrated with excitement, standing on the toes of her black leather half boots.

"It's him," she whispered to Jess as they stood behind the tall desk holding the Welcome Book that listed everyone who had ever visited the spa. "The pirate."

Oh, was it pirates today? She'd thought it trolls now. Maudie was given to odd fancies like that. She'd once proclaimed their friend Abigail Archer a mermaid in disguise, and she was equally certain Napoleon's agents were hiding in the Vicar Mr. Wingate's wardrobe. Her tendency to whimsy was one of the reasons the Spa Corporation had made Jess the official hostess of the spa a year ago instead of her older aunt. The other reason was pity, but Jess chose not to dwell on that.

"And where is this pirate?" she asked, attempting to look serious. "Do you mean Admiral Walsey there by the fountain? I could see him with a cutlass between his teeth." Perhaps twenty years ago. The four stone of pounds the good Admiral had gained since then might prevent him from climbing the ropes these days.

Maudie shook her head so hard her grey curls bounced

against her round cheeks. "Not the Admiral." She pointed at the man approaching through the crowd. "Him."

"Oh." It was all Jess could manage as she took in the confident strut, the cocky smile, the gleam in those brown eyes. Him? Now?

Maudie nodded as if she had noticed the change in Jess. "You see it, don't you? He's a pirate, a rogue. He's out to steal our greatest treasure."

Jess took a deep breath and raised her head. "Larkin Denby is no pirate. His mother and sisters live in Upper Grace. Very likely he's merely here for a visit."

Maudie dropped back onto her soles in a rustle of black bombazine as he came to stand on the opposite side of the mahogany desk from them. "Rubbish. He's here to cause trouble."

Jess was only glad Lark either hadn't heard her aunt or had decided not to answer. His head was bowed so that she could only see the crown of his golden-brown hair, and he seemed to be studying the names of the others who had come before him. Was he as nervous as she was at the thought of renewing their acquaintance? Or had he forgotten her completely in the eight years since they'd parted? Did men remember their first loves?

Best to remember her role now. She wasn't a girl on her first Season, unsure of herself and filled with awe of the world. This was her spa. She was the one in control.

"Good afternoon, Mr. Denby," she said, launching into her prepared speech. "Welcome to the spa at Grace-by-the-Sea. I am your hostess, Miss Chance, and this is my assistant Mrs. Tully. If you have any questions or would like an introduction, you have only to ask."

His head snapped up. Though he held her gaze only a moment, as was proper, she felt as if he were memorizing every feature, from the blond curls clustered around her face to her gloved hands resting on the table beside

the book. His smile bloomed, and something inside her bloomed with it. "Miss Chance. How nice to see you and your charming aunt again."

A simple statement, hardly threatening, yet a dozen ways to escape rushed in on her. She kept her smile in place. She had no reason to run. She'd welcomed nearly a thousand guests, first as a volunteer, then as an assistant to her father, and now in her own right. She arranged introductions, friendships, courtships! On any given day, she kept as many as three dozen people healthy and happy, and that didn't count her younger brother, Alex, or her aunt.

"And hostess now," he continued. "But of course you'd want to serve beside your father." He glanced around as if seeking the spa's physician.

Jess's throat tightened, but her voice came out all politeness. "My father passed away a year ago, sir. We are without a physician at present."

His gaze swung back to her, softening. "I'm sorry to hear that. Your father was a good man."

He'd been a great man, one sorely needed. She could never fill his shoes, and Alex did not seem to want to try.

"Thank you," she said. "Allow me to reacquaint you with the spa." She picked up the carefully worded pamphlet from the Corporation and offered it to him.

"The water is poured from nine to four Monday through Saturday, noon to three on Sunday. Bathing is on the low tide and by appointment. Tea is served at four Monday through Saturday and one on Sunday here in the Grand Pump Room, and we close early every Wednesday for an assembly in the evening in rooms just up the hill. I do..."

"Hope you'll join us," Maudie finished for her, and rather breathlessly at that.

Lark accepted the pamphlet from Jess. His fingers touched hers, as briefly as his glance. She had to fight to keep from snatching back her hand.

"I look forward to it, ladies," he said. He turned and continued his stroll about the room.

Jess took another deep breath, feeling as if she'd been wanting air for the last few moments. What was wrong with her? She'd been pursued by two other men in the time since Larkin Denby had shaken the chalk soil from his boots and ridden away from Grace-by-the-Sea. Neither of those courtships had been successful, of course, but she'd realized that her skill lay in matching others. And she had to deal with men every day—visitors to the spa, shopkeepers in the village. None were quite that handsome, that confident, but still.

She raised her chin. "Two hours yet until tea," she told her aunt, attempting to return things to normal. "Are you pouring today, or shall I?"

But Maudie started around the tall desk as if intent on chasing after their newest guest. "You can pour. I'll be watching Mr. Denby. I tell you, there's something odd about him."

Jess caught her arm to keep her from accosting him. Such a scandal would cost them their positions, and where would they be then?

"Mr. Denby will get on with the others famously," she assured her aunt, letting go of her cautiously. "Look, he's talking with the general like a gentleman." The two men chatted, strangers making idle conversation as so many of their guests did. Then Lark moved on, leaving the general smiling as he rubbed the paunch straining his waistcoat.

"Mr. Denby doesn't fit in the spa," Maudie argued. "He doesn't look the least bit ill. He has no limp, no squint, no sign of a scrofulous cough."

"Neither did most of our visitors to arrive this summer," Jess pointed out. "Not everyone comes to the spa because they are ill." She tidied the stack of pamphlets, noticed her hands were trembling, and shook them out. At this rate,

her aunt might suggest that Jess take the waters!

But Maudie had narrowed her grey eyes over her sharp nose. "We have few enough healthy ones. You have only to ask the Corporation."

She had no need to ask. The state of their visitors had been a constant topic of conversation at the monthly council meetings she was expected to attend. Famous spas like inland Bath or Lyme Regis farther along the coast brought people for the society as much as the healing waters. Despite improvements Jess had suggested and the presence of two great houses nearby, the spa at Grace-by-the-Sea had never achieved such fame among the wealthy and titled. They catered instead to the gentry and yeoman class. The reason remained more of a mystery than Lark's reappearance.

Though his reappearance was something of a mystery. He'd come alone, without mother or sisters. She spoke to them on occasion when they came to the assemblies. None had mentioned him being estranged from them. He'd originally left the area to seek his fortune. Grace-by-the-Sea had been too small for a man looking for adventure and advancement.

So, why return now? The only adventure here was the potential meeting of two hearts, and he'd forsaken that.

"Be that as it may," Jess said with a stern look at her diminutive aunt, "you may not harass the Newcomers. You promised."

Maudie humphed. She had developed the taxonomy of visitors years ago. Regulars were like family; Jess knew their stories, their reasons for coming each summer to the spa, their hopes and fears for the future. Irregulars had come often enough to be remembered; they were acquaintances with the possibility of becoming friends. Newcomers were the strangers, the ones first visiting the spa. It remained to be seen what would become of them.

She could not see Lark ever becoming a Regular. His story wouldn't be sad enough, his needs consuming enough, that their little company would satisfy, in the end. As before, he would be in her life as briefly as a wave cresting the shore. This time, she would make sure he left as little mark.

So, Jess was in charge of things now. Lark hadn't expected that. Just because he hadn't been ready to marry eight years ago at the tender age of twenty didn't mean another man wouldn't have leaped to offer for Jesslyn Chance in the meantime. She was pretty, she was clever, and she had a unique ability to tell people what they didn't want to hear, in a way that had them thanking her for it. Couple all that with a respectable family, and she would never lack for suitors.

Just not him. He'd been too young to settle down before, and his work was too dangerous now. He would not want to leave a wife behind the way his father had left his mother. Bad enough that she was a widow, but then, so was his oldest sister. The war tended to leave more than soldiers and sailors as casualties.

He excused himself from a conversation with a portly former general. While the fellow had admirable experience plotting strategy, his questionable health made it unlikely he was the man Lark sought. He was also far too obvious with his booming voice and portentous manner. The man Lark had been sent to discover would be subtle, used to living in the shadows, a spider awaiting a fly.

Perhaps that was why Lark had protested this assignment.

"Tarry in the spa? What possible good can that do?" he'd asked Commissioner Franklin at Weymouth only two days

ago as he'd stood before the man's desk in an office over-looking the harbor. "I was needed in Kent. There are two thousand ships and nearly one hundred thousand troops massing across the Channel. We cannot afford for smug-glers to pass information to them."

The commissioner had snorted, bushy grey brows bris-tling. "We've been told Napoleon brags about having smugglers in his pay, but it isn't just Kent that's in danger from his invasion. Smugglers ply the waters off Dorset as well, bringing out information and bringing in spies along with their duty-free goods."

"And you think that they sail from Grace Cove?" Lark pressed. "I've visited Grace-by-the-Sea some years ago, sir. It did not seem the sort of place to attract a criminal class."

"The very fact that you are known in the area is why you were chosen for this assignment," his superior insisted, thick body leaning back in his padded chair. "We've tried everything else—revenue cutters off the headland, dra-goons along the shore. It's time for something different, something unexpected, from the Excise Office. You're one of the best Riding Officers we have, you can pass for a gentleman, and your presence will not be remarked upon."

He wasn't so sure about that. His mother had moved him and his two younger sisters to the village just north of the area, Upper Grace, after his father had died. He'd spent his youth riding the Downs, sneaking off to the shore. And one memorable summer, he had accompanied his mother to the spa and met the golden-haired Jesslyn Chance. Some might recall that. Besides, if word got back to his mother and sisters that he was in the area and had failed to stop by, there would certainly be remarks.

"I am your devoted servant, sir," he told the commis-sioner. "But surely there are other ways to identify these smugglers than to spend my time sipping the waters."

"I don't care if you sip them, dunk yourself in them, or

pour them on the ground," the commissioner had replied, face tight and eyes steely. "Our source says the man we're after sails from Grace Cove, and we have reason to believe he moves among the gentry, perhaps even the aristocracy. Where else would you expect to find him but at the spa?"

Glancing around the Grand Pump Room now, he could not help but doubt the wisdom of this assignment anew. The spa at Grace-by-the-Sea was peace itself. Pastoral scenes decorated the arched ceiling; white wicker chairs waited with open arms along the blue walls. With the creamy stone fountain in one corner, waters sparkling in the sun shining through the nearby windows, and the white-lacquered harpsichord in another, the place resembled nothing so much as a conservatory in a great house.

The people crowding the space seemed just as benign. A few looked ill, their faces pinched, their shoulders stooped, their steps slow. More were intent on conversation and company rather than a cure. They laughed, they exchanged pleasantries, they took the waters. It was entirely too civilized. He wanted to shout at them, splash them with water from the fountain, throw the precisely folded pamphlets into the air, anything to wake them up to the impending danger.

"Is there something you need, Mr. Denby?"

It appeared he'd circumnavigated the room again. His booted feet had stopped of their own accord before the tall desk, the Welcome Book, and Jesslyn Chance. Her aunt, Mrs. Tully, had gone to pour some water for two elderly women who were obviously sisters. He had seen their names in the Welcome Book. He'd hoped the book would give him some clue as to a possible suspect, but the long list of names had only proven that the spa was as popular as his superior had intimated.

Jess might have been able to point him in the right direction. A shame he could not confide in her this time, but

the fewer who knew his purpose, the better. While many decried the lawlessness of smuggling, a good percentage welcomed the lower-cost commodities the Free Traders brought in. Those who worked for the Excise Office were not always appreciated, or safe.

But would Jess confide in him? She still looked as sweet as he remembered. Her thick blond hair was pulled back in a high bun, but curls danced about her cheeks. Her lips were as warm a pink as those little shells his sisters used to collect from the shore. Her curves showed to advantage in a high-waisted cotton gown printed in blocks of pink and white and topped with a modest white collar.

Yet it was her eyes that drew him. Large, wide-spaced, and a delicate blue, they made her look as if she were perpetually amazed by the world around her.

He and Jess had been close when he'd visited eight years ago, the only two people that young at the spa then. They'd spent every day together, talking, walking, dancing at the assembly, attending church. Nothing had come of it. Nothing could come of it. They were too different—her content with life, him determined to see and do more. Still, perhaps she would indulge in a little gossip now.

"Mr. Denby?" she persisted in that soft, lilting voice. "Might I be of assistance?"

He smiled at her. "I believe you may, Miss Chance. I'm staying at the Mermaid for a few days, and I find myself wondering what to do for entertainment."

"It depends on what you find entertaining."

Said in such a disarming tone, he should not hear iron beneath the words, yet he did. She was being polite but letting him know she expected him to respond in kind. This was no time for coy comments, teasing remarks. She was no longer the young lady looking for companionship to while away the summer.

He inclined his head. "I meant no disrespect. But Grace-

by-the-Sea always appears to be one of those quiet little villages where all seems placid, peaceful on the surface. I wonder whether there could be a current below."

"I believe it's called an undertow," she said with a bright smile. "And you will find none of that here. Grace-by-the-Sea is as sheltered as our cove. There hasn't been a murder in the area in more than sixty years, and our magistrate, Mr. Howland, hasn't had an offense worthy of holding over for the Assizes during his five-year tenure. I fear if you crave excitement, you shouldn't have returned."

He shared that fear, but he could only hope she was mistaken, for his future, the future of the village, and likely the future of the nation depended on there being something very wrong at Grace-by-the-Sea.

And it was his job to prove it.

CHAPTER TWO

JESS KEPT HER SMILE POLITE from long practice, but her insides boiled. How dare he intimate that something nefarious was going on at Grace-by-the-Sea! Their village was extremely well run and orderly. Neighbor helped neighbor; families supported one another. Mr. Wingate preached mercy and charity, and his sermons bore obvious fruit. Certainly the Spa Corporation would have it no other way. Visitors did not flock to spas where they felt threatened.

Despite her efforts, her outrage must have leaked through, for Lark bowed to her. "Forgive me, Miss Chance. I never meant to impugn your fair village. And I would be the last to encourage anything criminal. I will not monopolize you further. If you would be so kind as to introduce me to the gentleman standing by the hearth, I will leave you to your other duties."

Introductions she could manage. She knew every visitor, each merchant who catered to them, and all families in the village. But she could not help thinking that Lark had found a convenient way to excuse himself from her company and any unwanted questions. Perhaps that was why she was suddenly quite keen to ask.

Over the next while, she looked for her opportunity. But it soon became apparent she wasn't the only one interested

in the Newcomer.

"And what can you tell us about Mr. Denby?" Miss Montgomery, the eldest sister, asked over tea that afternoon.

Jess handed her a snowy white porcelain cup of the steaming brew from the wheeled teacart she or Maudie generally rolled from chair to chair. "His family lives nearby, a mother and two sisters."

"I think he's an equerry for a noble house," the other Miss Montgomery said knowingly. She reached for the cup Jess had poured for her. "He's here to determine whether his master will find the spa amusing."

Her sister nodded thoughtfully, but Jess could not agree. Lark had seemed destined for something important, something grand. An equerry hardly qualified. She hurried Maudie on to the next set of chairs before her aunt could ask questions.

But others were as eager to comment.

"Interesting fellow, this Denby," Lord Featherstone said as Jess poured the Regular his daily dose of the waters from the stone fountain later that afternoon. Lord Featherstone had been coming to the spa since she was a girl. Until Lark had returned, he had been the most likely to turn heads, with his tall frame, chiseled features, and charming address. Now he accepted the crystal glass with a deep bow, as if she were a great lady and not his impoverished hostess. Then he took a sip of the warm mineral water and managed to look as if he enjoyed it.

"Why do you call him interesting?" Jess asked.

The silver-haired lord smiled. "Because he asks more questions than he answers. A good listener is rare around here."

Jess followed his gaze to where Lark was even now conversing with one of their other Regulars, Mr. Warfield Crabapple. Mr. Crabapple was his usual animated self,

long arms waving about as he attempted to make his point. She'd always wondered how he could be so limber when he claimed to suffer from rheumatism. Perhaps it was the effect of the waters.

"Besides," Lord Featherstone murmured beside her, "I seem to recall seeing him here before. Some time ago, before the Winsome Widow arrived."

As if she had overhead his nickname for her, Mrs. Eugennia Harding laughed from her place near the windows. Her auburn hair piled up high, her considerable curves nestled in one of the wicker chairs, the Regular was holding court with a number of eligible bachelors, as she had so often in the last three summers she'd been coming to the spa.

"This is not Mr. Denby's first visit," Jess confirmed. "But he should not be considered a Regular."

Lord Featherstone stuck out his lower lip. "Pity."

Pity indeed. She'd had so much hope for him. She'd been eighteen, the first summer she'd been considered out, when she'd met Lark and fallen top over toes. His smile had been the air she'd breathed, his every word to be held close, considered, like some gem that had fallen into the lap of the fashionable gowns she had been determined to wear. His calm farewell had proven that he hadn't been nearly so affected.

"Thank you for everything this summer, Jesslyn," he'd said with that charming smile. "I'll be heading out for greater things shortly. I'm sure we'll see each other again."

She'd hung onto those words through the fall and winter, then the longer spring and summer that followed. But he had never returned to the spa, and she'd finally convinced herself that it had been merely a youthful infatuation.

When she truly fell in love, she'd thought she would do better partnered with a studious, self-effacing gentleman with an agreeable nature. But when such a gentleman had arrived at the spa, his stuttering courtship had left her

strangely ill-at-ease. And then there was Walter Vincent.

"Is something the matter, Miss Chance?" Lord Feath-erstone asked, and she realized she'd been woolgathering.

"No, not at all," she said brightly.

His puzzled frown did not leave his face. "Then why do I have the feeling you are about to seize up a sword and cleave someone in twain?"

Jess laughed. "Come now, my lord, you know me better than that."

"I do," he agreed, frown easing. "And I admit to being on occasion in awe."

"How kind of you to say so," she replied, but she moved away before she betrayed herself her further.

Her aunt was not so easy to dissuade.

"I have determined why Mr. Denby seems so out of place at the spa," she confided that night at dinner in their little cottage near the shore. Built from stone, it was tucked into the cliffside so that ivy grew over the roof and trailed down the sides.

Alex looked up from his portion of the fish stew Jess had kept simmering over the fire while she'd been up at the spa. "Mr. Denby? Do I know him?"

"No," Jess replied with a quelling look to Maudie. "He's a Newcomer."

Maudie didn't seem to notice the look. "I believe," she said, drawing herself up on the bench she shared with Jess, "that he is a French spy."

Jess sighed, but her brother raised his tawny head. Already nearly a foot taller than she was, he was swiftly becoming a man, though he seemed to be taking his own time decid-ing how to pursue his future.

"When did he arrive?" he asked eagerly, yanking a hunk from the loaf of bread she'd bought from the baker, Mr. Ellison.

"Do not encourage her," Jess warned him.

Alex looked abashed, but Maudie answered readily enough. "Earlier today. Why?"

Alex dipped his bread in his stew and gave it a wave, dripping some back onto the porcelain plate. "Spies arrive at night. Everyone knows that."

"Indeed," Jess replied, setting down her own spoon. "And did you learn that from the tutoring the Vicar Mr. Wingate gave you?"

Alex colored. "No, not exactly. But it stands to good reason. They're spies. We're at war. They aren't going to row into the cove in broad daylight and sashay into the spa."

Maudie slumped over her dinner. "No, I suppose not."

Jess almost felt sorry for her. Not enough to wish Lark was truly a French spy, of course. But Maudlyn could be, well, rather maudlin. She'd fallen in love and married a sailor before Jess was born. Mr. Tully had gone to sea and failed to return, and Maudie had never been right afterward, Jess's father had said. If her fancies sustained her, who was Jess to question them?

Her brother obviously felt the same way, for he reached across the table and patted their aunt's hand. "Never you fear, Aunt. We'll make sure no Frenchies land on our shore."

"Intending to fight them off, are you two?" Jess asked with a fond smile.

Alex pulled back his hand and raised his head. "If I must. You and Aunt have had to work too hard for our family, Jess. I'll be taking my turn soon."

She nodded encouragement, but she couldn't help thinking he and Maddie were both a pair of dreamers. She'd been that way once too. Thank goodness she had more sense now.

She had hoped Lark would decide the spa too peaceful for his tastes, but he was waiting for her and Maudie when they arrived the next morning. So was Mrs. Greer, wife of the Spa Corporation president, and her footman, and a full quarter hour before the spa was supposed to open. Only Lark looked apologetic.

"I'm sure Miss Chance did not intend to leave our guests standing about," Mrs. Greer simpered to Lark as Jess let them all in.

"I would gladly wait an eternity for a moment with Miss Chance," he assured her.

Jess nearly rolled her eyes, but Maudie seized Lark's arm and dragged him toward the wall clock, as if it held all the secrets of the world. Her aunt knew how challenging Mrs. Greer could be. The lady was lean and angular, and she appeared even taller by virtue of the fact that she held her head high. A shame her opinion of herself was even higher still.

Now she nodded for her footman to lay down the thick packet of pamphlets he held.

"What made Mr. Denby decide to visit us?" she asked Jess. "He doesn't seem ill."

"So everyone has noticed," Jess replied, fanning the pamphlets in a pleasing pattern on the desktop. The woman rewrote them at least monthly. Jess had tried to explain that most of the guests simply threw them away, but Mrs. Greer had ordered her to retrieve them from the rubbish bin as if they contained original Shakespearean sonnets instead of rather uninspiring instructions.

"And you have not asked?" Mrs. Greer pulled in air through her equine nose as if gathering a sufficient supply to blow the spa down. "I am certain, Miss Chance, that my husband has explained the importance of representing the spa in the best possible light. If a guest comes here for entertainment, you must determine how to acquaint him

with such. If he is unwell, you must ensure he receives the treatment he needs. How can you know what the guests *require* if you do not *enquire*?"

"Perhaps you'd like to ask him," Jess said, smiling. Her father had always said her smile was so sweet it attracted bees. "Just to show me how it's done, of course."

Mrs. Greer eyed her as if she suspected Jess was going to stick out her tongue behind the lady's back or do something equally impertinent. "No," she said at last. "You are the one being paid to perform your duties. I cannot imagine it will require much effort in his case. Such a handsome young man with a ready address is likely here to visit one of the important families."

Now Jess felt the sting. Once her family had been one of the important ones. "He hasn't mentioned them," she murmured, dropping her gaze.

"He may not feel the need to confide," Mrs. Greer replied. "You must make yourself ask. A woman in your position must be confident, Miss Chance. You may be a spinster, but you can still converse sensibly with the gentlemen clients. Here, now, see what you've done!"

Jess glanced down to find that she had crushed one of the pamphlets in her hand. "How silly of me," she said, smoothing it out. "I'll be sure to question him this very day. Was there anything else you needed, Mrs. Greer?"

"Only to remind you that you must send an invitation to our neighbors about the assemblies. I would not want the Howlands at the Castle or Lord Peverell at the Lodge to think we had slighted them. And don't forget our dashing naval hero recuperating in Dove Cottage."

Mrs. Greer and her husband took great pride in the town's connections. A shame they hadn't noticed how thin those connections were. The mighty Howlands avoided their ruin of a castle; the only family member who lived in the area was their steward and the local magistrate, James

Howland. The Peverells brought their own entertainments when they visited their lodge on the opposite headland, and they disdained to interact with the citizenry or the spa guests. And as for Captain St. Claire, he rarely stirred from his little cottage on the road out of town. In Jess's mind, they were all Newcomers, just like Lark. But then, Mrs. Greer had lived all her life in Grace-by-the-Sea, and she had never met the requirements in Jess's mind of a Regular.

Lark winced as the older woman shook a finger in Jess's pretty face. For a moment, he was quite glad he'd come to question the men instead of the women. He was considering a way to require Jess's rescue—falling into the fountain? Tripping over a chair?—when the woman swept from the spa. He could feel Jess's sigh all the way across the room.

Then he realized he was the only one in such a position. The spa was still empty of guests. Her aunt had pushed one of the wicker chairs behind the fountain and was napping, head tilted so that her grey curls squashed against the shoulders of her black gown. Jess moved closer to check on her, smile fond. Then she turned, long fingers skimming the collection of glasses stocked near the fountain as if she was counting them to determine whether she had an adequate supply. She must have seen his look, for she left off her counting to join him.

"The others will be here shortly," she promised with a smile. Today she was dressed in a fetching gown of blue trimmed in white that reminded him of the white-capped waves on the Channel. "Many of our visitors arrive around ten."

So he had her to himself for a few moments. "Perhaps you can answer some questions in the meantime."

"I'd be delighted," she replied, golden lashes fluttering. "And perhaps I might ask you some as well."

She could not suspect him. "Certainly," he said. "Tell me, how many people generally visit Grace-by-the-Sea over the summer these days?"

"Between a hundred and twice that," she replied.

"Still mostly older people?" he guessed.

She cocked her head as if considering the matter, and light from the windows shimmered along her hair. "I would say those established in their fortunes or professions are most able to afford a stay of a month or more."

People with that level of income did not generally turn to smuggling. He'd come to uncover a wolf, and all he could find were contented sheep!

"And what of my peers?" he asked.

Her mouth quirked, as if she found his question amusing. "Why, Mr. Denby, I thought you were without peer."

Was she flirting? His smile grew at the thought. But no, surely not. That face was all innocence. "You are too kind," he replied. "But you did not answer my question."

She tapped her chin with one finger. "Let me see. Your peer. Your height and build, do you mean? Or your vocation? Forgive me, but I don't believe you mentioned what profession you ended up pursuing."

For good reason. "I perform a minor service for the government," he said.

Her eyes widened as if he'd shocked her, and her hand fell. "What sort of service?"

"Copying papers, making reports, tabulating activities," he temporized. He did have to make two copies of his riding book, which documented his work each day, and provide one to the Riding Surveyor over his area.

Still, she looked surprised. "You left for adventure and advancement and became a clerk?"

Adventure he had seen, though not so much advance-

ment. He'd made a small contribution to the war effort while in Kent, but if he could uncover who was trafficking with the French to pass information about England and its defenses, he would count himself a success.

"I have done well enough," he demurred. "And what of the gentlemen who spend their time out-of-doors, say sailing? I saw more than one ketch in the cove."

"You likely saw fishing vessels," she explained. "We still have a ketch, but the only people who currently sail for pleasure are Mr. Wingate and Mr. Greer, the President of our Corporation."

He found it difficult to consider a vicar a smuggler, and, if Greer was anything like his wife, he wouldn't have soiled his hands with the work required to run a successful smuggling operation. Still, he'd seen stranger smugglers in his day.

Not Jess, of course. He'd watched her yesterday, flitting from group to group, individual to individual, and always leaving them looking happier than when she'd arrived. She tended the spa like a lady might tend her roses. Surely if there was the least hint of a weed in her garden, she would be the first to root it out.

Or had she only suspected? Did she too wonder about someone in the village? What secrets might lurk behind the blue expanse of her eyes?

He leaned closer. "Tell me, Miss Chance. Is there anyone in the area you find particularly intriguing?"

She pursed her lips, and he had to force his eyes away from the soft pink mouth. "At the moment," she said with her disarming sweetness, "I am most intrigued by you."

"Me?" Lark made himself smile. "I'm nothing remarkable."

"Yet everyone seems determined to remark on you." She took a step closer, and he straightened to retreat.

"You arrive with no notice after years away," she said,

ticking off her reasoning on her fingers. "You have family just over the hill, yet you are staying at an inn. You are obviously well. You haven't taken a sip of the waters or asked to bathe. From your conversation, your mind is sound. You don't seem to be searching for friendship. Why have you come to my spa?"

There was nothing but air surrounding him, but he had the distinct impression he had been trapped. "I simply decided to take a holiday."

His answer, unfortunately, did not appear to satisfy. "I'm delighted to hear that you wished to return to Grace-by-the-Sea for your holiday," she said. "I cannot help but feel compelled to make that holiday enjoyable."

All at once, he remembered another time, when being with her was all he had wanted. She had made his stay at the spa enjoyable at a time when he'd feared for his mother's health and wasn't sure about his own future. But now was no time to renew those feelings. If she knew the truth, she would only be in danger.

As if she saw his thoughts dart like swallows through his mind, she took a step back. "Let's start with reintroducing you to the village. I will be leading a walking tour at eleven. I'm certain you wouldn't want to miss it."

A walking tour? More inanities. He started to demur, but she put her hand on his arm. "Do join us, Mr. Denby. I promise you will be entertained."

Her smile was so hopeful, her look so wistful, as if his attendance meant the very world to her. How did anyone refuse her?

And why should he refuse? Going with her would further his charade, perhaps give him a better perspective of the village now. At the very least, he'd spend a relatively pleasant morning, which was more than he could say for his time at the spa so far.

"Very well, Miss Chance," he said. "I imagine I will find

it vastly entertaining. If you'll excuse me a moment, I have a call to pay before we go."

CHAPTER THREE

JAMES HOWLAND HAD NO IDEA his orderly village was about to be upended. He'd been reviewing the returns compiled by the parish constable, Mr. Keene. By the king's order, the lord-lieutenant for Dorset demanded each parish to record the number of horses, cattle, and sheep; the amount of grain stored; and the wagons, carts, boats, and barges available to transport them all inland in case of an invasion.

He found it hard to believe Napoleon would truly attempt to land. Even the power-mad Corsican had to see that crossing the Channel with thousands of boats was a fool's errand. Worse still was the requirement to raise a volunteer militia. The men of his village—fishermen, farmers, and shopkeepers mostly—were no trained fighters. If Napoleon landed, they might defend the coast for a time, but they would die in the process. He refused to aid in that. Indeed, he was under his own orders not to aid in that.

At the sound of a cough, he looked up. His secretary smiled apologetically from the doorway.

"A gentleman to see you, sir," he said. "A Mr. Denby. He brought a letter of introduction." Priestly ventured into the room, his coat as dark as the walnut bookcases around him, and handed James the sealed sheet across the polished desk before stepping back and awaiting a response.

"Give me five minutes," James said, "and send him in."

The secretary inclined his head and hurried out, shutting the door behind him as if fearing he'd interrupted something important. Some days, it seemed little James did held any importance. But then, his second cousins, the mighty Howlands, might disagree with him.

Though he looked enough like them with his blond hair and strong features that he often passed for a closer member of the aristocratic family, he would never inherit the earldom. Because he managed the million petty details of their holdings, however, the lords and ladies of the Howland family could spend their time playing in London and never give a thought to their moldering castle.

Very likely Denby was the latest in a long line of sycophants hoping to approach the Earl of Howland through James. He'd quashed the pretensions of any number of encroaching persons since becoming magistrate on reaching his majority five years ago. He knew how to smile while dealing their hopes a death blow. He leaned back in his padded leather chair, broke the seal on the letter, and scanned its contents.

And his carefully worded set-down evaporated from his mind.

They knew.

He sucked in a breath and read the letter from the Customs Commissioner at Weymouth again. Slowly, his pulse calmed. No, they didn't know. They only suspected. He still had time to keep things quiet. Thank the Lord for that.

He rose and went to the window, turning his back on the volumes of correspondence, the ledger books related to the castle's upkeep, the map over the hearth that laid out the holdings of his distant illustrious family. The window gave him a clearer view, showing him half of the crescent of the cove and the opposite headland where Castle How stood guard. Howlands had defended these shores since

before the coming of the Conqueror. He would do his duty, if not the way the lord-lieutenant or this commissioner wanted.

The sound of a door opening told him Denby had joined him. Turning, he eyed the man. He'd expected a fisherman, face grizzled, hands worn, coat no more than serviceable. That's the sort of person who generally agreed to serve as a Riding Officer. Denby was dressed like a gentleman and seemed comfortable in the clothes. His walk as he approached across the Oriental carpet was confident. Formal naval man perhaps? That could mean trouble.

James held out his hand. "Mr. Denby. I'm James Howland. How might I be of assistance?"

Denby's grip was swift and sure. "That seems a frequent question here in Grace-by-the-Sea."

"We aim to serve," James assured him. Disengaging, he waved to the chair before his desk. "Will you have a seat?"

"I won't take up so much of your time," Denby promised. "I trust you read the letter. I merely wanted you to know why I'm here and why I might have to come to you for help."

Help that would raise questions if it were refused. "Of course," James said with a nod. "But should you come to me for a warrant, do not bring me supposition, Mr. Denby. If you intend to accuse one of my neighbors of a crime, I expect you to bring me proof."

"Understood," he said. "For now, I'm merely asking questions, getting to know the area." He took a step closer, his gaze as sharp as a lance. "Have you noticed anything unusual, suspicious?"

James kept his face neutral. "Nothing out of the ordinary."

Denby nodded, stepping back. "Then I'll just have a look around. It may be our intelligence was in error." He grimaced. "So far, Grace-by-the-Sea seems remarkably

peaceful."

And there was more truth than Denby could know in the old saying that still waters ran deep. "Keep me apprised of any developments, Mr. Denby."

He bowed. "I will, sir. Thank you."

James waited only until the door had closed before going for his coat. He had a more important matter to attend to than the one on his desk, and this matter must be discussed in person.

Jess had wondered whether Lark's visit to the magistrate was merely an excuse to escape her offer of a tour. She wasn't sure why she'd insisted that he join her. Part of her was determined to keep her distance, even to build a wall between them. Still, it was her duty as hostess to see to his needs. Lark would likely be happier if he was kept busy.

She'd arranged yesterday to take Mrs. and Miss Cole, the mother and daughter from London, to visit the village proper. The elderly Misses Montgomery had proclaimed a walk too fatiguing, and the general had been more amused by a game of chess with Mr. Crabapple. The others would not be interested. After all, the Regulars had no need for a tour; they were instantly recognized and welcomed in every shop in town. The Irregulars also received a ready ear. It was the Newcomers who needed the introductions.

The Coles arrived at the spa at a quarter to eleven, but before Jess could collect them, Mr. Crabapple motioned her closer. His long nose was nearly buried in his crystal glass of spa water, but he managed to raise his head to blink bleary blue eyes at her. "What did Lord Featherstone have to say when you approached him?"

Jess noticed the water trembling in his glass and led him

to one of the padded wicker chairs along the wall. "He says you need have no concern. Mrs. Harding has refused his suit and is free to accept yours."

It had taken a hint from Jess, but the baron had agreed to cease his suit of the wealthy widow, knowing that his friend was keenly interested in the lady. That was another expectation of the hostess—to arrange romantic connections among the guests. Once she'd found it challenging, trying to match this fellow with that lady. Three couples this spring were being called in the banns because of her efforts.

Against her will, her gaze was drawn to the door, where Lark had entered. He looked to her, a smile curving up, and something fluttered inside her. She made herself call the Coles and took them to meet him.

"Mrs. Cole, Miss Cole, may I present Mr. Larkin Denby?" she asked.

The mother and daughter curtsied, and Lark bowed. The daughter's lashes fluttered like a sail in a strong wind. That would have to stop. Lark was at least a decade older and more interested in adventure than matrimony. At least, he had been. Her mind boggled trying to imagine him as a clerk. She truly hoped he hadn't become a fortune hunter. Poor Lord Featherstone didn't need the competition. He had yet to catch his heiress, for he was forever relinquishing his place for the good of the lady or another gentleman more enthralled by her company.

"Thank you for joining me on our tour," she said, leading them through the marble arch that separated the Grand Pump Room from the wide entry with its cluster of potted palms. "I believe you've had a chance to acquaint yourself with the spa. As you may have read in our pamphlet, the healing properties of our mineral waters were first discovered one hundred years ago by a prominent local physician."

"A Doctor Chance," Lark put in. "Your great-great-grand-father, if I recall, Miss Chance."

She didn't remember telling him that eight years ago, which must mean he had read the pamphlet. Mrs. Greer would be in alt! The Coles, however, were regarding her with open curiosity.

"That is correct," Jess admitted. "Many of the gentlemen in my family have been physicians and made use of the curative waters."

"Do you have a brother, then?" Miss Cole asked, eyes lighting.

Jess kept her smile in place. "I do indeed. However, he has yet to choose his path." And she wasn't about to go into details before Newcomers. "This way, if you please." She reached for the latch on the spa's main door.

"Allow me," Lark said and pushed open the door to hold it for the women.

Cheeks warming, Jess was the last to step through. Funny how the little courtesies moved her. Her father had always held the door for his patients, walked with them all the way from the door to the fountain and back again. Even after a year, memories bit hard.

"Everything all right?" Lark murmured as she crossed in front of him.

Those brown eyes were too knowing. "Fine, Mr. Denby. Do try to keep up."

There was nothing like a guide who knew and admired her subject. Lark found himself seeing the little village as if for the first time.

Oh, he had his memories from eight years ago, and he'd thought he'd paid attention when he'd rode in yester-

day. Attention to detail was a requirement for his job. A road, well maintained, cut through the chalk Downs and became the main street through the village. This High Street debouched on the shores of the cove, where boats bobbed at anchor. Church Street bisected the village into north and south and led first to the spa and assembly rooms and then past Mr. Howland's home to the stone tower of St. Andrew's. Castle Walk led in the opposite direction, and he could only conclude climbed the cliff to where Castle How had once defended the area from sea invaders.

Invaders that even now waited across the Channel.

He could not dwell on that. If he thought about the thousands of villagers huddling in little hamlets not unlike this one in Kent and Sussex, waiting for the fleet Napoleon was building to make landfall on their shores, he could not focus on his task.

A task he more and more doubted would have any impact on the war effort.

Despite his superior's hopes, the men at the spa did not appear a likely bunch. Perhaps he needed someone who'd lived here for ages, who had acquaintances among all strata of society. That sort of fellow did not seem to frequent the spa. And all he could do at the moment was continue his charade as if he hadn't a care in the world.

Jess cared, about her village, about her purpose. Her pride trembled in her soft voice, glowed from her expressive eyes.

"At Grace-by-the-Sea," she said as she led them past white-washed cottages with thatched roofs and gardens overflowing with bright flowers, "the entire village has come together to anticipate your every need from the moment you arrive. I trust you've found suitable accommodations?"

"The Swan is comfortable," Mrs. Cole said, but the sniff that accompanied her words implied she'd stayed in better.

"Have your maid open the window in the morning," Jess advised. "There's a row of lavender bushes across the back of the inn. The scent is heavenly."

Mrs. Cole stuck out her lower lip and nodded.

"Are you at the Swan as well?" her daughter asked Lark.

He resisted the urge to ruffle her brown curls as he would have done with his sisters once. Both had grown old enough that they no longer appreciated the gesture, and Miss Cole seemed of an age to be approaching her come out into Society. He knew she was attempting to flirt with him, but he could not take her seriously. It was a little hard to appreciate the bud that was Miss Cole when the blossoming rose that was Jess was standing next to her.

Mrs. Cole spared him a response. "Penelope, really," she scolded. "Such impertinence! You needn't answer, Mr. Denby."

"Oh, I think Mr. Denby is no stranger to impertinence," Jess said with an unmistakable twinkle in her blue eyes.

Lark put his hand on his heart. "You wound me, Miss Chance. I assure you, I am a most studious fellow, intent on serious pursuits."

Her mouth twitched. "Then you'll be delighted with our first stop." She waved a hand at the shop they were approaching on High Street. "Mr. Carroll's Curiosities."

Mrs. Cole and her daughter hurried through the door as if expecting to find an exotic bazaar inside. They were not too far wrong. Bookcases painted in bold colors eclipsed the walls and sagged with all manner of printed material, from clapboard books for children to leather-bound tomes with gilt lettering fit for the most learned of elders. Tables littered the center of the room and carried whimsical toys designed to impress children and adults alike. He spotted a mechanical parrot on a gilded perch, a telescope on a brass stand, and a miniature model of the solar system, planets slowly turning.

"Oh look, Mama," Miss Cole cried, "it's a stuffed hippopotamus." She grabbed her mother's hand and tugged her across the room to where a large, charcoal-colored shape dominated the corner.

"A very good likeness, I thought, based on a painting by Rubens," said a gentleman who had come forward from the back of the shop. A slight fellow with a balding pate, his round face and gentle smile offered an instant welcome. The eyes peering at Lark behind his spectacles, however, could only be called knowing.

The shopkeeper offered Jess a bow. "Miss Chance, how nice to see you again. And how kind of you to bring new friends."

"Newcomers," she advised as if the man would have thought otherwise.

But he nodded sagely, as if she'd given him insight into their characters. "I thought as much. And the gentleman?"

Jess glanced his way, and Lark found himself standing a little taller. "I'm not yet certain."

There was deeper meaning to their conversation. He was sure of it. Pulse quickening, he made a show of picking up a periodical and thumbing through the pages, head cocked to hear more.

Mr. Carroll did not disappoint. He stepped closer to Jess and lowered his voice. "I'm afraid the latest shipment from France has been delayed. Please give your aunt my deepest apologies."

Lark's muscles tensed. They were at war. Did Mr. Carroll count silk, lace, or even champagne among his curiosities?

"When may I tell my aunt you expect the goods?" Jess whispered back.

He nearly dropped the periodical. Jess could not be involved. People could change in eight years, but surely she would not cavort with the criminal element.

Perhaps she did not understand the dangers of smug-

gling. That was it. Too many people failed to realize the ramifications of purchasing goods for which no tax was paid. Taxes fed the army, paved the roads. And tea wasn't the only thing being carried on the waves. Some smugglers brought England's secrets to France.

Jess had to be an innocent. This shopkeeper was the villain. He obviously knew the people who frequented the spa, was a recognized member of the village. Everyone must come in the shop from time to time, if only to marvel at his latest offerings. And while a merchant would never be numbered among the ruling class, this fellow did have a way about him that could only be called noble. He could well be the Lord of the Smugglers Lark had been sent to find.

"They should be here Monday," Mr. Carroll said. "You can help me open them if you can slip away from the spa."

How easily the spider pulled her into his web. Lark would not stand for it. The shipment must arrive by water, very likely on Sunday night, if the shopkeeper hoped to open it on Monday. So, Lark would be at the shore Sunday night, to see who else the spider had trapped and bring them to justice.

CHAPTER FOUR

L ARK DID NOT APPEAR TO be as impressed with Mr.
Carroll's Curiosities as Jess had hoped. To her mind, it
was the most interesting of the shops. Of course, All the
Colors of the Sea, owned by her friend Abigail Archer, was
a close second. The neat white shop with its blue shutters
and multipaned windows sat across High Street from Mr.
Carroll's, and Jess sometimes thought the dolls and autom-
atons in his window looked longingly at the wonders in
Abigail's.

Her friend was a talented artist. There wasn't a home in
the village that didn't boast at least one of her watercolors.
Jess had two of the larger pieces at the spa and two of the
smaller ones at the cottage. And many a lady earned extra
money for her family by offering homemade goods for
the shop.

Jess had imagined Mrs. Cole and her daughter going
into raptures, and their reactions exceeded her expecta-
tions. She thought surely Lark would admire the intricate
ironwork contributed by their blacksmith, Mr. Josephs. But
he had been oddly quiet since they had left Mr. Carroll's.

Pulling the spotted painting smock off her slender, mus-
lin-clad frame, Abigail sidled up to Jess as Mrs. Cole and
her daughter debated the merits of two tatted collars. Her
ginger-colored hair, held high to keep it out of the way of

her work, winked red in the sunlight coming through the windows. "Isn't he…" she started.

Jess put a finger to her lips with one hand, then drew her friend further back among the paintings. "Yes, that's Larkin Denby. He claims to be visiting the spa."

Abby's green eyes lit. "*Claims*? Then you suspect he has another reason for returning. Oh, Jess, could it be you?"

Time to squelch that rumor. "No."

Abby deflated, but she wasn't defeated. Her coral-colored lips pouted a moment. "How can you be sure? You're a matchmaker. I know you can spot love when you see it."

"I can spot interest when I see it," Jess qualified, watching him wander through the shop. "And Mr. Denby's interests do not lie with seeking a bride."

As if to prove it, he picked up a lace collar and scowled at it.

Abby winced. "Mrs. Mance always prices her things too high. Excuse me." She hurried to Lark's side.

Jess followed more slowly, but his voice carried in the quiet shop.

"Hard to find French lace these days," he was telling Abigail.

"I concur, sir, but that isn't French lace," she corrected him. "That's good English lace, fashioned into a keepsake by a good English lady. Something for your sweetheart, perhaps?"

Jess tensed. Why? He had every right to find himself a sweetheart, even a wife. She could not understand why the shop was darkening. Had the sun gone behind a cloud?

"I was thinking more of my sisters," he answered. "But I do think they'd prefer French lace, if you have some."

Abby drew herself up. "We are at war, sir. You'll find nothing French in this shop."

He inclined his head. "Forgive me." He looked up and met Jess's gaze. "Perhaps Miss Chance could suggest which

of these to purchase. I have always held her opinion in the highest esteem."

Pleasure at his words pushed her forward before she could think better of it. "Something simple for Hester, I believe. Her daughter must be six now and keeping her mother busy."

His smile appeared, and the shop brightened. "She is six. I didn't realize you kept up with my sisters."

"Well, it was only polite," Jess demurred. "They come to the assemblies from time to time, after all." And she had not asked questions about him. At least, no more than might be expected.

"And what for Rosemary?" he asked.

Jess studied the fine work before her. It was certainly easier than studying him. "She is ever the innovator. Something more intricate for her, perhaps."

"Excellent suggestions," he said, selecting another. "I'll take both, and one for my mother. Thank you, ladies."

He beamed all around, but his gaze lingered on Jess. Easy to allow herself to fall into it.

Perhaps she led them through the rest of the village too quickly, for she found it difficult to catch her breath after that. Mrs. Cole and her daughter lingered before the display in the window at Beautiful Bonnets, run by Gladys Rinehart, and Jewels of the Shore, the jewelry shop run by Mr. Lawrence, the Corporation treasurer.

Jess had to shoo them out of the linens and trimmings establishment run by the Misses Pierce with the promise they could return at any time. Of lesser interest was the apothecary shop belonging to Mr. Greer, though Lark spoke at some length with the Corporation president about sailing of all things. They all skimmed past the tailoring and haberdashery Mr. Treacle took such pride in. But Mr. Ellison's bakery, where cinnamon vied with the sea to better scent the air, was a hit all around.

When she finally led them back up the hill for the spa, everyone was carrying packages. But though the ladies Cole exclaimed over what they'd seen, Lark still looked pensive, and she could not seem to draw him out.

"A traumatic childhood," Maudie predicted when Jess mentioned the matter that evening as the family gathered for dinner. "Tormented by a stepfather who kept a pack of ravening hounds on the moor."

"And set them loose every full moon," her brother agreed, grinning, "to savage the neighbors' sheep."

Maudie nodded wisely. "It's been known to happen."

"Nonsense," Jess said, rising to clear away the dishes. "There is no stepfather. His widowed mother moved him and his sisters to Upper Grace when he was a youth to live with her brother."

Alex eyed her. "Told you all that already, did he?"

Jess's cheeks warmed. "This is his second visit to the spa. And I speak to his mother and sisters on occasion when they attend the assembly."

Maudie wiggled her grey brows. "His first visit was certainly memorable."

Jess raised her head, prepared to defend her actions, but Alex merely smiled. "In league with the mermaids?"

"Trolls," Maudie said. "I tell you, he's a rogue, and he bears watching."

Jess sighed. "Rogue or not, I must find him something of greater interest here."

Alex swung his long legs off the bench. "I'll tell you what interests me at the moment: a stroll in the moonlight after such a fine meal. Don't wait up." He snagged his coat from the hook by the door and sauntered out.

Jess frowned after him. "Has he conceived a fancy for a young lady in town? I thought I saw him with the oldest Lawrence daughter last Sunday."

"She's taken up with that recruiting officer," Maudie

replied, head tilted as if to watch for Alex's shadow to pass the window. "It's the uniform. All that red goes to a girl's head."

Jess wasn't so sure. More and more, her brother distanced himself. He hadn't sought to apprentice himself to any of the village businesses. Though he'd learned to sail, she couldn't see him making fishing his trade. Despite his actions at the moment, he was a gentleman.

"Alex needs a purpose," she told Maudie as she poured heated water from the kettle into her largest pot so she could wash the dishes. When her father was alive, they'd had a maid to do such work. Jess and Maudie's salaries didn't cover such luxuries now.

"He should be a physician," Maudie said, going to fetch a towel so she could help. "Every male Chance has been a physician: my grandfather, my father, my brother."

"I know." Jess wiped the glass in her hand. "But we haven't the money to send him for training, and there's no physician in miles where he can apprentice. Besides, I'm not sure he wants to follow in Father's footsteps."

"He could be a tragic poet," Maudie offered, flicking the towel back and forth, eyes dreamy. "Writing of death and despair."

Jess wrinkled her nose. "I think there may be enough of that in the world already, Aunt."

"Not to my mind," Maudie grumbled.

"I'll speak to him when he returns," Jess said.

But Alex did not return before she was forced to put out her lamp and go to sleep. And he was still gone when she woke in the morning, so she could not be certain he had ever returned.

Her guests at the spa were no more accommodating. Several of the bachelors had finished their visit and moved on. She had no new arrivals that morning. But the Regulars were fractious. It didn't help that a misty rain had

turned the day grey.

"That is my seat from ten to noon," Mr. Crabapple whined to Jess, his hair hanging more limp than usual around his narrow face. "Lord Featherstone and I have an agreement." He nodded to where Lark was playing a game of chess against the baron at the board that sat near the fountain.

"I'm sure Lord Featherstone is only being polite to a Newcomer," Jess assured him. She leaned closer. "Besides, I see Mrs. Harding is all alone this morning, over there by the window. I'm sure she would enjoy your company."

Cheeks pinking, he cast a glance at the lovely widow, who was gazing out at the mist as if waiting for the right fellow to come along. "Do you think so?"

"Faint heart never won fair lady," Jess said with a jerk of her head in Mrs. Harding's direction.

Adjusting his cravat, Mr. Crabapple wandered closer. Mrs. Harding smiled in encouragement.

If only it was that easy to direct Lark. He finished his game of chess, refused Maudie's glass of spa water, and went to strike up a conversation with Admiral Walsey, another of their Regulars. Miss Cole's gaze followed his every move. Her mother took her arm and dragged her over to talk with Mrs. Harding and Mr. Crabapple.

Jess tried to busy herself with her other duties. Every month, the spa held at least one special event to entertain visitors and draw in more. The May Day Revels were over, but the Midsummer Masquerade in June required a great deal of coordination. She must make sure the Misses Pierce were ready to stitch costumes, Mr. Carroll had sufficient masks of various types in stock, and Mrs. Rinehart was willing to construct fanciful headwear. She must consult with Mr. and Mrs. Inchley, the grocers, and Mr. Ellison about refreshments; and Mr. Bent, the employment agency owner, about extra staff, including maids and valets

to help their guests. Perhaps she could see that Alex and Mr. Lawrence's daughter Patricia wore related costumes. A knight and his lady? That might bring the two closer. Lark wouldn't need a costume. He wouldn't be here that long.

Why did that draw a sigh from her? She prided herself on maintaining an air of calm, civility, and congeniality at the spa. She could gauge the climate of the room like a mariner gauged the seas. Lark was a storm cloud on the horizon, promising wind, rain, an upset to conditions. She simply wasn't sure what to do about it.

Biding his time, cooling his heels, that was all Lark could do until Sunday night, when he would be watching the shore for this cargo Mr. Carroll had mentioned. He'd spoken with Greer yesterday. The apothecary might know something about sailing, but he was as upright as they came. Lark would have to consider the vicar tomorrow. He just needed to get through today.

But Jess couldn't seem to leave be. It was as if he offered some sort of challenge. He caught her watching him as he moved from group to group. As the afternoon went on, she offered him teacakes iced with lemon, a book on the geologic wonders of the area, and a telescope with which to peer into the misty rain to spy the cove below. She introduced him to every person who set foot in the door. She was trying to distract him, as if she herself wasn't enough of a distraction.

Mrs. Tully sidled up to him for the fourth time that day, and he readied himself to once again refuse the hideous spa water.

"Blonde, brunette, raven, or red-head?" she demanded.

Lark tried not to frown at her. "I beg your pardon?"

She fluttered her lashes. "Grey, then. But I must warn you, young man, that my heart is already taken."

So, that was her gambit. Lark bowed to her with a smile. "Alas, madam, I will have to content myself with disappointment."

She drew herself up. "I never said anything about the rest of me."

Lord Featherstone was approaching, and Lark reached out to grab the baron's hand, feeling as if he clutched a lifeline. "My lord, how are you? I was just going for a stroll about the room. Join me?"

"If you wish," Lord Featherstone said, smile bemused.

Mrs. Tully huffed as they started off.

"I take it company is already wearing thin," the older man said, nodding as they passed Mrs. Cole and her daughter. The girl smiled at Lark. Her mother turned her toward the fountain, as if to admire the smooth white stone.

"The spa guests are a varied lot," Lark temporized. "But I expected something different."

"Ah." Lord Featherstone clasped his hands behind his back as they passed the great clock. "And what sort of activity do you pursue when you are in your own society?"

Best not to offer too much information. On the other hand, perhaps he could learn something. "I'm an avid boater."

Lord Featherstone sighed. "I had a lovely ketch on the Thames. She sank. Rot."

They came around the welcome desk. Jess had left her post to prepare tea. The cart didn't so much as squeak as she rolled it up to Mrs. Harding now.

The silver-haired lord cast him a glance. "Are you interested in travel, Mr. Denby? Perhaps to a foreign shore?"

A foreign shore? During a time of war? Lark's heart leaped, but he refused to give away his eagerness. Could he have been wrong about Mr. Carroll? Could he be speak-

ing to the Lord of the Smugglers even now? While Lord Featherstone seemed too old to cause such trouble, his witty conversation said he might be clever enough to have orchestrated it.

"Sounds intriguing," Lark said. "What did you have in mind?"

"Allow me to make inquiries," he said in his smooth voice as they passed Jess and steam from the teapot made a heart around her pretty face. "I should know more in a day or so."

"When the moon is dark," Lark guessed.

Featherstone's smile committed to nothing. "Just so." He stopped beside the fountain. "Thank you for an informative stroll, Mr. Denby. I shall not monopolize you further."

Lark inclined his head, and the aristocrat moved on. But he watched as the fellow spoke to this person and that, always moving closer to where Jess was pouring tea.

Lord Featherstone paused beside her, back partially to Lark. Around the fellow, he could just make out some of Jess's soft curls swaying, as if she was nodding her head.

Once again, warning bells rang. Could Jess oversee the smuggling? She knew every visitor, so she could choose ones who would carry goods deeper into the country. She had lived in this village her entire life and clearly knew everyone.

Yet, at the idea that Jess might be involved, his heart rebelled. Why? Was he still so taken with her? She'd been the first lady who'd ever fascinated him, the one who had stayed in his thoughts the longest. But he had steadfastly refused to consider courting until he no longer held a position that endangered his life. A wife should have some expectation that her husband would come home to her.

And Commissioner Franklin had some expectation of Lark's success. He must remain focused. Sunday evening could not come soon enough.

CHAPTER FIVE

JESS PUT LARK FROM HER mind long enough to corner her brother when he joined her and Maudie for dinner Saturday evening, after the spa had closed for the day. But their discussion was no more fruitful, and Alex ended up heading out for a stroll.

Maudie shook her head. "Silly time to go for a walk. The trolls won't be up until moonrise. And the mermaids are picnicking at the Durdle Door tonight."

The sweeping stone arch of the Durdle Door just down the coast was certainly picturesque, so she could almost see mermaids making a point of visiting. But she'd have given a great deal to know who Alex was visiting on his evening rambles.

For a moment, she considered following him. She had a dark winter cloak, still hanging on its hook near the door for all she wouldn't have to wear it for months. Easy enough to scamper from shadow to shadow. When she was a girl, she and Abigail used to pretend they were pirates, dashing about among the racks of drying nets along the shore, whacking at imaginary foes with wooden swords. Her father had taught her to sail his ketch, allowed her to wear trousers under her skirts so she could move easily about the craft.

But she'd put aside that adventurous girl the year she'd

come out, the year she'd met Lark. She was a lady now. She had a reputation to protect. And with Alex and Maudie's support resting on her salary, nothing was more important than keeping her job.

Besides, how much trouble could Alex get into at Grace-by-the-Sea?

Enough that he could not be bothered to rise for church Sunday morning. Jess called up to him twice and even climbed the ladder to poke her head into the loft. Tucked into the back of the cliff, with no windows, the rear half of the low room was dark, but enough light came from the small, round window at either end that she could see the pallet and mound of quilts and blankets that held her brother.

"Services start in an hour," she informed him.

A hand popped up from the crumpled mass. "Give my regards to the vicar."

Lips pressed tight, she climbed back down.

"Even the trolls attend services," Maudie grumbled as they walked up the hill toward the church, and Jess did not have the heart to ask her where they sat.

While Mr. Wingate prayed for the parish, the region, and the nation, she prayed for Alex and patience. She was not his mother. Her only right, if she could call it that, to ordering him about was that she supplied his room and board. She could not feel comfortable using that as an excuse to meddle in his affairs.

Yet even as she prayed about the matter, she felt as if a gaze was on her, like a butterfly hovering. She turned to find Lark seated on the other side of the narrow aisle. The dark wood box pews had always seemed warm and welcoming to her, but all at once her breath came easier. She smiled. He smiled. She turned to face the cross, surer of herself than when she'd entered.

It had been that way the first time too. Her father had

overseen the spa for some years, but she generally did not attend, not until she was considered out in Society. It had been rather daunting to walk into the august company, her hair done up, her body swathed in fine wool. What was she to say to them? How was she to respond if they spoke to her? She'd glanced around, meeting curious gazes everywhere. One man had gone so far as to raise his quizzing glass and squint at her through it.

And Lark had materialized out of the crowd, her father at his side.

"Jesslyn," her father had said in the voice he reserved for frightened clients, "may I present Mr. Larkin Denby of Upper Grace? Mr. Denby, this is my daughter."

Lark had bowed over her hand as if she were a member of the royal family. "Miss Chance, a pleasure to make your acquaintance."

Here she was, in her father's sphere at last, and Lark had been the one to make her feel as if she belonged. The spa had been her retreat after he'd left. She'd started a Newcomer, for all her father led the assemblage, and worked her way to Regular and now hostess. Yet one look from him still made everything seem in its proper place.

Her memories followed her from the church and up to the door of the spa. Lord Featherstone was waiting for her, and she swallowed her disappointment that it wasn't Lark. The other Regulars trickled in as well. Mrs. Harding went to take her place beside the windows. Maudie went to take her place at the harpsichord. The music seemed unnecessarily somber. Somehow, it fit Jess's mood.

Oh, no! She was not about to become her aunt, pining away for a lost love and prosing on about trolls and mermaids as a way to fill the hole in her heart. She had work before her. She had to confer with the innkeepers and Mrs. Kirby, the leasing agent, to determine who was coming to the spa and when; confirm the subscriptions they paid for

access to the spa with Mr. Lawrence. She had to manage the staff who cleaned the spa in the evenings and the caterers who provided food, dishes, and cutlery each day. She planned entertainments, amusements. She ought to see if she could find a young man for Miss Cole.

A noise caught her attention, and she focused on Mr. Crabapple, who was in close consultation with Lord Featherstone and Admiral Walsey. The Admiral thrust out his barrel chest, lined cheeks inflating. Oh, what now?

Jess joined them in a flurry of pink. "Gentlemen, might I interest you in a drink from the fountain?"

The Admiral's hard face softened. "You are only too kind, Miss Chance. I wish you would speak to Crabapple here." He turned to the scholar. "Grow a backbone, man!"

Instead, Mr. Crabapple folded in on himself further. "You would not understand, a man of your physique, your prowess, your fame. We lesser mortals are doomed."

"Nonsense!" The Admiral stumped off, cane smacking the tiled floors so hard she wondered they did not chip.

She put her hand on Mr. Crabapple's thin arm. "You mustn't let him fluster you, sir. I'm sure you can accomplish whatever you set out to do."

Mr. Crabapple's lower lip trembled. "No, I fear he has the right of it, Miss Chance. Despite your help, and the assistance of Featherstone, here, I cannot make any headway with Mrs. Harding. I am simply not the man for her."

"Nonsense," Jess said. "You haven't even applied yourself yet."

"She's right," Lord Featherstone said, voice kind. "You have much to offer the lady, Warfield. You are well established, respected, and you have a remarkably kind heart. She would be fortunate to attract a fellow of your standing."

Mr. Crabapple goggled. "Truly?"

"Truly," Jess agreed. She glanced to where the Win-

some Widow was gazing out the window. Her court had forsaken her for the moment, and her gaze was pensive, almost lonely.

Jess turned back to the men. "I have an idea. But I must know—what is it you want from the lady?"

Mr. Crabapple blinked. "Oh, nothing more than a dance at the next assembly. I would never presume to ask for more. Indeed, that is likely too much to hope."

Jess nodded. "A dance. That can be arranged. But you must be prepared to show your devotion, sir. Allow me to guide you. We will put our plan in place this very night."

Lark had joined the other occupants of Grace-by-the-Sea at St. Andrew's that morning. Since he had to wait until evening to catch Carroll or Featherstone or whoever was bringing in that illegal shipment from France, he should probably have ridden up onto the hill to attend services at St. Mary's in Upper Grace with his mother and sisters. But he had a job to do, and he couldn't feel comfortable breaking free until it was done.

First, he studied the vicar, a slight fellow who tended to bob his head when making a point, as if agreeing with his sentiments. He seemed a poor choice for Lord of the Smugglers. Wouldn't his countenance, his movements bear some evidence if he were routinely out all night? But his movements were sure, his voice commanding, and his look imploring as he read the sermon.

Perhaps he might learn more about the area. He retrieved his horse, Valkyrie, from the stable at the Mermaid and crossed from one headland around the cove to the other, looking for any signs of a landing—wagon tracks, bushes burned to light a beacon, an easy path up from the shore.

He found none.

So, he returned to his room at the Mermaid and kept an eye on the harbor. Noises rose from the public room, friends meeting. Admiral Walsey passed on his way from the spa. They all seemed miles away.

How many times had he sat in a room—here, at another inn along the coast, at the small house he rented in Kent— alone. He didn't remember it bothering him before. He had a job to do, a job that didn't admit friendships well. A Riding Officer was in the saddle for hours on end, covering four or more miles of coast as far inland as five miles. He was to note any disturbances, any suspicious activities, reporting them to his Surveyor. When matters warranted, he applied to use dragoons, who rode in, lances flashing, to stop the smugglers.

Each arrest brought a certain satisfaction. The smugglers were wily, clever. They had any number of tricks to prevent discovery. Why, one enterprising fellow had rubbed chalk on his face and played dead so that his cohorts might carry his casket, and the ill-gotten goods it held, past Lark's watchful eye. Besides, every smuggler caught made other families safer and England less vulnerable.

So why was he feeling the vulnerable one today?

As twilight wrapped the village, he slipped from the inn and edged his way toward the shore. All the shops were shuttered and dark, but light glowed from the cottages on either side. Voices tumbled out as someone opened a door. Lark stayed in the shadows.

Water splashed the pebbles, a sound soft and cool, as he stepped down onto the shore. The breeze carried the scent of brine. The creak and rattle directly ahead came from the boats riding at anchor, rocking on the incoming tide. To his right, squat shapes marked the sheds used by fishermen and the racks holding drying nets. No one was about.

Except there, where a stone cottage clung to the bank,

vines growing down to frame the window overlooking the cove. In the light from that window, three people stood in a tight knot on the path. Lark's heart started pounding harder.

He crept closer, watching, listening. Two men and a woman—he could see the swish of her skirts when she turned. And there! Light catching on silver hair. Surely the tallest was Lord Featherstone.

The woman pulled back, and Lark flattened himself against one of the sheds. As he watched, Jesslyn Chance ran up the steps and entered the cottage.

"No!" The word flew out of him, and Lord Featherstone and the other man glanced in his direction. He recognized Mr. Crabapple's long nose. Were they all in on it, then?

Lark squared his shoulders. Like it or not, he was here for a purpose. Stopping the Lord of the Smugglers was all that mattered. He must catch them now, before the rest of their gang arrived. He drew himself up to his full height, pushed off the shed, and strode down the shingle, reaching into his jacket for the pistol he had placed there.

"Stop!" he shouted, "in the name of the king."

Mr. Crabapple threw up his hands and burst into tears.

CHAPTER SIX

THE COMMANDING VOICE ECHOED ACROSS the cove, piercing even the stone walls of the cottage. Jess started, glancing toward the window.

Sitting in Maudie's rocking chair by the hearth, Mrs. Harding pressed her fingers to her generous chest. "What was that?"

"Banshees," Maudie muttered from the bench of the table.

Jess put a hand on her guest's arm. "Nothing to upset our chat, Mrs. Harding, I'm sure. You are kindness itself to wait on us here. Maudie and I don't get many visitors."

Mrs. Harding dropped her hand. "I was delighted to accept your invitation this evening and to offer my advice about the upcoming masquerade. I was a little surprised to find your home so far out of the way." She glanced around at the two-room cottage again. "A shame your brother is out. Are you certain all is safe?"

"I'll just check," Jess said with a look to her aunt. She closed the curtain before peeking out the door. She had worked for days to help Mr. Crabapple screw his courage to the sticking point. No one had better have convinced him otherwise.

The light spilled past her to illuminate the scene. Mr. Crabapple was collapsed against Lord Featherstone, while

Lark stood nearby, face set, feet planted, and one fist holding a pistol, the very picture of a determined highwayman.
What was this? Jess stepped out and closed the door behind
her.

"Gentlemen," she scolded. "What's happened? I thought
everything was arranged."

"So did I," Lark said, but his voice held doubt, and he
lowered his weapon. She heard the click as he uncocked it.

Jess frowned at him. "I was not told you were to join us
tonight, sir."

Mr. Crabapple wailed and buried his face in Lord Featherstone's waistcoat.

"His presence took us all by surprise," Lord Featherstone
admitted.

Jess came down the steps to the path that ran above the
shore and patted her Regular on the back. "There, there,
Mr. Crabapple. Compose yourself. All is not lost."

Lark's face bunched, his confusion obvious. Mr. Crabapple raised his head and sniffed bravely, one arm waving
about. "No, no, it was an impossible dream."

"Nonsense," Lord Featherstone averred. "Why, young
Denby here could be just the man we need. Baritone, I
believe?"

Lark glanced between them. "Baritone?"

"Your voice," Jess said. "And I believe you are correct,
my lord. But I have no idea of his abilities. Not all men can
manage it, particularly unaided."

Lark's chin came up. "I assure you, Miss Chance, I have
never been found lacking."

Now, that she could believe.

Lord Featherstone clapped him on the shoulder with his
free hand. "Good man. Do you know Burns?"

He blinked. "Burns?"

"*My love is like a red, red, rose?*" Jess prompted. When he
still looked blank, she sighed. "Well, hum if you must. Mr.

Crabapple, have you recovered sufficiently?"

He pulled away from Lord Featherstone and rubbed the back of his hand under his long nose. "Yes, Miss Chance. Thank you."

"Then I'll fetch Mrs. Harding to the window. When you see us, commence."

She looked to Lark, who nodded as if promising his utmost. At least he remembered to tuck the pistol away. It would hardly help Mr. Crabapple's cause. Whyever had Lark drawn it? By the moonlight, she could see nothing dangerous along the shore.

She slipped back into the house, shutting the door carefully.

"Mermaids in the cove, were there?" Maudie demanded. "I knew it."

"No mermaids and no banshees," she said. She turned to her guest. "But I believe you will want to see this, my dear." Taking the widow's hands and tugging her up, Jess led her to the window, then released her to draw back the curtains.

Like actors at a London theatre, Lord Featherstone, Mr. Crabapple, and Lark stood outlined by the light. The baron smiled, Mr. Crabapple fidgeted, and Lark glanced from them to the window, eyes narrowed, as if suspecting her of harboring French spies.

"What is this?" Mrs. Harding asked as Maudie tilted her head to see around her.

As if in answer, Lord Featherstone began in his warm bass.

"O my love is like a red, red rose
That's newly sprung in June;
O my love is like the melody
That's sweetly played in tune."

Mrs. Harding caught her breath as Mr. Crabapple stepped forward and took up the tune in his tenor.

"So fair art thou, my bonnie lass,
So deep in love am I;
And I will love thee still, my dear,
Till a' the seas gang dry."

Jess knew she should be watching the effect of their efforts on the Winsome Widow, but she couldn't take her eyes off Lark. She knew the moment he realized what was happening, for his brow cleared, his smile widened, and he sang with enthusiasm while making sure to give Mr. Crabapple pride of place. He was certainly well named, for he sang like a lark.

"Oh, how marvelous," Mrs. Harding breathed as the last echo faded across the water. Her hands fluttered as she applauded with gusto. Jess and Maudie joined in. Lord Featherstone bowed, then nudged his friend. Mr. Crabapple stumbled forward.

"Such praise is only your due, my dear Mrs. Harding," he called, voice catching. "All I ask is that you consider allowing me the honor of your hand in a dance at the assembly this Wednesday."

"Two dances," she called down. "And I will expect your escort, sir."

Even in the dim light, Jess could see her Regular turning as rosy as his namesake. "Delighted. Overjoyed. Such kindness, such condescension, such magnificence…"

"Perhaps the lady requires an escort back to her accommodations now," Lord Featherstone suggested, eyeing his friend.

Mr. Crabapple shook his head so hard his nose bounced. "Oh, I wouldn't dream of imposing. To have such a responsibility, no, no, it is too much to ask."

"A shame," the widow called, humor dancing in her voice. "I suspect I must then rely on Lord Featherstone or perhaps the handsome Mr. Denby."

Mr. Crabapple looked daggers at Jess's Newcomer, who

spread his hands as if well used to the attentions of the ladies.

And that was quite enough of that. "We'll all go," Jess said. "I believe Lord Featherstone and Mr. Denby have rooms along the way. Allow my aunt and me to gather our shawls, and we'll join you."

A few minutes later, they were strolling along the shore path toward High Street and Shell Cottage, which Mrs. Harding had rented for the summer. The widow walked with one arm linked in Lord Featherstone's and the other in Mr. Crabapple's, head turned first to the right and then to the left as she conversed with both. Maudie scurried just behind as if determined to overhear every bit of it.

"Two strings to her bow," Jess murmured with a shake of her head.

"Indeed," Lark said, walking beside her. "I regret that I blundered in."

She glanced at him. With the pistol safely out of sight, he no longer looked so dangerous. Indeed, he seemed the young man she had met at the spa eight years ago. She could not trust his thoughtful look.

"What *were* you doing down at the shore this evening?" she asked.

"Merely taking a walk," he assured her. "I thought the exercise might be healthful."

As if he could be any healthier. Even Lord Featherstone's shoulders were not so broad, his stride so firm.

"My father always considered exercise healthful," she allowed. "Though he favored walking along the cliffs when he could and in daylight."

"Yet he decided to take a house right at the shore," Lark mused, taking her arm as they stepped off the shore path and onto High Street. The touch sent a tingle up her arm, as if she had put a hand in the cool of the sea on a hot day. "That wasn't where you lived eight years ago."

"No," Jess said. "The cottage used to house the constable. The Spa Corporation decided it was better for lodging the staff. I was raised in Shell Cottage, the house Mrs. Harding is now renting. I could not keep it after Father died." There, she sounded regretful, not bitter. Lark wasn't the only one who could hide his feelings under polite conversation.

"I'm sorry you lost your father," he murmured, "and your home. That had to be a double blow."

It had been, but she was thankful she had a place to live. "The cottage suffices for me, my aunt, and my brother."

"Ah, yes, your brother," he said. "He was only a lad when I was here before, and I don't believe I've met him yet this time. What does he do?"

"Alex has yet to decide on his vocation," Jess said, and left it at that.

The slope of the street was gentle as they passed through the shuttered shops. There was no reason for him to be holding her hand, but he didn't pull away.

Neither did she.

But she paused as they reached Shell Cottage. Though Mrs. Harding's servants had left the lamps burning, Jess did not need the light to see it. Her memories provided too many visions. The welcoming smile on her father's face as he came in the front door with its fan light shaped like a cockle shell. The laughter around the damask-draped dining table that could seat twelve comfortably yet never felt too large for the four of them bunched on one end. The warmth of the fire in the white marble hearth of the parlor on a night when the wind rattled the panes and her father teased Maudie about her ghost stories.

Now Mrs. Harding stood on the porch, wiggled her fingers in farewell, and glided inside, where her maid and footman were waiting. Jess bit back a sigh.

Mr. Crabapple's sigh sounded far happier as the door closed. Then he whirled so fast, Maudie scrambled back

with a shriek.

"Oh, Miss Chance!" he cried, eyes wide and hands once more gesticulating. "You must help me. I'm to take Mrs. Harding to the assembly. What should I wear? What shall I say?"

Lord Featherstone laid a hand on his shoulder. "All matters for another day, my good man. Bid your hostess good night and thank her for her help."

"Oh, yes, yes, of course." He dropped his hands and blinked owlishly. "Thank you so much for your assistance, Miss Chance, and you as well, Mr. Denby." A smile spread. "I'm to escort Mrs. Harding."

"Good for you," Maudie encouraged him.

Lord Featherstone stepped away and nodded to Lark. "Be a good chap, Denby, and see him home. I must have a word with Miss Chance and Mrs. Tully."

She felt the shift in Lark's body, closer to hers, protective. What did he think Lord Featherstone meant to ask her?

"It's quite all right, Mr. Denby," she said. "Lord Featherstone has known me since I was a child."

"Well, perhaps a young lady," Lord Featherstone demurred.

"Me too," Maudie said, and the older lord looked hard-pressed to maintain his smile.

Left with no other choice if he wanted to keep the appellation of gentleman, Lark inclined his head and went to walk with Mr. Crabapple. Lord Featherstone waited only until they passed the next house before bending his head to look Jess in the eyes.

"There is something decidedly odd about Mr. Denby," he pronounced. "Nothing but questions, and then he barges in on Crabapple's assignation."

"Hardly an assignation," Jess protested. "You and I and Maudie were there."

Maudie nodded agreement.

"We were invited," Lord Featherstone reminded her. "He was not. Be very careful, Miss Chance. I begin to believe he has designs on you."

Jess reared back. "Me?"

"Indeed," Lord Featherstone said, straightening. "Though I would not admit it before the Widow, I have on occasion considered myself as acting *in loco parentis*, Miss Chance. Your father was alive when previous gentlemen attempted closer acquaintance with you. I'm sure he gave you wise counsel. I only hope to do the same now."

Her father had had both a discerning and a protective nature. He had eased her sorrows when Lark had departed the first time and confirmed her concerns about the next fellow she had thought she might come to love. But he had missed the last dastard entirely.

"Thank you for your concern, my lord," Jess told Lord Featherstone. "But never fear. I know exactly how to deal with a gentleman who finds himself in over his head."

"Dunked in the sea?" Lark stared at Mrs. Tully the next morning. It had not been a good night. First, he had learned nothing about the shipment supposedly coming in, then he had nearly given himself away at the shore, and finally there had been so much celebration in the public room of the Mermaid that he hadn't been able to fall asleep until nearly dawn. The final nail had been pounded into his coffin when he had encountered Mr. Carroll on the way through town to the spa.

"Please let Miss Chance know the shipment has arrived," he had told Lark with a pleasant smile.

Lark had stopped in his tracks, shocked by the brazen statement. "Shipment, sir?"

"Fashion magazines," he'd explained. "Monthly. Late, of course, because of the war and duties, but so popular at the spa, particularly with Mrs. Tully."

French fashion magazines, duty paid. Perfectly legal. Another day wasted.

And now Mrs. Tully expected him to go dunk his head.

"It's part of the spa's treatments," she said, stabbing a boney finger at the pamphlet. "Very efficacious for puss-filled protrusions." She peered closer. "Have you any puss-filled protrusions, Mr. Denby?"

"None whatsoever," Lark informed her. "So I see no reason to avail myself of a cure."

"But being dunked would allow you to keep an eye on the cove," she pointed out, straightening.

Lark made himself shrug. "And why would a gentleman like me have any reason to watch the cove?"

Mrs. Tully slapped a hand against her black bombazine dress. "I wish I knew! Lord Featherstone seems to think you have nefarious designs on my niece."

Nefarious? He met her gaze. "I would never do anything to harm your niece."

She nodded. "I'm more inclined to believe you're in league with Napoleon."

Lark eyed her. He'd spent all this time considering Lord Featherstone, Mr. Carroll, and even Jess, and the leader might have been right in front of him all along. Did Mrs. Tully just play at being mad?

"Have you met many people in league with Napoleon?" he asked cautiously.

"Dozens," she declared, disgust lacing her voice.

He edged closer. "Oh? Who?"

She leaned toward him and lowered her voice. "The ones on the cove." She nodded sagely.

"The fishermen?" he pressed.

She straightened and gave him a pitying look. "Of course

not the fishermen. Some of them haven't the sense God gave a goose. Why else would they keep dropping their nets overboard?"

Why else indeed, if they weren't actually fishing? "Then one of the Spa Corporation leaders," he guessed. "Someone with a fast ship at his disposal."

She tapped her nose with one finger. "Now you're thinking. Have to be fast to keep up with them."

"Who?" Lark nearly winced at the begging tone.

"The French, of course," she said, clearly exasperated with him. "I saw Old Boney himself, on the headland by Castle How, only last month."

And wouldn't the commissioner sit up and take notice at that report? Lark puffed out a sigh, straightening. A shame he couldn't believe her story. Napoleon wouldn't set foot in England without his elite guard at his back and a thousand ships behind them, ships Lark was thankful were still on the other side of the Channel. For now.

"Perhaps you should have threatened to dunk him," Lark said. "That would have frightened him back to France."

Mrs. Tully laughed, just as her niece wandered closer. Today, Jess's curls had been confined in a severe bun at the back of her head, and he had to tighten his fingers to keep from reaching out to tug one free. The lack of frills on her dove grey gown only added to the feeling that she was being strict with him.

"Dunking isn't a threat, Mr. Denby," she said with that pleasant smile she reserved for difficult answers. "It's a special treat. We only do it a few times each summer now that we have no physician to oversee the process."

He seized on the excuse. "I would certainly want a physician on hand before trying it."

"Why?" Mrs. Cole asked as she and her daughter joined them. "Is it dangerous?"

"Not in the slightest," Jess assured them. "The water is

bracing."

"Freezing," Lark amended.

She did not so much as spare him a frown. "And every bather is attended by two strong assistants."

Her aunt raised her hand. "I volunteer to assist Mr. Denby."

"Of the same gender," Jess hurriedly added.

Mrs. Tully dropped her hand.

"And can we see the other bathers?" Miss Cole asked with a glance to Lark through her lashes.

"No," Jess said with rather more vehemence than might have been warranted. "Men bathe on one side of the cove, women on the other, and the bathing huts prevent any sightings."

Miss Cole sighed.

Lark stepped back. "I wish you all great fortune. I'll be at the spa when you return."

"Nonsense, Mr. Denby," Lord Featherstone said, coming up and pressing a hand against his back as if to prevent Lark from fleeing. "You must have come to Grace-by-the-Sea hoping for a diversion. Saltwater bathing is highly diverting. Even our noble king and his family avail themselves of the opportunity when it is offered."

Mrs. Tully's eyes narrowed. "Have you something against the king, Mr. Denby?"

They were all watching him. Jess was the only one who looked amused, the light sparkling in her blue eyes.

He forced a smile. "Not at all, Mrs. Tully. Since he approves of it, who am I to disapprove? As Lord Featherstone reminded me, I came to experience the spa, even if that means jumping into the sea."

CHAPTER SEVEN

LARK'S DUNKING DID NOT HAVE the effect Jess had hoped, at least on him. After his initial hesitation, he went willingly enough, attended by Mr. Inchley, the grocer, and Mr. Josephs, the blacksmith and owner of the livery stable near the Swan.

"A good sport, he was," the burly blacksmith assured her when she accepted the invoice for his time. "Smiling all the while."

That she did not have to imagine. She'd been overseeing the ladies' bathing when she'd caught her aunt up on the bank above the shore with her father's spyglass pressed to her eye.

"Stop that at once," Jess ordered.

When Maudie paid her no heed, she lifted her skirts and clambered up the chalky bank herself. "Maudlyn Tully, lower that glass."

Maudie let the spyglass fall into the lap of her black bombazine gown. "Someone must oversee the gentle-men's bathing."

"Mr. Josephs and Mr. Inchley have helped us before. I see no need to interfere. Besides, I promised our guests they would have privacy."

And privacy was not too difficult. Grace Cove was cupped by grass-topped headlands, like arms embracing

the clear waters. A narrow opening was all that gave access to the Channel. Mr. Josephs lent her his horses, which he hitched to the six bathing huts. He knew exactly how to position them so that the ten-foot-square boxes blocked the views from each other. The attendants walked the horses out into the water to the ordained spots, until the waves lapped at the second step, then unhitched the horses and returned the beasts to shore.

Inside the huts, her guests changed into muslin smocks that covered them from shoulders to knees. When they were ready, they stepped out, and their attendants helped them down into the cool waters, dunking them in the waves. Lark was right—the waters were generally as crisp as an autumn morning, but the treatment only lasted a few minutes. Then the attendants helped the bathers back into the huts, and the entire process was reversed. It was all very civilized.

Well, except for the fact that her aunt was intent on spying!

"Protecting the village is more important than privacy," Maudie insisted, fingers turning the spyglass in her lap as if she just couldn't wait to put it to her eye again. "I want to know what Mr. Denby is doing."

"Oh, for pity's sake." Jess snatched up the glass and put it to her eye. "Mr. Denby is just coming up from the sea. He isn't doing anything the least…"

He stood in the water, waves up to his waist, the bathing smock clinging to his arms, his chest. He shook drops off his handsome face and gazed directly at her, smile lifting.

Jess whipped down the glass. "Help me with the ladies," she told her aunt, starting down the bank. And if she slipped twice on the way, it was only because of the soil.

All her guests retired to their lodging after the dunking, but it was still hard for Jess to meet Lark's gaze the next day. She knew he couldn't have seen her across the cove while

he had been bathing, but she could not shake the feeling they had shared something personal. She was simply glad Lord Featherstone monopolized his time with helping Mr. Crabapple prepare for the assembly on Wednesday.

Jess had convinced the would-be Romeo that the baron would be a far better guide than she would in matters of dress and etiquette when it came to impressing the ladies. Lord Featherstone, in turn, enlisted the aid of the Admiral ("that military bearing is always impressive") and Lark ("a younger man quite obviously in the know about these things"). The four spent most of Tuesday strolling about the spa pontificating with Mr. Crabapple, who carried a small notebook and pencil and kept nodding and writing, nose nearly pressed to the page.

The spa closed just after tea on Wednesday so that her guests could dress for the event and she could prepare the assembly rooms at the top of the hill behind the spa. Designed in the Palladian style, with tall columns at the front, the solid, square building held an elegant hall for dancing, a narrower room for a supper served at midnight, and several retiring rooms and a kitchen at the back. The blue of the walls inside recalled the sea at sunrise, and the cornices above had been carved to resemble whitecaps.

Mr. Inchley and his family served as caterer and cleaning crew. He and his wife were waiting at the rear door when Jess opened the rooms. While she consulted with them, their son lowered the massive, multi-tiered crystal chandelier in the center of the high plastered ceiling of the main hall so Maudie could replace the candles.

"Still beeswax," Mrs. Inchley said with a nod of her dark head as she eyed the pair through the doorway to the kitchen. "I expect I'll hear from Mrs. Greer about the cost."

"Very likely," Jess commiserated. "But we'd both hear of it if tallow dripped on any of our distinguished guests."

"Or her," Mrs. Inchley agreed.

And their guests did look distinguished. Jess smiled in greeting as she stood by the doors to receive them that evening. Lord Featherstone was splendid in a dark blue cutaway coat, wine-colored waistcoat, and buff breeches. The pristine white cravat in a complicated fold drew attention to the silver of his artfully waved hair. Only he and Jess knew the diamond winking in the folds of that cravat was paste.

Mr. Crabapple looked nearly as impressive. Somehow Lord Featherstone, Lark, and the Admiral had convinced him to wear a wasp-waisted bottle-green coat that made his narrow shoulders look broader. She only hoped that wasn't padding under his white stockings. The things were notorious for moving during activity. Mrs. Harding would scarcely thank him for his escort if his manly calves ended up on his knees.

The widow herself was in carmine, with rubies at her ears and throat and ostrich plumes in her piled-up hair. Jess had a few fashionable gowns from when she was younger, but styles had changed. She was thankful the Corporation had decided its hostess must do the spa credit, for the Misses Pierce at the linens and trimmings shop had been given leave to construct three ballgowns for her, which she rotated wearing at the assemblies and major events.

Tonight, it was the lilac-figured muslin with an over-skirt of embroidered tulle. She'd embroidered the stars and flowers herself in white, cerulean blue, and silver, and they caught the light as she moved. Would Lark like it?

That didn't matter. Of course that didn't matter. Still, she found herself glancing around for him as the rest of her guests streamed into the hall.

"No sign of Mr. Denby," Maudie reported, as if she had read Jess's thoughts. "Or Alex, for that matter. How does that boy expect to continue the line if he refuses to do the

pretty?"

"Perhaps because he is still more boy than man," Jess reminded her. "Nineteen is young to be setting up a nursery."

Maudie sniffed. "What about thirty?"

Jess followed her gaze to where James Howland was approaching. His coat and breeches were an unrelenting black, his waistcoat a silvery grey. Even his evening pumps were unadorned. The look on his face was nearly as severe. Had she done something to offend?

Jess dropped a curtsey and lowered her gaze. "Magistrate."

"Miss Chance, Mrs. Tully," he acknowledged as she rose. "A good turnout tonight."

Jess glanced around the room. The assemblies generally attracted those who did not sully their hands to make a living, but the village had decreed that the members of the Spa Corporation Council and their families, no matter their background, should be included. The five current members of the council—Mr. Greer, Abigail, Mr. Lawrence, Mrs. Kirby, and Mr. Bent—had arrived and stood clustered at one end of the room. Mr. Wingate was in attendance, although he seldom danced. All their spa guests were accounted for as well, except one. She tried not to sigh.

"Yes," she said brightly, "a fine showing indeed. I'm glad you could join us."

His gaze was also sweeping the room. Who could he be searching for? "I believe the dancing will commence shortly. I was hoping you'd favor me."

Despite her training, she stepped back, brows up in surprise. He never danced, and certainly not with the spa hostess.

"I don't dance," Maudie informed him, nose in the air. "It will have to be you, Jesslyn."

His mouth quirked, but he did not go so far as to laugh at her aunt's assumption. "Miss Chance?"

Impossibly rude to refuse him. And she would be expected to start the dancing in any event. At private balls, the highest-ranking lady led the dancing. At Grace-by-the-Sea, the spa hostess ranked highest, if only on assembly night.

"I'd be delighted," she assured him.

The string quartet began playing exactly as she had requested, and she took his arm to join the others for the first dance. It was the same set of dances each time; she merely had the quartet vary the order. She'd had complaints from time to time that she was no innovator, but it was easier for their guests to join in when they knew what to expect.

Mr. Howland surely knew what to expect, yet he danced stiffly, head up, shoulders back, as if marching to the beat of a military tattoo. She wasn't sure what to say to him when it came time for them to stand out at the bottom of the set.

"And how are your latest Newcomers faring?" he asked. "Any particularly challenging?"

Lark came immediately to mine, but she hardly wanted to confide her conflicting feelings to the magistrate. "They all seem to be finding friends among our Regulars."

"And what of this Denby fellow?" he pressed. "Miss Archer and Mr. Carroll have remarked that he asks a great number of questions. What is he trying to accomplish? Who is he trying to implicate?"

"Implicate?" She stared at him. "Do you suspect one of my guests of a crime, Magistrate?"

"Not your guests," he hedged, but he took her arm to lead her back into the dance.

The figures required their attention, and she did not have an opportunity to question him further before the set ended. Then she latched her arm onto his.

"What could Mr. Denby have done to raise your concerns, Mr. Howland?" she asked.

He smiled, but it did not reach his eyes. She turned to see who he was intent on greeting, only to find Lark approaching.

He was as well dressed as Lord Featherstone, if as dark as Mr. Howland. Yet the black coat only brought out the reddish threads of his golden-brown hair and made his brown eyes darker, more mysterious. He bowed to them both.

"Miss Chance, Mr. Howland, a pleasure to see you here."

As if she'd be anywhere else.

"Denby," Mr. Howland said. But he did not go so far as to question Lark.

Oh, why did gentlemen have to be so circumspect all the time? The trait was particularly vexing when she was attempting to arrange a match. So was a lady's reticence. Sometimes she just wanted everyone to speak the truth and get on with things.

"I believe you wanted to talk to Mr. Denby, Magistrate," she said.

Either Lark did not wish to speak to Mr. Howland, or he missed her pointed hint, for he turned to her. "I was hoping to offer myself as your next partner, if you haven't already promised the dance to another."

She looked to the magistrate. He merely nodded. Oh! Must she arrange everything?

She transferred her hand from Mr. Howland's arm to Lark's, only to find a similar tension there. "I'd be delighted, sir."

He hadn't planned to ask her to dance. It seemed wrong to be enjoying himself when others were hunkered down

in their villages, fearing the French might invade at any moment. He'd come to the assembly mainly because he'd wondered whether his quarry might attend, a forlorn hope at best. But he'd spotted the usual group from the spa—Lord Featherstone, the General, the Admiral, the Misses Montgomery, Mr. Crabapple, Mrs. Cole and her daughter, and Mrs. Harding. He'd also recognized the Greers and Miss Archer. He had considered leaving, until he'd seen Howland and Jess together.

And then the blue walls of the elegant assembly rooms had turned rather green.

Ridiculous feeling. He and Jess were not courting. They had been slightly more than friends eight years ago, and he wasn't sure what they were now. But he could not deny the sense of purpose that came over him as Jess placed her hand in his keeping. Indeed, it was with a triumph as profound as if he had defeated Napoleon himself that he led her out onto the floor.

He'd forgotten how light she was on her feet. She skipped through the steps of a country dance, her gloved hands lifting her lilac-colored skirts. The twinkle was back in her blue eyes, as if she encouraged him to smile along with her. He was almost disappointed when it came their turn to stand out.

"Are you enjoying our little assembly, sir?" she asked.

He almost asked her to call him Lark again, but he stopped himself. Such a request implied continued association, and he could not promise beyond tomorrow. "A fine showing," he told her.

She watched the couple threading their way toward them. "Particularly fine tonight. Mr. Howland does not always grace us with his presence."

Interesting. "Odd that a prominent fellow like the magistrate would avoid Society," he commented. "Why do you think he came tonight?"

Her sweet smile held just a hint of an edge. "I have no idea, but he seemed as interested in talking about you as you are about him. What have you done, sir?"

Lark pressed a hand to his black satin-striped waistcoat. "Me? I scarcely know the man."

"Perhaps."

He was only glad the dance prevented private conversation for the remainder of the set. He was prepared to spin a tale if needed as he escorted her from the floor, but she excused herself to see about supper.

He ought to see to his duties as well. Howland had been questioning Jess about him, it seemed. Why? The magistrate was the only one who knew the true reason for his visit. If he had questions, he could ask Lark. Yet, as Lark looked around, he could not spot the fellow. It seemed Howland had danced with Jess and left.

Her aunt sidled up to him just then. "Dark of the moon tonight. You should be headed for France."

Not again. "I am not a French spy, madam," he reminded her.

She nodded sagely. "Smuggler, then. I thought I caught the scent of brine. The tide won't turn until near dawn, worst luck."

Lark frowned, pulled into the story despite himself. "Why should I care when low tide falls?"

She cuffed him on the shoulder. "How else are you to sail into the caves?"

He certainly needed to sail somewhere at the moment, for he felt all at sea. "Caves?"

"The caves, the caves," she scolded, obviously exasperated with him. "Under the headland, below Castle How. My goodness, but you must be terrible at your craft. Small wonder you must work as an equerry to pay your bills. You will never amount to anything unless you apply yourself, sir."

"So it appears," he said. She started past him, and he shifted to block her way. "Tell me, Mrs. Tully, are there other smugglers using those caves? I wouldn't want to run into competition."

"Smugglers have used those caves for centuries," she informed him, as if she'd lived to see it. "More than one drowned attempting it. See that you do better." Head high, she embarked for the supper room.

Could he believe her story any more than the tale she'd spun about sighting Napoleon on the headland? Who could he ask to confirm it? Surely not the magistrate. If the caves lay beneath Castle How, Howland might not want to admit it. Few of the others he'd met would be in a position to know the local legends.

Except Jess.

The air in the assembly rooms smelled sweeter, as if a cool breeze had blown in from a newly mowed field. He might have a clue at last. He had only to speak to her about it.

He kept an eye out for an opportunity through supper and the last set of the night. But she was a butterfly, impossible to catch, flitting here and there, making sure everything was going smoothly and everyone was happy.

Who made sure she was happy? Aside from him and Mr. Howland, no one had asked her to dance. She'd spent a few moments with Miss Archer, the painter, but all other conversations had been fleeting. No one singled her out for attention. Surrounded by acquaintances, she seemed all alone.

He shrugged off the feeling. She had a purpose, prosperity, the respect of nearly everyone in the village. Who was he to pity her?

Except, why hadn't she wed? Surely the village held some eligible bachelors. There were even one or two in Upper Grace, from the letters his sisters sent. Howland was of an

age to marry. Had none of them noticed the gem managing the spa? Or, because of the death of her father, had they all assumed she was beneath them? His fists bunched just thinking of it.

Perhaps that was why he made sure to be waiting at the door when she ushered out the last attendee. An older man, coat sleeve pinned to his side where he'd lost an arm, was escorting a group down the hill under the light of an ornate lamp held high on the pole he carried. A young man was lowering the crystal chandelier, very likely to snuff out the lights. Her aunt came toward them, eyes bright. She'd darted from group to group all night, and she still walked with a lilt in her step.

He turned to Jess. Her aspect was nearly as bright as her aunt's. Tenacity must run in the family.

"Might I have the honor of walking you home?" he asked.

Lightning flashed in her eyes a moment before she dropped her gaze, and he wondered how he had finally incurred her wrath.

"No need, Mr. Denby," she said.

Why had she put a wall between them? He could feel it looming up, shutting him out.

"Well, I'll accept your offer," Mrs. Tully said, latching onto his arm. "Perhaps you might keep a bit of lace for me, or do you deal in spirits?"

Jess followed them out the door, leaving her caterer to the cleaning. "Mr. Denby isn't a merchant, Aunt."

"I know that," Mrs. Tully threw over her shoulder. "He's a smuggler. I'm simply trying to determine what sort."

"He isn't a smuggler either." Jess came up beside him with an apologetic smile and detached her aunt's grip from his arm. "Forgive us, sir. We won't detain you further."

Perhaps it was the late hour, perhaps her aunt's folly, perhaps his frustration or desperation that forced the words

from his mouth.

"*Are* there smugglers in Grace-by-the-Sea?"

Her pink lips tightened. "Certainly not. We have been fortunate to escape that blight. Now, goodnight, sir." She took her aunt's arm and marched for the cove.

With a sigh, Lark watched the glow of the lamp carrier's lantern fade down the hill. As darkness gathered closer, stars popped into view, twinkling. One burned brighter, and it was a moment before he realized what he was seeing.

High on the headland, where Castle How stood guardian, a light flickered. Had the mighty Howlands returned at last?

Or was someone else bent on using their grounds, perhaps illegally, despite Jess's assertion? Is that why Howland had disappeared from the assembly early, to light the lamp that would guide smugglers to Grace-by-the-Sea?

CHAPTER EIGHT

"**Y**OU MUST LEAVE MR. DENBY alone," Jess told her aunt as they hurried down the hill. Her feet protested. She loved the excitement of the assemblies, but she was always tired afterward. It didn't help that Lark had asked to walk her home, as if he were a suitor. Did he simply not realize the ramifications? He had two sisters, one who had been married and widowed. Surely he knew how such a request would be viewed, by her and anyone else who noticed.

She was just thankful to reach the cottage, until she spotted Alex warming himself in front of the fire. Instead of the coat and breeches of a gentleman, he wore a rough wool jacket and striped trousers favored by the local fishermen.

"What are you doing?" Jess demanded.

He shifted, and water ran off his clothes to pool on the floor. "Some of us went swimming for fun."

Jess shook her head. "In the dead of night, in your clothes?"

He shrugged. "Too cold for bare skin."

"You need tea," Maudie declared, bustling for the sideboard and the tin kept there.

"I'm fine, Aunt," he protested, before lowering his head and his voice to Jess. "Check the tin before she does. I left you something." He straightened and set about pulling off

his things.

Jess went to intercept her aunt, taking the red-lacquered tin from Maudie before she could open it. "You must be tired, Aunt. Start for bed. I'll come help you undress shortly."

Likely it was the late hour that made Maudie nod and head for the bedchamber she shared with Jess. As soon as the door shut behind her, Jess pulled off the lid on the tea canister.

They were getting low on the dusky leaves. In the fire-light, she could see the flash of tin below. Something brighter glimmered on top. Reaching in two fingers, she drew out a gold coin.

She whirled toward the hearth. "Where did you get this?"

But her brother had already climbed the ladder to the loft, leaving the jacket and trousers behind. The wool steamed by the fire as water puddled around them on the floor.

She set the tin aside and went to the foot of the ladder to peer up into the darkness. "Alex?"

"Sorry, Jess," he called down. "I'm worn. We can talk in the morning."

No point demanding answers now. Even if he responded, she'd only bring Maudie into it. She didn't need to hear more of her aunt's dark fancies. Hers were dark enough at the moment.

Jess rose early in the morning, but Alex was already gone. Once again she climbed the ladder to confirm as much. She walked to the spa with Maudie, feeling as if her legs had weights on them. She couldn't help remembering

Lark's question last night, flung at her with desperation on its wings. But smugglers? Here? Grace Cove was small. Surely someone would have noticed strange vessels coming in. And why did Lark care? He could not wish to consort with smugglers! Nor could he be the French spy her aunt named him.

Could he?

As if ready for her questions, he was waiting for her at the spa door. His blue coat was neat, his cravat simply tied, but that look of determination was back in his eyes. She thought hers might be just as determined as she inserted the key in the lock.

"Early again," she commented.

"Perhaps I'm just eager for the company," he said, pushing the door open for her and her aunt to enter. "And good morning to you too, Mrs. Tully."

"Did you bring me something from your haul last night?" Maudie asked.

He followed them as Jess headed for the desk. "Alas, my only haul was in dreams, and none interesting enough to relate."

Maudie sucked her cheeks a moment, then nodded. "You will have better luck tonight. I saw the light."

Lark went still. "Light?"

"In the castle window." She leaned closer and hissed, "It's a sign."

Jess was so out of countenance today she could not appreciate Maudie's whimsy. "Perhaps you could check on the glasses, Aunt," she suggested. "I'll start the impeller. You would likely enjoy seeing the mechanism, Mr. Denby. Gentlemen find it fascinating."

He looked every bit as eager, but somehow she didn't think it was because of the fountain's inner workings. His question proved as much as he followed her to the stone basin.

"Did you see the light too?" he asked.

"Alas, no," she told him. "Did you?"

She was sure he would deny it, but he nodded. "I did indeed. Someone lit a candle in Castle How. Have the Howlands come to visit, perhaps?"

"Doubtful." She pointed to the lever sticking out below the lip of the fountain before bending to pull on it. "This is connected to a pump designed after ones created in Rome. It uses water pressure to push the water up from the springs below the spa into the fountain."

"Are you sure?" he asked, leaning closer.

Jess frowned at him. "Certainly I'm sure. I've crawled down into the inner workings with my father."

"Not about the impeller," he said as the mechanism woke up and began its low ticks and clanks that heralded the arrival of the water from the spring. "The light."

Jess straightened. "The Howlands haven't visited since I was a child. The castle is shut up. Mr. Howland inspects it from time to time, but certainly not in the middle of the night."

"And the caves below the headland? Are they closed as well?"

She hadn't thought about the caves in years. How did he even know about them?

"Not to my knowledge," she allowed. "But they might as well be. You need a narrow boat with a shallow bottom to enter from the sea and as the tide is turning. And you'd have to know the channel well. Otherwise, you'd wreck on the rocks near the entrance."

"Who knows the route so well?"

She felt as if his words pressed her against the unyielding stone of the fountain. "Most of us who were raised in Grace-by-the-Sea," she told him over the splash of water bubbling out of the fountain's mouth. "It's something of an honor to be able to say you sailed in and out unscathed.

But that has nothing to do with the light in the castle."

"Doesn't it?" he challenged.

Jess raised her head. "No. No one would be foolish enough to sail those waters after dark. And the passage from the caves up into the castle has been locked for decades."

He eyed her. "All I know is that a light was shining like a beacon from Castle How last night. There must be a reason."

A reason she feared to discover in front of him. Could Alex have tried to sail into the caves and overturned the boat? Was that why he was soaked? Better that he was trying to prove himself a man than that he was in league with smugglers. Yet, where had he earned that gold?

"If there was a light, it is none of our affair," she told Lark. "The waters should be at full strength in a few moments. May I offer you a glass?"

"No, thank you." He turned and strode away.

Jess pressed her hands against the cool stone to keep them from shaking. She had no idea why he cared, and he clearly cared more than someone looking for gossip. No, Lark was looking for a smuggler, and she feared he may have found it, in her brother.

James Howland stood gazing out the window of his study toward the castle his ancestors had built. His great-grandfather had been earl, but James' line descended through a number of second sons until there could be no thought of inheritance, only service. His was the key to the castle, the right to inspect quarterly. He hadn't been inside since the storm in March.

But someone had. Priestly, his secretary, had reported seeing a light last night. James would be up there inves-

tigating now if not for the appointment he had early this morning.

Jaw working as he tried to stifle a yawn, Priestly showed the fellow in now. The timing of the assembly had been arranged with an eye toward keeping their guests entertained. Heaven help the person who had responsibilities the next morning. James wouldn't have attended except he'd had an itch to learn how Larkin Denby fared. Nearly a week now, and he was still in Grace-by-the-Sea. What did the fellow hope to prove?

"Major Stiverson, sir," his secretary said.

James turned from the view and his thoughts. "Thank you, Priestly. That will be all."

His secretary left, shutting the door behind him.

James studied the major. Rugged face, with a hint of a scar along one sharp cheek. Lank brown hair held back in a queue. But that red uniform gave him an authority. Or maybe it was the glint in his green eyes.

"Major Stiverson," he said to James, voice hinting of a land farther north. "Recruiting Agent for the King."

James gave him a brief smile. "I heard you were in my district, Major. I'm afraid you've wasted your time. We have men serving as Sea Fencibles to protect the coast from invasion, but we have no young men capable of fighting in the king's army."

The officer went to take a seat in front of the desk as if making himself at home. "Pity. But perhaps I might be of service to you."

James crossed to the desk. "How?"

Stiverson leaned back. "By passing along a warning. His Majesty's Army isn't the only one looking to recruit. There's word of a press gang making its way along the coast. You might tell your young men they'll get a fairer deal from me."

A press gang. He'd heard of the bullies forcing men to

serve in the navy in bigger towns with wide harbors. Portsmouth. Poole. Weymouth. But here, in Grace-by-the-Sea?

"I'll alert the village," he told the recruiter. "But I can't promise anyone will volunteer to take the king's shilling."

"If they volunteer, there's a reward for you," Stiverson reminded him. "If we don't get them to volunteer, we'll have to forcibly conscript them. You know the law. If enough men between the ages of seventeen and thirty, without young children, volunteer, you spare yourself the ballot."

"And if they don't, you can use that ballot to draft any man from seventeen to fifty-five into the regular army to fight the king's wars," James finished. "Our farmers and tradesmen would die in the first battle."

Stiverson spread his hands. "There's an easy solution. Raise a volunteer corps here in Grace-by-the-Sea."

There it was. He was a Howland, a leader born and bred. Of course he must champion his people. Indeed, as the highest-ranking permanent resident in the area, he was the only one who could. A shame his family had ordered it otherwise.

Your work on my behalf is entirely too necessary, the earl had written. *It would be inconvenient for you to be out leading wastrels who had nothing better to do anyway. Never fret. I will make the arrangements with the government. You will not be troubled further.*

He did not doubt the Earl of Howland could arrange anything he liked, regardless of what James liked. He had a hostage, after all. James' mother resided with the earl, companion to the countess. People spoke of the earl's benevolence, his kindness to support a poor widow. None of them knew that she was surety against any rebellion. If James did not comply with every request, each edict, the earl's favor would be withdrawn, their lives made miserable. The Earl of Howland had made that patently clear.

James met the officer's gaze. "I regret, Major, that leading a volunteer corps isn't an option."

"Then you leave me no choice." Stiverson reached inside his coat and drew out a piece of parchment, offering it to James. "This is an order from the Home Secretary. You're to compile a list of all able-bodied men between the ages of seventeen and fifty-five."

James took the paper and tossed it onto his desk. "When I have the time."

Stiverson shook his head as he rose. "Do yourself a favor. Complete the list yourself. If I compile it, I may end up listing those you'd prefer to leave off."

James eyed him. "I am a magistrate and a Howland, Major Stiverson. Neither disposes me to take threats well."

The recruiter bowed. "Meaning no disrespect, sir. I'll be back this way in a sennight." He turned and left.

James squeezed two fingers to the bridge of his nose, where a headache was building. Castle How wasn't the only thing under attack, it seemed. How could he protect his neighbors, his friends? He could not look Mr. Carroll in the face, knowing he'd put the man's name on the list. The savvy shopkeeper would never have lifted a gun to kill, even if his life depended on it. And Alexander Chance, just barely a man? And Quillan St. Claire...

He dropped his hand. His old friend would have to wait. First he must discover who was using the castle and why, and all while keeping Larkin Denby away from the truth. Only then could he determine how to keep the villagers of Grace-by-the-Sea from going to war.

The spa was quieter that day. A shame, for Lark could not quiet his thoughts. Most of its denizens were recover-

ing from the exertions of the night before. Mrs. Cole and her daughter talked in hushed tones. Lord Featherstone avoided the chessboard as if fearing he'd disgrace himself. Only Mr. Crabapple and Mrs. Harding remained oblivious to the tension, sitting in each other's pocket at one of the tables and murmuring low.

The peace roared at Lark like waves pounding the sand. So close, so close! His conversation with Jess had only made him more eager to search the castle.

And find the caves.

She was busy at the welcome desk. Two more guests had arrived. Another mother and daughter, it appeared, by the similarities in the women's patrician faces and crimped brown hair. This time, the daughter was older than Lark, the mother beyond Mrs. Tully's years and leaning heavily on her daughter's arm. Jess straightened as he approached.

"Mrs. Barlow, Miss Barlow, you must meet Mr. Denby, another recent visitor to our fair shores."

Lark inclined his head. The mother managed a smile, but even that little effort seemed to pain her. The daughter spoke for them both.

"Mr. Denby. How refreshing to find a gentleman. By the article in the Upper Grace newspaper this morning, we assumed all men had enlisted in the militia and were off training."

"We must be prepared for invasion," her mother added. "I told Susan that when she insisted on coming. Too close to the Channel."

Her daughter patted her arm. "But the physician said you would benefit from the waters, Mother. And it is so nice to be out in company again."

"Napoleon will never land near Grace-by-the-Sea," Jess put in brightly. "Not while men of Mr. Denby's character protect us."

He refused to preen at her praise. Besides, he wasn't being

much of a deterrent to Napoleon's plans when he could not find one dangerous smuggler. "And where might these lovely ladies reside?" he asked.

Surrey, as it turned out. He made polite conversation, feeling as if he could hear the great bronze clock across the room, ticking away the moments. Finally, Miss Barlow led her mother off, leaving Jess alone. Lark watched as she began rearranging the pamphlets on the desk.

"Can you be certain there are no smugglers in Grace-by-the-Sea?" he asked.

Her head snapped up. "Why are you so insistent, sir?"

Lark held up his hand. "Forgive me. I have no wish to quarrel with you, Jesslyn."

She hissed. "I did not give you leave to use my first name."

She had, once. That time was clearly over. He bowed. "Forgive me. I can see that Grace-by-the-Sea remains a bucolic, peaceful place. But someone is using it, most cruelly if I am correct. I only seek to right that wrong."

"There is no wrong!" She threw up her hands, and the pamphlets fluttered in protest. "There are no conspiracies here, no danger. I wish you would simply accept that."

The spa door banged open, and Miss Archer hurried in. Her fashionable feathered bonnet was askew, reddish curls peeking out as if attempting to escape. She clutched the welcome desk with her gloved fingers, green skirts settling about her trembling frame.

"Jesslyn," she breathed as if Lark wasn't there. "I just heard, and I had to come warn you. They are plotting against you!"

CHAPTER NINE

WHAT! JESS COULD NOT SEEM to grasp her friend's words, but she knew where her duty lay: defending the spa. She reached out to take her friend's hand. "Slow down, Abby. Mr. Denby will think something terrible has happened."

It was a warning as much as comfort. Lark already saw smugglers around every corner. Jess hardly wanted to fuel that obsession. And surely no one in the village would attempt to do her any lasting harm, Mrs. Greer's interference aside.

Abby blinked her green eyes, glanced at Lark as if noting his presence for the first time, and then turned resolutely to Jess.

"But something terrible *has* happened. I knew it the moment I ventured into the emergency council meeting and you were not there."

Jess withdrew her hand. "An emergency meeting? I was given no word."

Her aunt must have noticed their conversation, for she hurried over to join them. "What meeting?" she asked, glancing among them.

"The council met early this morning," Abigail explained. "I thought at first Jesslyn must be unable to tear herself away from the spa, but I was soon disabused of that notion.

They scheduled the meeting so that they could discuss the spa without you. Jess, I fear they mean to replace the two of you."

Maudie gasped, clutching her chest. The floor tilted like a ship on the wave beneath Jess, and she lay her hand on the Welcome Book to steady herself. As if he'd seen the change in her, Lark stepped protectively closer.

"I was not informed that my performance was lacking," she told her friend. At least, they hadn't said so in so many words. Mrs. Greer was never pleasant, with anyone.

"It isn't you," Abigail said. "They want a new physician to take charge, a man." She spat out the last word and looked to Lark, as if it were somehow his fault.

"A man," Maudie echoed, eyes narrowing. "Well, I suppose it's better than being replaced by a mermaid."

Jess drew in a breath. "We have needed a physician for some time. But any worth his salt will want to spend his time examining patients, prescribing cures. He won't want to attend to the little details of running the spa."

Maudie nodded sagely, hand dropping.

"But you can be sure he'll tell you how to do it," Abigail insisted.

Jess's father had accepted her suggestions about the running of the spa, but she understood why her friend was wary. Abby's father had been a domineering sort. A retired military man, he'd brought his family to live at Grace-by-the-Sea for the quiet. Until the day he'd died three years ago, he'd never understood his daughter's love of painting or her ambition to pursue it as a profession. Her mother was a cowed little woman who tended to jump at the least noise. Because of Abby's talent and tenacity in pursuing her dream, she could support her mother now.

"It might not be so bad," Jess temporized. "I'm certain we could work something out."

Abigail shook her head, ginger hair catching the light. "I

urged them to consult you on the matter, but they refused to consider it. They fear you will be prejudiced, because of your father. You will want a man like him, or none at all."

She might indeed. Her father had set a noble standard for what to expect from a physician. He had been calm, considerate, compassionate. He'd listened to any complaint, from the spurious to the serious. He'd prescribed remedies where he could, dealt out kindness where he couldn't. She'd never understand how he could have succumbed from a bout of pneumonia one of his patients had brought to his door. He'd seemed so healthy, so vibrant.

So needed.

"There is no man like my brother," Maudie said, nose in the air. "We won't stand for his memory to be tarnished by a Newcomer. We'll stage a revolution. Down with tyrants!" She thrust her fist into the air.

Jess caught it and tugged her arm down. "Hush, Aunt. This isn't France. And we have no right to dictate the running of the spa."

"I disagree." It was the first Lark had spoken in the conversation, and his tone was firm. "You know more about the running of this spa than anyone. Failing to consult you about a change is a grave oversight. I will tell Mr. Greer so myself."

Hope surged up, then promptly fell. The Greers would never listen to the word of a guest, not unless he came with a title and funds to support it.

"Thank you," she told him. "I will speak to Mr. Greer and the other members of the Corporation myself." She looked to her friend. "I appreciate you coming to tell me, Abby. At least I am warned."

"Forewarned is forearmed," she agreed. "Just know there are many behind you. This village was built by a Chance; this spa exists because of a Chance. It makes no sense to drive out the last of the Chances."

The last of the Chances. A shiver went through her. God willing, there would be many more Chances at Grace-by-the-Sea, for generations to come, if she could convince her brother of the folly of his ways before something terrible truly did happen.

Were they all blind? Lark shifted on his feet, fighting the urge to march down to the apothecary shop and tell Greer he was a fool. He had dealt with a few physicians in his life. After his father's death, his mother had had heart palpitations that did not ease as time went by, even with the move to Upper Grace and her brother's household. Learned men of medicine in Kent and Dorset had examined her, prescribed remedies that either left her sleeping much of the day or walking about in a daze. He'd been a youth, then, someone none of the physicians had deemed savvy enough to comment on much less complain about the treatment she was receiving.

Jess's father had been the one light of hope. He'd talked with Lark's mother, advised a change in diet and walks on the Downs after they'd left the spa. The time away, in such a caring atmosphere, had done wonders. Could there be another physician so kind, so reasonable?

Certainly not one who could devote himself the way Jess did to making every guest happy. What better welcoming presence than a pretty, sweet, intelligent young woman? He'd seen Jess put each guest at ease, from military men with bristling mustaches to girls on their first Season. A physician, no matter how well schooled, would be hard-pressed to fill the role.

"I should return to the gallery," Miss Archer was saying now. "Just know you have my friendship and admiration,

as always." She gave Jess's arm a squeeze before she hurried toward the door.

Mrs. Tully hitched up her black gown by the shoulders. "So, it's war."

Jess shook herself. "It is not war, Aunt. I will speak to Mr. Greer at the first opportunity. For now, we have duties to perform. We will continue to perform them to the best of our ability until we are told otherwise."

"Bah!" Her aunt stalked off toward the fountain.

Lark refused to move from Jess's side.

"The shopkeepers and the tradesmen aren't the only ones behind you," he told her. "I'm sure I speak for all your guests when I say it is impossible to think of this spa without you in it."

The smallest of smiles brightened her lips. "Thank you. Now, if you'll excuse me, I should see to my responsibilities."

He wanted that smile to grow. "Always water to be poured," he teased.

It inched wider. "Water to be poured, guests to entertain, receipts to be cataloged, arrangements made."

He leaned closer. "And what weighty arrangements are you managing now?"

Her brow wiggled as she dropped her voice conspiratorially. "The Midsummer Masquerade."

"Ah, a masquerade. And how will you dress?"

She tapped his fingers. "Fah, sir, I cannot tell you that. It must remain a mystery. The gentlemen and ladies must guess each other's identity. It's part of the fun."

Somehow, he thought he'd recognize her whatever she wore. Her smile, those sparkling eyes would be difficult to hide. And he would have given a great deal to hear her laugh, to take her hands and whirl her in the dance.

But midsummer's night was more than three weeks away. Surely his supervisor would protest if Lark hadn't discov-

ered the Lord of the Smugglers before then.

Which brought him back to his purpose. "The Midsummer Masquerade sounds delightful. But I'm interested in another sort of entertainment in the meantime. I'd like to go sailing. Can you recommend a captain who would take me, for a fair price, of course?"

She cocked her head. "Perhaps my brother. He maintains my father's ketch in the cove. And he could use a reminder that there are gainful ways of making an income."

Interesting. Was her brother given to less gainful ways of earning a living? Smuggling, perhaps? No, surely not a Chance.

"Sounds like the perfect choice," Lark acknowledged. "Would he be available today?"

"The tide's coming in," she said. "That's a difficult time to leave the cove."

Or enter the caves, from what he'd gleaned. "Then perhaps at the change in the tide," he said.

She stiffened. "I see your plan, sir. You're still fixed on those caves below Castle How. No one will take you there. It isn't safe."

"It's safe for some," he insisted.

"You're thinking about that light," she accused him.

Lark shrugged. "Someone put it in the window."

Her nose wrinkled, making her look years younger. "And why should you care if they did?"

Best to dance around that. "It's a mystery, like your masquerade. Think how much fun it would be to solve."

"Fun? You have no concept of the dangers of sailing into those waters. The area is called the Dragon's Maw for good reason."

What, had her aunt named the spot? "The Dragon's Maw?"

She thrust up two fingers. "For the rocks that guard the entrance. And the waves pounding the cliff give off a sort

of roar. Besides, only Mr. Howland could give you permission. The caves are on his family's property."

A fact that gave him pause even now. "And does every youth in Grace-by-the-Sea get permission from the magistrate to sail into the caves?"

"Well, no," she admitted, reluctance lacing each word. "But I would not feel comfortable recommending anyone to take you unless Mr. Howland approved the visit."

Frustration made him shift on his feet. "I had hoped not to trouble the magistrate."

Her chin came up. "I'm afraid I must insist. If you are determined to know the source of that light, you have no reason to visit those caves, sir. You need only tour the castle."

Her face was set; her eyes snapped fire. And the color that had fled when Miss Archer had brought the news of the council's plans was returning in force.

"Let us approach this logically," she said in a surprisingly calm voice. "You wish to discover the source of that light in Castle How. I'd like to keep my guests entertained. What if *I* approach Mr. Howland? If he saw this light in the window last night, he must be curious as to how it came about."

Or he may well know how it had come about, but Lark couldn't share his thoughts aloud, not until he had some sort of proof.

"We can accompany him on his inspection," she continued, tapping her chin with one finger. "He can let us into the castle. That way, we are not at the mercy of the tides and can go whenever it is convenient for him."

What was convenient for Magistrate Howland could well be convenient for the smugglers too. But then, it was doubtful they could erase all evidence of their passage. What Lark needed was sufficient proof to bring to Commissioner Franklin in Weymouth. With his approval,

dragoons would ride, and ships would sail. This Lord of the Smugglers could find a revenue cutter waiting off the headland on his next trip.

"Very well," Lark said. "Ask Mr. Howland. If he agrees, we can join him on a tour of the castle and see what we can discover." And if he refused, that alone might be telling.

CHAPTER TEN

JESS WAS MORE THAN A little surprised when her politely worded note to Mr. Howland was met with an equally polite response agreeing to take her and Lark up to the castle that very afternoon. That gave Jess just enough time to slip down to the village and speak with Mr. Greer. Having made sure all her guests—Regulars, Irregulars, and Newcomers—were safely busy, she put on her bonnet and hurried down the street for the apothecary's shop.

Mr. Greer was tall and gaunt. His hair had slowly receded, like an outgoing tide, until only sandy fringes remained hugging his ears. He walked with his head thrust forward, his hands clasped behind his back, as if he were pondering weighty matters. Perhaps that was the reason he'd been elected president of the Spa Corporation five years running. Every family in the village had a share in the profits from the spa, and any person above the age of five and twenty who had paid his or her tithes to St. Andrew's and taxes to the Crown was eligible to be nominated for the board. Board members were elected yearly, at harvest time. Her father had attended each meeting, advised and recommended each action. Now she attended the meetings, though her recommendations were not always heeded.

Mr. Greer was just handing Mrs. Bent a cone of brown paper as Jess entered the shop.

"One a day, no more," he told the wife of the employment agent. "And no sharing with others."

"But kitty is so fond of it," she protested.

He looked down his long nose at her, and she sighed, clutching the paper closer. "Oh, very well." Turning, she sighted Jess and smiled. "Good afternoon, Miss Chance. I trust everything is going splendidly at the spa."

"As usual," Jess assured her. "And how is kitty getting along?"

She shot the apothecary a look. "She has aches and pains, as would anyone her age. Not everyone understands." With a nod to Jess, she sailed from the shop.

"Are you unwell, Miss Chance?" Mr. Greer asked, long face settling into concern.

Jess stepped up to the tall wooden counter. His lean body was framed by the blue and green bottles on the shelves behind him. "I am physically sound," she told him, "but a bit distressed by a rumor that came my way. Have I failed to give good service as hostess?"

He busied himself with wiping out a clear glass jar, long fingers flexing on the rag. "I have never had any complaints about your service, Miss Chance. Yet the spa continues to lose patronage since your father passed."

"We have had fewer visitors this year than last," Jess acknowledged, trying to see up under his gaze. "But that could be the fault of this war and the stories of invasion."

He pulled out the rag and squinted into the jar, as if he could spot the last trace of a stain. "We on the Spa Corporation Council believe it has more to do with our lack of a physician. We have sent out a request to the College of Surgeons in London to see if anyone might want to relocate to Grace-by-the-Sea."

Jess hid her shudder. "A surgeon? An anatomist? Why would the spa need one of those?"

"We need a gentleman of learning," Mr. Greer insisted.

"We have had no luck with the medical college in Edinburgh or with writing to physicians elsewhere in Dorset. No one wants to move closer to the coast right now, particularly when they might be conscripted into the army."

"But whoever you attract will not wish to manage the day-to-day operations of the spa," Jess protested. "Can you see a surgeon filling cups from the fountain?"

"Perhaps our guests can fill their own cups," Mr. Greer hedged. "The fact of the matter is that the spa is losing money, and we must find some way to staunch the bleeding. For now, carry on as you have. We can discuss your position further when we know a physician is coming."

And what could she say to that? She thanked him for his time, trudged back up the hill, and put on her smile for her guests.

"May I have your attention?" she called. Though her voice had never been strident, it nonetheless had the effect of halting every conversation as all gazes swung her way. "We have been granted a rare privilege—a tour of Castle How by the magistrate himself. The party leaves at a quarter past, and the spa will close to allow all to take part. Please gather your things and join us."

Lark regarded her. "We're taking all of them? Magistrate Howland may not be willing to allow so many in the house."

"I did not specify a number," she replied, smiling as Mrs. Cole and her daughter came up to them.

"Will the Howland family be in residence?" the mother asked hopefully.

"Is it true the castle is haunted?" the daughter asked with equal anticipation.

"Mr. James Howland will be leading the tour," Jess answered. "And I do not recall any stories of hauntings."

"I do," Maudie said, wandering closer. "The Hound of the Headland—great white beast with glowing red eyes.

And who can forget the Lady of the Tower, wailing on stormy nights for her love lost at sea."

Miss Cole sighed happily. Lark's sigh sounded of something else.

Mr. Howland raised his brow when he found them all assembled a short time later. Besides Lark, the Coles, and most of the Regulars, Miss Barlow had decided to join them. Her mother, the Admiral, and the general had chosen to retire to their rooms at the Swan. The Misses Montgomery had left for home that morning. Such was the way of the spa—some came for a few days, others a week or two, still others the entire summer. A rare few, like Lord Featherstone, remained the entire year. Economizing, in his case. Residing in Grace-by-the-Sea was far less expensive than living in London.

"I should have brought a carriage or three," the magistrate said now, glancing around as if counting heads.

"There was considerable interest in acquainting ourselves with the home of your illustrious family," Jess explained.

"Hound and all," Maudie agreed.

"I am honored," Mr. Howland said, though he looked more bemused to Jess.

It was a short walk from the spa across High Street and up Castle Walk onto the headland. Deer-cropped grass, emerald green on the sunny day, lay on either side of the white-graveled drive, with wildflowers clustered beyond. Ahead, Castle How stood erect and proud, a square block of lichen-darkened stone four stories high, with a rounded turret at each corner another story taller. If that had not been enough to make the Howland's hunting lodge appear a true castle, the narrow windows and crenelated roofline completed the picture. Easy to imagine gentlemen on fiery chargers jousting on the lawns to the cheers of their ladies.

Lord Featherstone seemed equally at home. He walked with Mrs. Cole and Miss Barlow, nodding to the castle and

pontificating on its provenance. His voice trickled back to Jess. "A fine example of gothic architecture."

Just behind him, Miss Cole was listening with wide eyes to Maudie's fancies.

"And then the hound pounced!" her aunt proclaimed.

Miss Cole would likely need a cup of warm milk to soothe her to sleep tonight.

Mr. Crabapple did not appear concerned. He had Mrs. Harding on his arm and a strut to his step, like a peacock who had discovered his tail.

That left Jess to walk with Lark. His head was also high, his gaze swinging over the landscape as they approached the castle.

"Perhaps you could show our guests around," he ventured, "while Howland and I look for the source of the light."

Was he still trying to deter her? "Oh, I'm sure my aunt would be delighted to do the honors," Jess told him. "She visited the house many times when she was young and remembers a number of tales."

"Of that, I'm sure," he muttered.

Jess patted his arm. "My aunt takes some getting used to. But she means no harm. I think sometimes she's simply trying to find an excuse to converse. It can be lonely at the spa in the winter months when few come to visit. Not everyone attends to the spa hostesses."

His gaze was thoughtful. "It must be lonely for you as well, then."

"On occasion," she admitted. "Oh, Mr. Carroll will always welcome me with a cup of tea and scones. And Miss Archer can be persuaded to stop her painting and visit. But everything changed when Father died, and I don't feel as if it's settled yet."

"Worried about the Corporation?" he asked, kicking a stone off the drive.

She should not confide in him, yet the urge was so strong she allowed herself the luxury. "Yes. We are dependent on my position at the spa for our income, the use of the cottage. I'm not sure what we'd do if all that went away."

He nodded, sunlight reflected in his tall black hat. "I remember what it was like when my father died. My mother moved us all to Upper Grace, and my uncle did his best to support us. Still, it was some years before I felt we were on stable ground."

"You should bring your mother and sisters to the spa," Jess suggested. "I'd be delighted to show them around again, introduce them to some charming gentlemen."

His smile inched up. "You're very good at that."

Her face felt warm, and she knew it wasn't the sun slipping under her bonnet. But she'd believed fine words and tender looks before, and she'd lived to regret it. "I greatly enjoy my position. There is something satisfying about making sure people have what they need to be healthy and happy. And what of you? Working all this time in Kent, I believe?"

"Yes," he said as the main entrance to the castle loomed up. Stone steps led to an arched entry surmounted by a circular window. "Though I come home from time to time to visit my mother and sisters, make sure their investments are providing for them."

And never once had come to see her. She shook off the disappointment. "Did you leave a wife waiting for your return?"

My, how polite she sounded, as if she didn't tremble to hear the answer.

He shook his head. "Alas, no. I have been too busy working to consider taking a bride."

First adventure, now work. Was he the sort of man who could not give his heart?

And why, oh why, was her heart still so eager to offer

itself to him?

She was a wonder. He had never met a woman so poised, so self-assured. Jesslyn knew what mattered to her—helping others. He could only commend that.

In front of them, James Howland climbed to the wide stone veranda that spanned the front of the house. Everyone gathered around, crowded close.

"Castle How," he said, glancing from face to face, "was built in 1610 and remodeled several times over the centuries."

"In 1698 and 1795," Mrs. Tully supplied, as if she'd seen both occasions.

He inclined his head in her direction. "Just so. Most of the furnishings are covered for protection against dust, but you will note the various architectural features as we go inside. I regret I cannot accompany you through every room, but Miss Chance—"

"Mrs. Tully," Jess corrected him sweetly.

He frowned and glanced at her aunt before continuing, "Mrs. Tully will lead you."

Her aunt stepped up beside him. Her head came only to his shoulder, but she somehow managed to loom over him, even in her black dress and bonnet.

"That's right," she declared. "And I cannot abide stragglers, so keep up. I should not want the Castle to take another life."

"It is quite safe, I assure you," Howland insisted.

"If you discount the moldering ramparts and the vermin-ridden moat," she agreed.

"There's a moat?" Miss Cole asked, glancing over the stone balustrade toward the clipped lawns they had crossed.

"If there was a moat, it has long since been filled in," Howland assured her.

"With the bones of their enemies," Mrs. Tully added.

"With good English soil," Howland snapped.

Jess took pity on him and stepped forward. "Mrs. Cole, Miss Cole, Mr. Crabapple, Mrs. Harding, and Miss Barlow, please follow my aunt. Lord Featherstone, I will count on your good escort."

The baron inclined his head graciously as Howland busied himself with unlocking the massive wood door.

"You rely on Lord Featherstone," Lark said to Jess as they followed Howland into the house. The fact should not bother him as much as it did. He certainly wasn't in a position to allow her to rely on him.

"He has proven a good friend over the years," she acknowledged, gaze going heavenward.

He looked up as well. They had entered the Great Hall, which stretched from the front door to the back of the castle. The ceiling was delicately veined in white, the walls carved with hunting scenes. Antlers stuck out here and there from wood mounts. Mounds of white cloth likely hid a long table and chairs. The white marble hearth, big enough to roast an ox, stood empty and bare.

"This must have been quite the place," he murmured, but his voice still echoed.

Howland arched a brow.

Mrs. Tully drew the others deeper into the Great Hall, already spinning tales of the wonders that had unfolded here. Howland started for the broad stairs on one side. Lark moved to intercept him.

"You must want to determine the source of the light the night of the assembly," he said.

Howland pulled up short. "What light?"

"I asked the same question," Jess said, joining them. "I did not see it, but both my aunt and Mr. Denby assure me

a light was shining in the window of the castle last night."

From the other side of the hall, Mrs. Tully's voice rose.

"And then the trolls besieged the castle."

Howland cocked his head and eyed Lark.

He would not allow the fellow to rattle him. "I know what I saw, Magistrate. Someone is using your castle."

Howland straightened. "I highly doubt it, but I would like to confirm the matter."

"So would we," Jess said with a polite smile. "For the good of the village and the spa, of course."

Left with little choice, the magistrate inclined his head and led them up the sweeping stairs for the chamber story. The upstairs corridor was marked by suits of armor dulled by dust. More dust puffed out to sparkle in the air as they walked along the thick blue carpet. Howland did not appear to notice. The windows were few enough that it wasn't easy for Lark to get his bearings. But the view out of the bedchamber to which the magistrate led them clearly showed the village, including the assembly rooms and the Mermaid. It could easily have been the source of the light. Yet, nothing seemed out of place. The big bed was draped in white cloth, speckled by grey dots of dust. No lamp stood on the side table or the tall dresser against one wall.

Howland frowned down at the windowsill, where drops of white marred the wood. Jess removed her glove to fleck off a piece with her finger and brought it to her nose for a sniff.

"Beeswax," she said. "Most families in the village use tallow, I imagine."

Howland nodded. "Most likely."

"A candle from the castle, then," Lark surmised.

"We had them all removed some time ago," Howland said. "Less opportunity of attracting mice. Whoever used that candle brought it in himself."

"Or herself," Jess replied. "Who cleans the castle quarterly for you?"

"I asked Mr. Bent's employment agency to supply the help," he allowed. "But whoever he assigns would generally come in during the day, with no need for a candle."

"True, but the person would also have a key that could allow access at other times," she said with a look to Lark.

Clever. She was right. But then, she often was.

Howland turned from the window. "Regardless, it appears you are correct, Mr. Denby. Someone unauthorized has been using Castle How. I will see to the matter."

And he was clearly supposed to be satisfied with that.

Jess appeared to be. "Thank you, Magistrate," she said, turning for the door. "I'm sure it's nothing but youthful high spirits, someone's idea of a prank. I appreciate you allowing Mr. Denby and me to have a look with you."

Lark put himself in Howland's path. "I cannot believe this is merely the work of pranksters."

Howland's mouth quirked. "If you have something to say about the matter, Mr. Denby, I suggest you consider what brought you to Grace-by-the-Sea."

Was that a warning not to give himself away? Jess was already glancing at him with a frown.

Lark squared his shoulders. In for a penny, in for a pound. "Forgive me, Magistrate, Miss Chance, but this could well be the work of someone in league with smugglers, lighting the way to a safe harbor. There's been word of a noted villain in this area—calling himself the Lord of the Smugglers. What better place for a lord to land than a castle?"

Jess's smile returned to its usual pleasant state. "Oh, if that's all, then we have nothing to worry about."

CHAPTER ELEVEN

L ARK WAS STARING AT HER. He couldn't know her
relief to hear there was a recognized band of smugglers
in the area. Surely Alex would never align himself with
people like that. This could have nothing to do with her
brother. All they need do was locate the villain, and everything would return to normal.

"I fear I must disagree," Mr. Howland said, crossing his
arms over his chest. "We cannot tolerate such crime. I will
not allow it on my property."

"I would not ask you to tolerate it," Jess assured him.
"Surely you can capture the fellow."

Lark had recovered. "We'll lay a trap here at the castle.
Meet them when they come in."

"We can certainly try," Mr. Howland allowed. "But word
will get out that we were here today. They may not return
to this spot."

Lark's face darkened, and she would not have been surprised to hear him grind his teeth.

"I can understand Mr. Howland's concern for lawful
behavior," she told Lark. "He is the steward of this castle
and a magistrate sworn to uphold the law. You called this
a mystery, yet you seem inordinately determined to solve
it. Why are you taking such an interest in local affairs, sir?"

The magistrate eyed him, head cocked, waiting, but the

smile hovering told her he knew the answer already. She sucked in a breath, narrowed her eyes at Lark.

Pink crept into his firm cheeks, as if he had been caught pouring his glass of spa water into a potted palm. But he straightened his spine and met her gaze.

"I am a Riding Officer, Miss Chance. I was sent to Grace-by-the-Sea to stop a smuggler."

Disappointment washed over her, stronger than the waves on the shore. He hadn't come for the spa or to reacquaint himself with their little village. He would never be a Regular or even an Irregular. Why did she persist in hoping otherwise?

"I see," she said. "And you thought to find this smuggler at my spa?"

Her words echoed in the room, sounding all the more accusatory with the repetition.

"I did," he confessed. "Or at least my superior believed the spa might be involved. The man leading this smuggling ring considers himself a gentleman. He may even pass for one in public. Where better to conceal himself than with other gentlemen at the spa?"

Exasperation sent her hands into the air. "Oh, certainly. We have any number of gentlemen, as you have noted. Perhaps the villain is Lord Featherstone. He's never sailed a day in his life unless it was as a passenger on a fancy yacht, but why consider such trivial matters? Or Mr. Crabapple. I'm sure the local fishermen would rally around him. No, no, the Admiral or the General, who could not accompany us today. I'm sure the Admiral's excuse that his corset is too tight to allow him to climb the headland is merely a ruse."

He ducked his head, but his abashed look did not ease her frustration. "I grant you there were more likely candidates elsewhere," he allowed.

"I quite agree," she said, lowering her hands. "The most likely fellow in Grace-by-the-Sea to be a smuggler is you."

He reared back, but Mr. Howland nodded, lower lip thrust out.

"She's right, you know," he said thoughtfully. "Strong man who knows something about sailing, highly interested in the cove and the local population."

"Sneaking about at night," Jess put in.

"Is he?" Mr. Howland tutted. "And we have only that letter to prove he is who he claims to be."

"Letter?" Jess asked, but Lark took a step back.

"Now, see here," he said, chin up once more and eyes flashing. "I am an agent of the king."

"Perhaps," Mr. Howland said. "But perhaps I should lock you up until I can write to Weymouth for confirmation."

"That is your right," he allowed, "but I hope you will reconsider. Time is of the essence if we're to catch these smugglers."

He was so intent on seeing justice done that it was hard to keep her temper hot. Already she could feel it cooling, like a boat stuck in calmed winds, sails hanging slack.

"I agree, Mr. Howland," she said. "Locking up Mr. Denby, however satisfying in the moment, would hardly serve the purpose of stopping the smugglers, if there truly are any in Grace-by-the-Sea. And he could not have put that light in the window last night. Though he arrived late, he was at the assembly until it closed, and the light apparently appeared around that time."

Lark drew a breath as Mr. Howland nodded again. "Very well. On Miss Chance's good report, I will refrain from confining you, Mr. Denby, for now. But I must ask. How are we to identify and stop these smugglers?"

And what would she do if the trail led to someone she cared about? Impossible! Unthinkable!

Lark opened his mouth to respond, but Jess spoke before he could. "I am certain it can be no one in Grace-by-the-Sea. Mr. Denby and I will investigate the area. We will

bring you a report within a week's time."

"*We* will not," Lark put in with a look to her. He turned to the magistrate. "However we decide to proceed, Miss Chance cannot be involved. It could be dangerous."

"It could be more dangerous without me," Jess protested. "You do not know our ways, our traditions, sir. Why, you suspected Lord Featherstone!"

"Not for long," he admitted.

Mr. Howland held up his free hand. "Miss Chance is right, Denby. You've been blundering around in the dark. Time to enlist the aid of someone who knows the area."

"Then let it be you," he said. "You can make some excuse for my presence. The fewer who know my true purpose, the more likely they'll be to answer our questions. And I refuse to endanger Miss Chance's reputation, her business, or her life."

He was so fervent on her behalf that she could not help but be touched. Not enough to back down, of course.

Mr. Howland was less moved. "I see no need to endanger her. You will go about in full daylight. Take Mrs. Tully with you if you feel you must have a chaperone. I will explain to the Spa Corporation that I have requested Miss Chance's and your help to confirm the returns we must submit to the lord-lieutenant for Dorset."

"Some suspect Mr. Denby of being an equerry," Jess told him, "so the excuse is plausible."

"Then your position will be protected until you feel the need to reveal it, Denby," Howland agreed. "And with you at Miss Chance's side, I'm sure she'll be safe."

Jess nodded. "You see, Mr. Denby? All perfectly logical. Now, we should return to the others. I'll develop a plan of action for you. We can discuss it at the spa first thing."

Maddening, the pair of them. He could understand Jess's desire to be involved—these were her people, this was her home, and she understood the dynamics better than anyone. But surely Howland could see the potential problems. Whoever had placed that light in the window had access to his family estate, was abetting the smugglers. That person would not take kindly to discovery.

Unless Howland thought Lark and Jess could not discover that person.

The thought remained on his mind as they descended the stairs for the great hall. Howland went first, with Jess behind and Lark in the rear. Over the musty scent of the castle, he became aware of a trace of lavender in the air. Was that what she used to wash her hair? Her high bun bounced with each step, and he had to fist his hands at his sides to prevent himself from reaching up to touch the silky strands that broke free.

He forced himself to consider the situation instead. Jess now knew his secret, so at least he no longer needed to posture with her. That fact brought an unexpected rush of relief. And Howland was giving them a reasonable story for their investigation, though he pitied anyone who truly thought he spent his time as a sycophant to the royal household.

Jess had intimated the sort of fellow they were looking for, and the magistrate had used the same metric. The Lord of the Smugglers could only be a strong, healthy man who knew something of sailing and could inspire the aid of the locals. Howland looked strong enough—he was of a height with Lark and had shoulders nearly as broad. Having lived all his life in Grace-by-the-Sea, he likely knew something about sailing, and who better to rally the locals than their own trusted magistrate? Besides, he had access to the castle and had left the assembly early, giving him

ample time to signal his cronies from the window.

Did all that mean that Lark's ally was in reality his enemy?

He watched the magistrate as they returned to the main rooms of the castle. Mrs. Tully must have led her group up the stairs as well, for he could hear her voice above them. "And then she threw him from the window."

Howland grimaced. "I never realized my family had led quite that colorful an existence."

Jess gave him a commiserating smile. "She means well. I'm sure you can correct any misperceptions."

He inclined his head. "You think more highly of my abilities than I do, Miss Chance." But he went to fetch Maudie and her group.

Jess wore a slight frown as they started back to the spa. Miss Cole was bubbling to her mother about a painting they'd seen and whether she might have a portrait of herself in a similar pose. Mrs. Harding and Mr. Crabapple were discussing the appropriate size and furnishings of a home. Mrs. Tully had her hand glued to Miss Barlow's arm, as if to prevent her from escaping further musings on the tragedies the castle must have seen. Mr. Howland and Lord Featherstone were deep in conversation at the head of the column.

"We should speak to the vicar first," Jess said.

"Beg pardon?" Lark asked as they turned for the path down to the village.

"Mr. Wingate," she explained, lifting her skirts to descend. "He interacts with everyone in the area and may have heard rumors. He also organizes our Sea Fencibles."

He knew the term. The navy was relying on a network of local boat owners to be the first in the line of defense between England and Napoleon's ships.

"I have the utmost respect for the trained, skilled sailors who make up the Sea Fencibles," Lark said. "But I doubt most would be taken as aristocrats."

"True, but one may be sufficiently full of himself to think to call himself a lord," Jess said. "Oh, and we should talk to Jack Hornswag as well. He runs the Mermaid, but everyone knows he escaped the navy. He's been ducking the press gang for years."

Hornswag held possibilities. The position of the inn near the shore and the ability to pass cargo to travelers headed inland would offer ample opportunities for a smuggler. Landlord, Lord of the Smugglers, perhaps?

"I thought no one in Grace-by-the-Sea could be involved," he told her.

She shuddered. "I don't like thinking of anyone in our village being involved. But someone lit that candle and placed it in the window of the castle." She glanced his way as they came around another turn in the switchback path. "And you're certain this Lord of the Smugglers sails from Grace Cove?"

"So Commissioner Franklin at Weymouth said."

She raised her chin. "Well, I do not recall anyone from the Excise Office visiting the spa before, so I doubt he could be much of an authority on Grace-by-the-Sea. And neither are you. You've been away too long."

Lark inclined his head. "Agreed. I look forward to learning what you advise, Miss Chance."

She sighed. "If we are going to work together, perhaps it would be best if we called each other by our first names. For the sake of efficiency, of course."

He'd wanted to use her first name since near the moment he'd met her again. He'd already slipped up once. Accepting her excuse was easy now.

"Of course," he agreed, admiring the pink in her cheeks as she glanced his way.

It was difficult to pretend the rest of the afternoon that nothing had changed. The spa guests chatted about their tour with the others who had rejoined them, exclaimed

over what they'd seen, the stories they'd heard. Yet the sound was oddly desultory after his agreement with Howland and Jess. He kept catching her eye as she went about her duties. She always returned a commiserating smile, as if to promise *soon*.

Lark found himself glancing around the common room at the Mermaid that evening, wondering which of the hearty fellows present might be secretly transporting goods from France. It was all he could do not to confront Jack Hornswag as he poured ale. A bear of a man as broad as he was tall, with a reddish beard that hung to the middle of his barrel of a chest, he joked with his customers and shouted commands to his serving staff. Rather merry fellow for a smuggler, but then, what said a smuggler had to be grim?

He had reached no conclusions by morning and was once again standing by the door of the spa when Jess and her aunt arrived.

As soon Jess opened the spa door, she pulled a piece of parchment from her reticule and held it out to him.

"You suspect Lord Peverell?" he asked, scanning the tasks she'd outlined.

"No, but using the Lodge is as logical a choice as putting a light in the castle window," she replied.

"Choice?" her aunt asked, standing on tiptoe to see over his arm at the list.

Lark lowered it to hold the ink against his buff trousers. "For a gentleman's gentleman."

She dropped down. "Ah, you're looking for a valet. Who's the lady?"

Lark managed a smile. "I strongly believe a gentleman owes it to himself to present himself well, regardless of whether he's courting."

She snorted. "Not every mermaid would agree."

"Aunt," Jess said, "would you check the glasses? I'm not sure Mr. Inchley brought us a clean set."

With a nod, she toddled off.

Jess stepped closer. "We could check the Lodge and keep an eye out for any activity on the Downs. If that light welcomed smugglers on Wednesday night, shouldn't we still be able to see evidence on a Friday?"

"No. Smugglers usually work faster than that. Whatever they brought in on Wednesday has likely already reached London and been sold."

Her brows went up. "They *are* organized. Still, it wouldn't hurt to check the other headland, see what we can find." She started for the welcome desk.

She was so determined the villains had to be elsewhere. "Do you have a horse?" he asked, following her.

"No," she admitted, stowing her things in the desk. "But it's an easy walk from the spa."

He could not help his smile. "Isn't everything?"

"Are you certain that isn't a list of French agents?" Mrs. Tully asked, reappearing at his side.

Lark tucked the paper into his coat. "Quite certain, thank you."

"Magistrate Howland would like Mr. Denby and me to assist him in preparations to defend the coast," Jess told her. "I may need to be away from the spa on occasion the next day or so."

Her aunt nodded. "I'll handle things."

Jess smiled at her. "Thank you, Aunt. And you won't be alone. I'll ask Mrs. Harding to help with hostess duties."

Mrs. Tully raised her chin. "She can't," she said with a sniff. "She's still mourning the death of her husband." She lowered her voice and leaned closer to Lark. "I hear he was her third, and they all died under mysterious circumstances."

"You know very well she was only married once," Jess reminded her. "And I am delighted she's taking Mr. Crabapple's suit seriously."

"For now," Mrs. Tully muttered, straightening. "But I've been giving him an extra dose of spa water just in case."

"And do we have sufficient glasses?" Jess asked.

"No," her aunt grumbled. "Come see for yourself."

After Jess excused herself and went to the fountain with her aunt, Lark drew out the paper again. Besides checking the Peverell Lodge on the opposite headland, she'd listed speaking with several members of Grace-by-the-Sea, including the vicar, Jack Hornswag at the Mermaid, and Quillan St. Claire, a retired naval officer. Not a promising start. Still, he could think of two other men who might have been able to shed more light on the situation if they were questioned thoroughly. Of course, Jess might be equally cautious about suspecting the magistrate.

And Lark could think of any number of reasons why she might hesitate to include her brother.

CHAPTER TWELVE

JESS HAD PUT THE VICAR at the top of the list and left a note on the parsonage door on her way to the spa that morning to alert him to her and Lark's upcoming visit. Answers to these vexing questions about smugglers in the area could not come soon enough. Alex had never returned that night. Jess had paced the floor until she was forced to retire. Even then, she had tossed and turned, waking to the least noise. She must discover this Lord of the Smugglers, make sure Alex had not fallen under his influence. She owed it to her brother, her father, and herself.

Because Maudie had protested Mrs. Harding's help, Jess approached Miss Barlow instead. She wasn't sure how the Newcomer would take her request, but the lady brightened, lashes fluttering.

"Oh, I'd be delighted! Being the hostess of the spa seems a wonderful position. Everyone admires and esteems you."

It felt like that, most days. Jess thanked her, settled her Regulars, and left them and any Newcomers to the good graces of Maudie and Miss Barlow. Then she put her bonnet back on, collected Lark from a conversation with the Admiral, and started for the door. It felt odd to be leaving the spa in the middle of the day, as if hands reached out to clutch at her and hold her close.

"I'm not sure how they'll function without you," Lark

said as they started up Church Street.

"I am not indispensable," she told him. "Ask the Spa Corporation."

Mrs. Norris, wife of their barber, came out of her cottage, basket draped over one arm, and waved to Jess. Jess waved back.

"Not everyone is blessed with vision," Lark countered.

"I can't think much of the vision of your superior," she said as they approached the long white church with its three-story tower and slender silver cross that had been a gift of the Howlands. "Why would he suspect Grace-by-the-Sea of harboring criminals?"

He held open the wrought iron churchyard gate for her. "You have an excellent cove, a remote location, and skilled sailors."

"A cove that can be seen by nearly every house in town," she reminded him. "And sailors who are honest and loyal to their country. More than one has been trained as a Sea Fencible, to anchor off the shore and prevent a landing by the French." She pointed him around the side of the church for the neat vicarage attached there.

"Well," he allowed as they reached the blue-lacquered door, "to do my superior credit, he did search elsewhere first."

"Obviously not hard enough." She raised her hand to knock.

Mrs. Mance, the vicar's housekeeper, opened the door, white hair like the seeds of a dandelion about her wrinkled face. "Miss Chance, Mr. Denby, how nice to see you." She stepped aside to let them in.

Jess had visited the vicarage any number of times over the years. The wood-paneled walls were warm, the lamplight soft. Easy to imagine curling up somewhere with a cup of tea and a good book. Mrs. Mance led them to the withdrawing room, where the vicar was waiting beside a

scroll-backed chair with a needlepoint seat. Her mother had stitched the roses herself, before she'd died trying to birth Jess's little sister when Jess was fifteen. Her father had blamed himself, of course. Maudie had been the one to focus him on his remaining children.

"Do you want the fairies to come for them?" she'd threatened. "That's what happens to unwanted children. Changelings, all of them."

"My children," her father had said, "will never be unwanted."

She shook off the memory now as the vicar smiled in welcome.

"I was delighted to receive your note, Miss Chance," he said in his reasoned voice. "You have always been a light of hope in this village. I have been awaiting this day for some time."

"I'll get the cider," Mrs. Mance proclaimed, hurrying out.

Lark glanced to Jess, brow up in obvious confusion, but she wasn't any surer of the vicar's purpose.

"Had you expected me to call previously?" she asked, taking the seat opposite him. Lark settled on the chair next to hers.

"Oh, any number of times," Mr. Wingate assured her as he sat, brown eyes shining. "I had thought perhaps Lord Featherstone might sway you, but I'm glad to see you understood that his attentions were fatherly. And there was that nice Mr. Vincent from London. Whatever became of him?"

Cold rained down on her. "Mr. Vincent returned to his wife and family."

The vicar's face crumbled. "Oh, my dear, I am so sorry. We were all deceived."

Lark was studying her. It hurt to keep her smile. "Yes, we were."

The vicar rallied. "But not about Mr. Denby here, eh?"

He expected an answer, one she could never give. Indeed, she wasn't sure she could even speak. As if he saw her struggle, Lark leaned forward and met the minister's gaze.

"We seem to have given you the wrong impression, Mr. Wingate. Miss Chance and I are not courting. Magistrate Howland asked us to confirm some facts related to a report he's compiling for the defense of the coast."

Mrs. Mance bustled back into the room, carrying a silver tray with four crystal glasses filled with amber liquid. "Shall we toast the happy couple?" She glanced from the vicar's face, which was turning red, to Jess's, which was likely white.

"Perhaps not," she said and left, taking the cider with her.

"Defense of the coast, you say?" Mr. Wingate asked, usually firm voice wobbling. "Against invasion?"

Lark cocked his head. "Invasion, smuggling, that sort of thing."

The minister nodded. "Of course."

"Then you suspect the area harbors smugglers," Lark pressed.

She had recovered sufficiently that she wanted to protest the assumption, but she kept her lips shut. She'd suggested they speak to the vicar. She must see this through.

"I could not say I suspect anyone of smuggling," the vicar replied, leaning back, "but I'm not surprised to hear you mention it. These are difficult times. Any man might be tempted to turn to dishonest means to support a family."

"The navy is recruiting," Lark said, voice hardening. "The army is always looking for able-bodied men."

"Men who must leave hearth and home," the minister protested. "Men whose pay would mostly go to their own provisioning. Men who would have few reliable ways to send money home to needy families. There are brave souls who have trained and are ready to confront our foes, but

I can see why others less brave, less capable turn to smuggling instead."

Jess blinked. "You almost sound as if smuggling is a common practice. Not in Grace-by-the-Sea."

"Perhaps not here," he allowed. "The trade from the spa supports many, if not through direct work than through subsidies. But we cannot forget our brothers and sisters in Upper Grace and along the shore."

She shot Lark a look. He was still focused on the minister.

"Surely you're not condoning breaking the law," he said.

"I cannot condone it, but I understand the need that drives it. Besides, the laws are specious at best. Champagne, lace, silk—the law punishes those who bring them in and refuse to pay tax but not those who gladly accept the so-called free trade goods."

"And what of those who traffic in more than goods?" Lark challenged. "Information to the enemy, the transport of French spies."

Jess gasped. "You cannot be serious."

"No one in Grace-by-the-Sea would betray the king," Mr. Wingate agreed.

Lark would not let the matter go. "And yet they send no word to the Excise Office," he accused. "Tubs of brandy, bolts of silk, casks of tea—all have been found not far inland from your village, Mr. Wingate. Whispers of French spies appearing from Dorset. Did no one see them passing through?"

"I have heard nothing," the minister promised him. "But it doesn't surprise me that no one alerted the government. Preventers are generally seen as the enemy."

"And why?" Lark demanded. "Riding Officers are good Englishmen, looking to uphold the law and protect our shores from invasion."

"Some," the minister allowed. "Others accept bribes for

looking the other way or, worse, blackmail those involved. It is a sad state of affairs. But I must repeat that Grace-by-the-Sea is immune to such things, for which I thank God daily."

Jess nodded, but the sinking feeling in her stomach told her she was no longer so sure.

Lark left the vicarage with more questions than when he had arrived. How could a man of the cloth take such a lax view on crime? Were the members of his parish working with the smugglers? Did he know? Was he a willing partic-ipant? Or did he simply refuse to see the truth?

And who was this Mr. Vincent whose name had made Jess curl in on herself like a flower withering in the heat?

"Lark, wait."

He hadn't realized he was walking so fast. He slowed his steps past the gravestones of the churchyard to allow her to catch up. "Forgive me."

"No need," she assured him as they exited the yard. "I could understand why you'd want to distance yourself from that visit. The vicar's conversation was unsettling at best. I wonder how many others share his views."

"Too many," Lark said. When she looked at him askance, he shrugged. "I've seen it. The tax on goods from France is high for a reason. We are at war, and taxation is one way to bring an enemy to its knees."

"Those purchasing the goods as well," she reminded him. She nodded toward a lane leading up onto the head-land behind the church, and Lark fell into step beside her.

"The tea tax hurts us all," he acknowledged as they started up the hill through bushes clinging to the chalky soil. "But silk and champagne are hardly necessities. The tax is meant

to be ultimately borne by those who can afford such luxuries. Smugglers take all the risks; the wealthy enjoy the spoils. It isn't right."

She sighed, her skirts swaying with her step as made the first switchback on the path, where a simple stone bench looked out to sea. "No, it isn't. And your concern about French spies only worsens the matter. Is it true? Are we in danger? Maudie has been claiming spies have infiltrated the area for years, and none of us believed her."

"Well," Lark said with a smile, "she has claimed to have seen Napoleon and mermaids too."

The smile she returned was a ghost of its usual self. "There is that." She looked away from him, toward the blue of the sky at the top of the hill. "Do you suspect Mr. Wingate of being the Lord of the Smugglers, then?"

Lark shrugged. "He is a possibility, and one I would not have considered but for you."

She pressed a hand to her chest. "I'm not sure that was a compliment."

"It was," he told her. "You have a rare gift for understanding people, Jess."

They had reached the top. The Downs stretched before them, the breeze whispering through the spring grass, setting it to rippling like an inland sea. In the distance to their right, white-faced sheep bent their heads to crop. To the left, the waters of the Channel sparkled silver blue. Closer still, a copse of trees hid the Lodge from sight.

She sighed as if the pastoral scene brought no comfort. "I wish you were right. Sometimes I don't understand people at all."

She sounded so weary he had to ask. "The mention of this Mr. Vincent upset you. Who was he?"

She dropped her gaze and turned onto the path that led toward the Lodge, as if the dusty white soil held some secret she was determined to uncover. "He came to the spa

just before Father died. He seemed thoughtful, considerate. Several remarked on his attentions to me. It was easy to believe he was smitten. No one but my father and me understood why he left so suddenly. Some said I should have encouraged him, that I'd kept him at a distance, that I was as frigid as the waters of the Channel."

"Those people obviously cannot know you well," Lark said.

Her hand fisted at her side. "Neither did he. He pretended to be a bachelor, you see, but Father exchanged letters with his physician, who had advised him to take the waters for a minor ailment. It seems Mr. Vincent had a wife, children. His attentions to me were only a diversion."

He had never met the fellow, but he had an overwhelming desire to plant him a facer. "Stupid," he said.

Her gaze snapped up to his, and lightning flashed from those delicate blue eyes. "When you have lived for six and twenty years and are considered a spinster with no hope of changing your circumstances, sir, you may have earned the right to judge me, but not before."

She started for the Lodge at a fast clip, skirts flapping, and he sprinted to put himself in front of her. She pulled up short, chest heaving.

"You mistake me," Lark told her. "The stupidity belongs to Mr. Vincent, for even thinking to dally with the kindest, sweetest lady it has been my pleasure to know."

She glanced up at him again, and this time the blue swam with tears. It was all he could do not to gather her in his arms.

She sucked in a breath, as if pulling in dignity with the air. "Thank you, Lark. Forgive me for assuming the worst. I thought I'd put it all behind me, but Mr. Wingate's words caught me off guard." She sniffed bravely. "You too, I think. That was a very spirited defense of the Excise Office."

He should brush it off, claim he was only defending his

vocation. But if she could share her deepest pain, so could he.

"Supporting the Excise Office is a matter of some pride to me. The vicar is right—the officers are often treated as pariahs in their own villages. My father was a Riding Officer. He had a four-mile stretch of coastline in Kent. It was his job to note oddities, arrange for support when he identified smugglers in the area. My mother heard mutterings against her whenever she came into the village. Someone once spit on her."

She blinked away the last of her tears. "How unkind."

"Like your minister, there were those who felt smuggling was a just and equitable vocation. When I was twelve, my father ran afoul of smugglers near the village. They captured and beat him and left him for dead. My sisters found him. He didn't recover."

Her hand shot out, gripped his. "Oh, Lark, how horrid."

When he could not find the words to respond to the compassion in her eyes, she put her arms around him and held him.

And he could only marvel.

He was supposed to be brave. He believed in his mission, his duty. He'd been trained to hunt down ne'er-do-wells, bring them to justice, restore order. His job was to safeguard communities like Grace-by-the-Sea from criminals so that no family must endure what his had.

Yet he hadn't been able to muster the courage to hold her when she needed comfort. Now she defied convention, propriety, to comfort him.

This Vincent fellow truly was stupid. But his betrayal hadn't stopped Jess from reaching out. She deserved better.

Lark drew back. "Thank you for that. But these are far too dismal thoughts for such a beautiful day."

She sniffed. "The day may be beautiful, but we have work that must be accomplished."

"Work?" He raised his brows. "Why can't we enjoy ourselves as well? When was the last time you felt the wind in your hair?"

She started laughing. "Really, sir, what a question to ask a lady! Why do you think we wear bonnets every time we go outside? To protect our faces and hair from the wind."

He frowned. "Why? Feeling the wind on your face is one of the ways you know you're alive."

Her look was all doubt.

"Here, let me show you." Before she could protest, he reached under her chin and tugged free the ribbons holding her bonnet in place. The straw bonnet fell back easily, and the breeze immediately reached for her curls. He caught her hand as she reached up as if to cover them.

"Now," he said. "Run with me."

He tugged on her hand. She resisted at first, then her eyes lit, and she gathered her skirts with her free hand.

They dashed along the path, sun warm, cool salty air filling their lungs. As they neared the trees, he caught her in his arms and spun her in a circle.

"There!" he proclaimed, swinging to a stop. "How do you feel now?"

Her cheeks were pink, her eyes sparkling. "Much better," she admitted. "How extraordinary." Her wonder was so bright, like sunlight on the sea, that his spirit couldn't help rising to meet it. He was bending closer before he thought better of it.

Her gaze snapped past him toward the trees beyond. "Who is that?"

Lark jerked upright, his purpose slamming into him. Turning, he saw a man through the trees, standing on the drive in front of the Lodge. His movements were slow, cautious, and he kept glancing around as if expecting someone to protest his presence. Lark took Jess's hand again and pulled her behind a tree.

"Do you recognize him?" he whispered.

She was frowning. "Not at this distance. Lord Peverell generally sends his staff ahead to open the house when he intends to visit. I hadn't heard he'd hired a caretaker."

Interesting. Lark chanced a glance around the tree. The fellow had disappeared, at least from their vantage point.

"Wait here," he told Jess.

She caught his arm. "No. I'm coming with you."

He opened his mouth to argue, and she held up a finger. "Listen. I know each entrance to the Lodge, and, should we find a way inside, I can lead you through the interior. Father and I visited several times over the years."

Knowing the layout of the house might give him an advantage. He ought to be thankful, but all he could think about was the possible danger to her.

"All right," he agreed, "but stay behind me."

She nodded, and they set out.

Lark crept from tree to tree, always watching the circular gravel drive up ahead. He saw no movement, heard no voices. He stopped at the edge of the trees and gazed out.

Unlike most of the white-washed cottages in the area, the Lodge was made of red brick that could only have been brought in from a distance. The builder must have had as whimsical an outlook as Mrs. Tully, for the three-story house had turrets and bowed windows a-plenty, with short wings sticking out either side and at one corner. All in all, the place didn't seem to know what it intended to be—fortified castle, rustic hunting lodge, or grand manor house.

He edged out of the trees. "I'll try the door."

Her boots crunched on the gravel as she followed. "It's likely padlocked. Try the kitchen door. It's around the back."

"Can I help you?"

The rough voice came from the corner of the house.

An older man in a wool coat and the striped trousers of a fisherman stood frowning at them. A little shorter and lighter than Lark, he had unruly reddish-brown hair that matched his beard.

"Mr. Bascom." Jess was graciousness personified as she stepped around Lark to venture closer to the fellow. "I had no idea you were helping at the Lodge. How clever of you to figure out a way to do that without interfering with your fishing."

He shifted on his feet, as if he wasn't sure how to take her praise. "Wasn't too hard. Fish bite in the mornings. Lodge needs watchin' at night."

"Quite right," she agreed with a nod. "I trust there's been no sign of trouble?"

He wiped his bulbous nose with the back of one hand. "None. Did his lordship send you to check? Is he coming back sooner than expected?"

Odd. Jess might know more about Grace-by-the-Sea than anyone else in the area, but if this Bascom was truly the caretaker, surely Lord Peverell would contact him before Jess. And there was a tone of worry under the fisherman's words.

"I have not heard he is returning before the Season ends," she assured him. "I doubt we'll see him before August, at the earliest. Forgive our intrusion. We were just out for a stroll. We won't detain you further. Please give my regards to your dear wife."

He nodded, but he didn't take his eyes off them as Jess returned to Lark's side and linked her arm with his. She drew him back into the trees and the path to the village.

"Waste of time, then," he surmised.

That frown was gathering on her brow again. "No, indeed. I sincerely doubt Lord Peverell would hire Henry Bascom to watch the Lodge. I sincerely doubt his lordship is aware that Henry Bascom even exists."

Lark fought the urge to glance back. "I'll come back tonight, see what I can find."

She shivered, as if the idea troubled her. "No need. I know someone else who can likely answer our questions. I propose we go see Mrs. Bascom, preferably before her husband can get home."

CHAPTER THIRTEEN

WHAT AN ODD DAY. JESS could not seem to find her equilibrium as they descended the path to Church Street. She hadn't intended to share the story of Walter Vincent. It did no one any credit. She still wasn't sure how she, the town matchmaker, had been so easily taken in by him. She only knew she must be more careful in the future. So, why open herself up to Lark?

He strolled along beside her as they made their way along the street, smile as bright as the day and nearly as carefree. How? If her father had died under such circumstances, she wasn't sure she'd ever be able to forget. But then, he hadn't forgotten, had he? He'd gone into the same profession. Small wonder he was so determined to catch the smugglers he thought lived in the area.

"The Bascoms live down along the water," she told him as they neared High Street.

"Of course." He shot her a grin. "Are you certain you want to keep investigating today? How will the spa survive your absence?"

The spa! For a few moments, in his company, she'd completely forgotten her responsibilities. What if Mr. Crabapple needed advice on courting? What if a Newcomer arrived and wanted introductions? Would Maudie remember to put out the seed cakes Mrs. Inchley had brought for

tea? Would Miss Barlow find herself out of her element? Jess still had to send the invitations for the Midsummer Masquerade.

Her thoughts must have flittered across her face, for he put a hand on her arm. "I was teasing. Your efforts are exceptional, but surely you are allowed time away on occasion."

Jess drew in a breath. "You'd be surprised how infrequently. But Maudie sometimes served as hostess when my father was alive. And she has Miss Barlow to help her today. I just can't shake the feeling I'm derelict in my duty."

"Magistrate Howland must have spoken to Greer by now," he said. "Surely the Spa Corporation will understand."

She was not nearly so sure. But Lark's work was important too, and it might be the only way she'd finally learn what her brother was up to.

"Perhaps if we hurry," she said.

They set off down the hill.

"So, which one?" he asked as they reached the first of the shops. Abigail stood in the window of her gallery. She pointed to Lark, then the fourth finger on her left hand. *No,* Jess mouthed.

"Sorry," she said aloud to Lark. "Which what?"

"Which house do the Bascoms own?" he clarified.

"Ah. They're across the cove from us." She nodded to Mr. Lawrence, who was rearranging the collection of wedding rings in the window of the jewelry store. He winked at her. She ignored the look.

"Good location for a fisherman," Lark observed. "Bit inconvenient for reaching the Lodge."

"Very inconvenient, but he's more interested in profit." She thought for a moment how to share the rest of what she knew. Between her guests at the spa and those at the assemblies, she was privy to a great deal of gossip and did

her best not to pass on any of it. However, Lark needed to know all if he was to put together the pieces of this puzzle.

"I have noticed that Mr. Bascom tends to increase his prices for fish when the other fishermen are having a difficult time finding any," she explained as they passed the linens and trimmings shop. The younger Miss Pierce came out, white satin ribbons draped over one arm, and waved them at her. Jess did not need white satin ribbons, the kinds used by brides. She shook her head at the seamstress, whose face fell.

"Not necessarily a crime," Lark mused as they approached the barber. Mr. Norris was lounging on his front stoop. He straightened to gaze at Lark and stroked his chin with two fingers. Lark did not appear to notice the offer of a shave.

"It may not be a crime," Jess said, "but it's not fair to his neighbors or the others in his profession. And he's not above getting out ahead, even if it means sailing at night."

Lark glanced her way, in time to miss the look Mr. Treacle shot him through the window of the haberdashery. "So, he might have been willing to try the caves under the castle after dark."

Jess shrugged. "That I'm not so sure about. Perhaps it would be best if you let me lead the conversation on this one."

Another man might have bristled. He merely nodded. "I am yours to command."

And wouldn't that be nice? She could imagine coming home from the spa to a dinner with him across the table, sharing stories of their day. He'd laugh over something a Newcomer had said. She'd marvel over the villains he'd brought low. She blinked until the image disappeared.

"This way," she said as they reached the shore.

Henry Bascom and his family lived in a cottage at the very end of the row. He had a son about her brother's age, another a few years younger, and two daughters, one still

on leading strings. They found Mrs. Bascom and the girls out in the small yard in front of the stone cottage, hanging clothing on the line to dry.

"Good afternoon," Jess said with a smile to the girls, who ducked behind their mother's blue skirts.

"Miss Chance," Mrs. Bascom acknowledged, but her look darted to Lark.

"This is Mr. Denby, a Newcomer to our shore," Jess explained. "He's interested in sailing, and I thought your husband might like to discuss the matter with him."

"I pay in gold," Lark put in with a charming smile.

Mrs. Bascom brushed down her lace collar before bending to pick up an apron from the basket at her feet. "My Henry's very busy."

"He certainly is," Jess agreed. "Why, half the tables in this village would be empty but for the fish he brings in."

She did not brighten as she flipped the apron over the line. "He's a hard worker."

"Oh, my yes," Jess said. "We recently encountered him up at the Lodge, but I didn't think to ask him until afterward. I understand he's the caretaker there now."

Her body tightened, but she kept working, hands smoothing the fabric. "He helps out when needed, same as me. I'm not sure when he'll be home today." Sunlight glinted on the pins holding up her brown hair.

"Then we'll take no more of your time," Jess said. "I hope to see you in church on Sunday."

Mrs. Bascom nodded, and Jess led Lark away toward the village.

"Disappointing," he said. "But perhaps we can get more out of him on Sunday, as you noted."

"Her husband rarely attends services," Jess told him as they followed the path to the street. "But something isn't right. Henry Bascom works hard, and he does sell his catch all over town, but with so many mouths to feed, he strug-

gles to make ends meet. I've collected a Christmas and Easter basket for him three years running. Yet those pins in Mrs. Bascom's hair were gold. I'm certain of it. And she didn't buy that lace collar in the shops here. The Misses Pierce haven't stocked French lace in years. Neither has Abigail, as she noted to you."

"But to wear them so openly," he protested.

"She wasn't expecting us," Jess pointed out. "And their cottage is the last in the line before the headland, so she likely thought no one would notice."

"Which means we can't cross him off the list yet," he surmised.

"No, indeed. Though it is quite possible he's having a better year than usual." Jess sighed. "Oh, but I cannot like suspecting any of our neighbors. Surely your superior was mistaken. This Lord of the Smugglers cannot live in Grace-by-the-Sea."

Yet even as they started up the hill, her brother came to mind once more. But Alex, being taken for a lord? He still forgot to wear his coat on chilly days. And he hadn't settled on a profession. No, thinking of him leading hardened smugglers was too much. Even Maudie would laugh at such a tale.

"Perhaps we can convince the commissioner to look elsewhere," Jess said, lifting her lavender skirts to climb the hill. "You've found no one to suspect."

He lowered his voice as they came past the shops. "What of this Quillan St. Claire, the retired naval officer?"

She aimed a smile at Mr. Carroll, who was sweeping off his stoop. He smiled back, jerked his head toward Lark, and raised his brow in question. Oh, not another one. Jess shook her head emphatically no.

"He arrived eighteen months ago, claiming to be recovering from a war wound," she explained as Mr. Carroll's eager look turned to one of disappointment. "He's leasing

Dove Cottage, on the hill between here and Upper Grace. It's an easy walk to the assembly rooms, yet he rarely joins us. His manservant does the marketing and brings him the paper and other reading materials from Mr. Carroll. He never attends church services. If he is truly in pain, why not at least come to the spa?"

He chuckled. "I admire your loyalty to the waters."

"I am loyal because I have seen them work," she insisted as they passed the last shop. "People come with pale faces, worried countenances. They leave with robust color and a smile. How else would you explain it?"

He smiled. "That's not from drinking the waters. That's because they met you."

Once more the admiration in his gaze held her tenderly. She could not look away. Perhaps that's why she stumbled.

He caught her before she fell. "Careful. Perhaps we could both do with a drink from the fountain."

Assuredly. But somehow she didn't think that would cure her of her returning feelings for him.

Jess was anxious to check on the spa, so Lark agreed they would continue their efforts on Saturday.

"Perhaps we should ride out along the cliffs," he said as they continued up the hill. "It might give me an idea of where they are landing their goods, if not Grace Cove. Shall I ask Mr. Josephs for a horse for you?"

She laughed. "No, please. I never learned to ride."

Lark stared at her. "Never? How do you get about?"

She waved a hand toward the little village. "There is nowhere I need to go that I cannot walk, sir."

He could not imagine being so hemmed in. "Leave this to me. We'll meet at the crossroads above the spa at half

past nine tomorrow. I'll bring a gig and the appropriate chaperone."

She looked at him askance, but they had reached the spa, and he opened the door for her.

He removed his hat as they stepped inside the columned space. Lord Featherstone nodded a welcome. Mrs. Tully went so far as to wink at him. As Jess hurried to check with her, Mrs. Cole and her daughter came over to ask about his health, his plans. It had been a long time since anyone asked after him.

And he could not see that anything had changed during Jess's absence. Miss Barlow seemed quite eager to please, peppering her with questions and offering suggestions. But he could not deny he enjoyed having Jess to himself. He excused himself from the spa to make the arrangements for Saturday.

He was waiting for Jess at the crossroads above the spa the next morning. Her lavender skirts swished over her brown leather half-boots as she approached the curricle and pair he had borrowed from Mr. Josephs at the livery stable. Miss Archer gathered the reins in one hand and waved at Jess with the other.

"Abigail," Jess greeted her warmly before turning to Lark. "It seems you thought of everything, sir."

Lark inclined his head. "Miss Archer graciously agreed to accompany us. She'll be driving the carriage. I'll be riding alongside. We'll stop and walk as it pleases us."

"And I can paint," Abigail put in with a smile.

Indeed, he was rather counting on that.

He stepped forward and gave Jess his hand to help her up into the carriage. The scent of lavender brushed his

nose. He would not inhale like some love-struck school-boy, however tempting it was. As if she'd felt his scrutiny, she blushed prettily as she settled herself into the seat. He had to force himself to walk to his sorrel mare and mount. Miss Archer clucked to the pair on the curricle, and they all set out up the hill for the cliff road toward West Creech.

The day was warm and clear. Chalk puffed from the horses' hoofs to hover in the air. Mrs. Tully would probably have claimed it was pixie dust. He could imagine it spar-kling in Jess' hair, which was once more confined inside a straw bonnet. He longed to pull the bonnet free, as he'd done yesterday, but she wouldn't have allowed it today. She was being a proper lady, chatting with him and her friend and flashing smiles brighter than the sunlight that was anointing the fields with gold.

After a time, he slowed his horse Valkyrie to a trot, then urged her off the road. Miss Archer pulled the curricle to the side of the road as well. Beyond the grass, the Channel filled the horizon, deep blue melding with the blue of the sky in the distance.

"Where are we?" Jess asked as if they had reached another land.

"About halfway to West Creech," he said, dismounting and taking up Valkyrie's reins. He nodded toward a field of wildflowers bursting with pink, scarlet, and azure. "Would you care to walk, Miss Chance?"

Miss Archer pulled a sketchbook out from under the seat. "I'll be here when you need me."

Singularly accommodating woman. He must remember to thank her.

He helped Jess down and walked with her and the mare toward the cliff. "I thought we could start here," he mur-mured, head close to Jess', "and make our way back toward the castle, looking for draws that lead up from the shore."

She beamed. "Excellent suggestion."

He felt very clever.

She glanced back at her friend. "A shame we cannot invite Abigail. She's drawn these cliffs more time than anyone and might notice something we missed."

He tucked her hand in his arm. "I would rather not share my profession with her if possible."

"Of course."

They had reached the edge of the land, and she craned her neck to see over the cliff to the shores below. "No easy way down here. That's what you seek, isn't it? How this Lord of the Smugglers is coming ashore?"

He still suspected the fellow was using the caves under Castle How, but it wouldn't hurt to look elsewhere.

"Yes," he allowed. "Though it's possible he never comes ashore. There are a number of ways to land a cargo. Some of the larger vessels sail down the Channel, and smaller boats go out to meet them. Others come as close to shore as possible and in shallow enough water that men can form a human chain from ship to shore and pass the goods by hand."

"Well, I certainly haven't seen that on Grace Cove," she assured him.

Reins in one grip, her hand in the other, he led the horse along the cliff. "It could have happened in the dead of night, while you slept."

"You forget. I live on the cove. Either Maudie or I would have heard something."

Interesting that she didn't mention her brother, but perhaps he was a heavy sleeper. "You'd be surprised how quietly they can move. Some use a specially designed harness on their horses to muffle the sound."

"I had no idea," she marveled. "You must have to go to great lengths to catch them."

Easy to feel confident in that assessment. "It can be challenging."

Suddenly, she stopped, pointing. "There, where the cliff slumps? Are those wagon tracks?"

CHAPTER FOURTEEN

IMMEDIATELY, HE WAS ON THE alert. She could only liken it to the way her mind snapped to attention when she spotted interest between a lady and a gentleman at the spa. He handed her the reins, heedless to the fact that she had never held them before, and scurried to where the grass had been disturbed.

The horse eyed her, brown eyes wary.

"Well," Jess said, "I suppose we should follow him."

The mare seemed to agree, for she ambled closer to Lark, then bent her head to nibble at the grass, nearly tugging the reins from Jess's fingers.

"Yes, you're right," Lark said, striding along the track to the draw in the cliff. "At least two wagons by the lines in the soil and deeper in one set of tracks than the other, so they likely arrived empty and left full."

She would not have thought to check for such things. "Did the smugglers come up from the shore, then?"

She was almost sorry she'd asked, for he was leaning precariously out over the cliff. "There's a good path up, though I can't see the bottom with the high tide. Still, very promising."

She drew in a breath as he moved toward her, his eyes bright. He nodded back the way they had come. "It looks as if the smugglers joined the cliff road there. I'll be sure to

note that in my report."

His report? "You don't intend to chase them?"

"Unfortunately, they could be anywhere by now." He held out his hand, and she surrendered the reins to him. "But I'll see that the Riding Officer for this stretch of coast is alerted to keep watch. When he detects a pattern, he can call in the dragoons and capture the lot of them." He clucked to the horse, and they continued along the shore.

The breeze tugged her bonnet back, and sunlight warmed her cheeks. Jess breathed in the brine-scented air. Every direction she looked, the view went on for miles, from spring-green grassland to rolling sea. Abigail and the curricle were tiny in the distance. How vast the world seemed, just over the hill from the village.

"Hungry?" he asked, and suddenly she was. As if he saw the answer in her eyes, he drew up in a patch of shorter grass surrounded by wildflowers, which bobbed their heads in greeting. From the saddlebag, he pulled a blanket and handed it to her. "Will you set the table?"

Smiling, she took the soft wool and arranged it on the grass. He busied himself bringing a pouch, a tin, and a metal flask.

"Where did you get all this?" she asked as he spread them on the blanket.

"Jack Hornswag and Mr. Ellison were surprisingly accommodating," he replied as his horse bent her head once more.

She settled on the blanket. Dropping down beside her, he popped open the lid on the tin and held the canister out to her.

"Oh, strawberries!" Jess plucked out two, red and juicy. "We must save some for Abby."

He set down the tin and opened the pouch. "There's also cheese and rolls as well as lemonade."

"How thoughtful." She shifted on the blanket to find a more comfortable spot on the bumpy soil.

"Lean against me," he offered, positioning himself partly behind her.

The view before them, food between them, her shoulder brushing his. What more could she want?

His arm draped around her waist, warm, solid. Ah, that. She could not stop the happy sigh that bubbled up.

They did not speak for a time as they partook of their feast, and she hoped he felt as content in the moment as she did. But their purpose could not fade away completely.

"You've found your smugglers, then," she said between bites of strawberry.

"I've found *evidence* of smuggling," he corrected her. "I still haven't identified the Lord of the Smugglers or those helping the French."

She shook her head. "Is it always this difficult?"

"It can be. All smugglers are breaking the law. They understand the penalty if they're caught, so they do their utmost not to be caught. Knowing he's betraying England, this Lord of the Smugglers must be doubly careful."

She swallowed her mouthful of lemonade. "How many have you captured?" She glanced at him to find his face inches away. Flecks of gold brightened his dark eyes. So easy to press her lips to his. She held herself still.

As if unaware of her look, he gazed off over the waves, clearly calculating the results of his efforts. "Fifty in the last few years," he said.

Jess raised her brow. "Kent must be terribly lawless."

He chuckled, gaze coming back to hers. "No more so than any place along the Channel." He sobered. "Sometimes I wonder how much of a difference I've made."

She could not help it. She lay a hand on his cheek, so warm and firm. "Fifty fewer smugglers, sir. And you must have given the others pause to find you so diligent. Small

wonder your supervisor sent you on this assignment."

His gaze held hers, soft, sweet. She lost her breath.

He broke away to rise. "I should return you to Miss Archer and the village. They will flounder without you."

She was floundering now. One moment in his company, and she was willing to throw caution, even prudence, to the wind. Much more of this and she would be blurting out how much she'd missed him, how badly she wanted him to stay.

But was she really willing to take a chance on love again?

Despite his best intentions, they did not reach the village until late that afternoon. Jess had insisted that they walk the rest of the way along the cliff, as if determined to prove to him there were no landing places closer to Grace-by-the-Sea than the one they'd discovered.

Or perhaps she was as loath to part company.

Miss Archer had kept to the road, running parallel to them and always within easy shouting distance. He had scarcely noticed her. Jess had been so understanding, so interested in his work, that he'd found himself prosing on. Then, that one moment, when their gazes had held, he'd nearly kissed her. But a kiss implied commitment, promise of a future, and he could not be sure of his.

So, he walked beside her, leading Valkyrie, and talked of commonplaces—the school his sister Rosemary had opened in Upper Grace, how his niece Rebecca was growing up as kind-natured as her mother, Jess's ambitions for the spa. They found no other sign of a landing. As the cliff curved closer to the castle, he convinced her to rejoin Miss Archer and ride to the top of the hill above the spa. It was for her comfort. He'd have far preferred to take her

up with him. On horseback, he could have held her in his arms and dreamed for a moment of what might be.

"I'll return the curricle to Mr. Josephs," Miss Archer offered as they reached the village.

"You are too kind," Lark told her. "I cannot thank you enough for your assistance today, Miss Archer."

She smiled. "I can play matchmaker nearly as well as some, sir." With a wink to Jess, she guided the horses toward the livery stable.

"A matchmaker, eh?" Lark asked as he and Jess started down the hill toward the Mermaid. The shops were closing, and the village was quiet as they strolled through.

"What else is she to think when you ask her to play chaperone?" Jess pointed out.

"I've only fanned the flames of speculation, then," Lark mused.

Jess made a face. "I'll explain to her another time. She'll understand."

He could only hope she was right.

"We won't be able to do much on Sunday," she said as they reached the bottom of the hill. "Perhaps we should regroup on Monday, determine how to proceed."

"Very well," he allowed, trying his best to hide his disappointment.

She put out a hand to stop him from continuing on to the Mermaid.

"Perhaps you could join my family for dinner Sunday evening," she ventured with a sidelong look his way. "I think my brother might have something to add to our conversation."

Indeed, he might. Did she suspect him of consorting with smugglers? Simply asking might put her back up.

"Oh?" Lark asked instead.

Her cheeks were turning that delightful pink again, and she fidgeted. "He knows many of the younger people bet-

ter than I do. Perhaps one of them has mentioned seeing a smuggler."

Or being one.

"I'd be delighted," Lark said.

She smiled. "Then I'll leave you here. Thank you so much for today, Lark. I won't forget it."

Neither would he. He was smiling too as he led Valkyrie toward the stables.

He spotted no light from the castle that night, though he looked for it until past midnight. Much as he had enjoyed the day with Jess, he knew he must show progress or be recalled. Even the commissioner's certainty must be flagging by now. He would have to make a report, and soon. And that meant leaving Grace-by-the-Sea.

And Jess.

She remained on his mind as he ventured to church the next morning. Just the sight of her in the nave raised his spirits. She sent him a smile and tipped her head as if beckoning him to join her. He slid into the box pew. Mrs. Tully nodded a greeting. Jess beamed. He knew he must be grinning as the service started.

Worship came easy. Indeed, thankfulness was welling inside him. How could he not be grateful for Jess at his side? Paisley shawl draped about her shoulders, head bowed to pray, she was only an inspiration. He had to force himself to focus on the minister.

As the service ended, Lark glanced around for the Bascoms. The wife and children had attended church near the back, and neither the gold hairpins nor the lace collar had come along. Might she just have been self-conscious of the gifts or think them too proud to wear before her Savior?

Still, the oldest lad narrowed his eyes at Lark when he caught him glancing their way.

He wasn't the only one to shoot Lark questioning looks as people turned to leave. A young lady requested a moment of Jess's time, and he gathered it had something to do with a certain gentleman who was courting her, so Lark went ahead so they might have privacy. Mr. Carroll gave him the eye before putting up his head and marching past. Miss Rinehart, the milliner, sniffed in his direction as if she found his beaver top hat objectionable. Even the vicar refused to meet his gaze as Lark thanked him at the door for his efforts. If Jess hadn't agreed to partner him, he shuddered to think of the reception he would have received.

As he waited for her by the churchyard gate, Magistrate Howland moved in beside him.

"Progress?" he asked, gaze on the stones of the path.

Lark glanced around, but the other villagers were giving him wide berth. "Not much, but we still have other avenues to pursue."

"How are the villagers reacting to your questions?" he asked.

"Noticed the looks being directed my way, did you?" Lark countered. "I imagine few villages welcome strangers, particularly ones asking difficult questions."

Mr. Howland eyed him. "It's not the questions, Mr. Denby. Miss Chance is greatly admired. They are wondering about your intentions."

Lark reared back. "My intentions? Mr. Wingate made the mistake of assuming Miss Chance and I were courting because we showed up together to question him the other day, but surely not everyone—"

"Everyone," Howland said. "I've had three complaints sworn out so far."

Lark frowned. "Complaints? I've done nothing illegal."

His mouth worked a moment before he spoke. "Mr. Lawrence accused you of loitering. Miss Pierce was certain you bore a strong resemblance to a highwayman said to be preying on the roads hereabouts. And Mr. Carroll insisted you were only impersonating a gentleman. All were concerned you had wronged Miss Chance."

Lark leaned closer. "I would not wrong Miss Chance if it meant saving my own life."

Howland nodded slowly. "Good to know. Then I suppose I should tell anyone who asks your intentions are honorable."

Lark straightened. "My intentions are to find the Lord of the Smugglers. Nothing more." He turned his attention to Jess and her aunt, who were approaching. Offering each an arm, he escorted them toward the spa.

"Something wrong?" Jess asked with a frown his direction.

He pasted on a smile. "How could anything be wrong on such a lovely day?"

She smiled back, but he felt her doubt.

Still, she was her usual efficient self at the spa, moving from group to group, welcoming, encouraging. An odd tension hung in the air even there, like the murmur of thunder in the distance. He could not determine the source, but he feared as if it might be inside him.

At least he could look forward to the dinner that evening. He walked Jess and her aunt to the foot of High Street, then tarried a few moments at the Mermaid to give them time to set their house in order. The company in the public room held no interest. Perhaps that was why he arrived before the appointed hour. He certainly hadn't been able to slow his steps along the path from the inn.

Mrs. Tully answered his knock, black skirts partially blocking the door. "Brandy?" she demanded.

"Never drink the stuff," he assured her.

She pouted, then shrugged. "Well, I suppose it's good you don't consume your wares."

"Aunt!" Jess's voice speared out. "Mr. Denby doesn't deal in brandy. He isn't a smuggler."

"Says you," she muttered, but she stepped aside and let him in.

He wasn't sure what he had been expecting after seeing the outside of the house the other night, but the simple, two-room cottage did not do Jess justice. Oh, someone had hung landscape paintings of the sea along the white-washed walls, and the cupboard beside the stone hearth held finer china than generally graced such a place. Combined with the rocking chair near the fire and the thick blue-and-green carpet on the plank floor, the house had a welcoming feel to it. Or perhaps it was the lady standing by the fire, pink skirts brushing the floor.

He pulled off his hat. "Miss Chance, Mrs. Tully, thank you for inviting me."

"You needn't stand on ceremony, Lark," Jess said, straightening to bring a platter to the table in the center of the room. "We agreed to call each other by our first names."

Her aunt sidled closer to him. "You may call me Hepzibah." She wiggled her grey brows.

"Her name is Maudlyn," Jess said.

"It suits you," Lark told her aunt.

"Bah," she said, but she stomped to the table.

A thump sounded overhead a moment before a young man came down a ladder on the other side of the hearth from the cupboard. He jumped the last three rungs to land with another thump, then turned to stick out his hand. "Mr. Denby, I'm Alexander Chance."

So, this was Jess's brother. He was tall and lean, but those arms looked strong enough to sail a bark in a storm and intelligence sparkled in his blue eyes.

Lark moved to take his hand. Firm grip, confident smile.

But as Alex pulled away, Lark spotted the discoloration of callouses on his palm. Now, what had young Mr. Chance done to earn those?

"A pleasure," Lark said, watching him. "It was very kind of you all to host me."

"Oh, Jess hosts strangers all the time," her brother said, going to snatch a floret of broccoli from the bowl Jess had added to the table. "Newcomers from the spa, people moving into town. We're used to strays."

She rapped his fingers with a wooden spoon as he reached for another floret. "Mind your manners, if you please. Lark will think you weren't raised properly."

"I wasn't," he said, looking to Lark with wide, innocent eyes so like his sister's. "Ask Aunt Maudie. I was bought from the gypsies on a full moon and thrown in the sea at the first opportunity."

"Both true," his aunt said with a nod.

"Neither true," Jess corrected them, adding a bowl of golden cheese sauce to the table. "Though you did start sailing at an early age."

"Best way to meet mermaids." He winked at Lark.

Maudie brightened. "Oh, will they be joining us too?"

"No," Jess said, finality in her voice. "If you'd all be seated, dinner is served."

Maudie and Alex sat on one side, Jess on the other. The only empty place was at the head of the table or beside her on the bench. Lark sat beside her. His boots brushed her skirts. Once more, he caught a whiff of lavender.

As if unaffected by his presence, Jess clasped her hands and bowed her head, and he joined the others in mimicking her.

"Dear Lord," she said as if talking to a good friend, "thank You for the food before us, the friends and family around us, and the affection between us. May we remember Your blessings, now and always. Amen."

"Amen," echoed Maudie and Alex.

He'd said a blessing most of his life, but thankfulness pushed his head up once more. Smiles flashed. Laughter rang out. Conversation passed as quickly as the bowls from hand to hand. Newly caught fish, golden and firm. Broccoli fresh from the farm with a sharp cheese sauce to cover it. Apple cider from last year's press, still crisp and tart. And Jess beside him, as if she belonged there.

This was the friendship, the camaraderie he'd thought they'd once shared, the closeness he'd missed. It was as if he'd found a home he'd never known he'd sought.

Was he truly willing to risk it all by questioning the one person who most intrigued him, her brother?

CHAPTER FIFTEEN

WHY DID DINNER SEEM MORE companionable again? She glanced to the head of the table, where her father had sat from before she was born. None of them had felt comfortable taking that seat. But she could not deny how pleasant it was to have Lark at her side now, as if he belonged there.

Guilt tugged at her. Truth be told, she hadn't invited him just for his company, however pleasant she found it. She'd been hoping Alex would make an appearance, and she'd only been relieved when she'd risen to attend church and found his dirty clothes sticking out of the wash basket. She'd plucked out the trousers, noting the mud along the bottom. And was that a strand of seaweed?

"Alex?" she'd called up the ladder.

"Too tired for services," he'd called down. "You can tell me what happened later."

Her mouth had tightened. "We'll be having company for dinner tonight. See that you're dressed and presentable. No excuses."

She must have sounded as determined as she'd felt, for Alex had been home when she and Maudie had returned from the spa. There too, things had been a bit rough. Miss Barlow appeared to be conscientious in her duties, if perhaps a bit too zealous, but the other guests seemed restive,

and only her constant reassurances had calmed the waters. All she could hope was that her brother's conversation with Lark would give her insights into what he was doing and how she could help him. Then they could finish locating this Lord of the Smugglers, and things could return to normal.

Lark's boot bumped her skirt as he shifted on the bench, and suddenly the food she'd worked so hard to prepare tasted like ash. When they found the smugglers, life would indeed return to normal, and Lark would leave.

"So, you started sailing at an early age," he ventured to her brother now, his fingers tearing open a crusty roll.

Oblivious to her conflicted feelings, Alex grinned. "I was four, no less. Father claimed I was precocious."

Jess rallied. "Which was his way of saying you needed to be kept out from under foot."

Alex shrugged. "Well, you didn't start until you were six, so I beat you there."

Lark turned to her. "You sail?"

Something tingled through her at the avid interest in his gaze. Once she might have denied it. There had been a time when being seen as a lady was all important to her. It still was. Hoydens did not host spas. But surely she need not posture with him.

"Yes," she admitted. "Father wouldn't have had it any other way. He said just because we lived on the shore didn't mean we shouldn't learn to respect the sea."

Alex nodded, flaking off some of the fish. "Sailing is in a Chance's blood, just like living in Grace-by-the-Sea."

"And becoming a physician," Jess reminded him.

"And dancing around toadstools," Maudie added as Alex shoved the fish into his mouth.

"I have never danced around a toadstool," Jess told her with a smile. "And I doubt you have either."

Maudie nodded. "I might surprise you." She bit into her

roll.

"You all surprise me," Lark put in.

Alex laughed. "Stick around Grace-by-the-Sea long enough, and nothing will surprise you."

"Lark was asking about going sailing," Jess said, trying to get the conversation back on topic that might inform her. "I thought you might take him, Alex."

Alex shook his head. "Sorry. Busy. But you could take him out, Jess."

Had he forgotten she had a job now, responsibilities? And while many of the inhabitants of Grace-by-the-Sea might look the other way when their beloved physician instructed his young daughter in the fine points of sailing, they might not be so forgiving if their spa hostess took up the tiller. She hardly wanted to give the Spa Corporation another reason to replace her.

"I stopped sailing ages ago," she said.

Alex turned to Lark. "You should have seen her, Mr. Denby. Father let her wear trousers under her skirts when she was young, but when she decided to play the lady all the time, she couldn't sail as well."

"It isn't easy tying off a sail in petticoats," Jess retorted. "You try it."

"No, thank you," Alex said, holding up his hands in surrender. "And I meant no disrespect. Petticoats must have their purpose."

"Easier to dance around toadstools," Maudie said.

Jess gave it up and laughed. Lark's smile only made the moment sweeter.

"And to show my respect," Alex continued, "I will tell you that she's being modest, Mr. Denby. She was good. She even sailed into the Dragon's Maw. She was so determined to prove her skills that she nearly wrecked the ketch on the rocks."

Her brother would have to mention that. Jess busied her-

self with spooning out more broccoli, as if she had nothing more important to do.

"I wasn't the one guiding the ship," she said. "And we both lived to tell the tale and no one the wiser."

"Your father didn't know?" Lark asked.

"No," Jess admitted.

"I knew," Maudie put in. "I always know when Alex is lying. His ears twitch."

Alex dropped his fork and clapped a hand to each ear. "They do not!"

"I certainly never noticed," Jess assured him. Though she would be on the watch for it now. "And I don't see how you could be too busy to take Lark out, Alex."

She eyed her brother, who looked to Lark as he dropped his hands. "Truly, Mr. Denby, you need someone else. I tend to stay on land these days."

Terribly wet land that appeared to grow seaweed. His ears twitched. Jess narrowed her eyes.

"So, who would you suggest?" Lark asked, forking up the broccoli. "Henry Bascom, Quillan St. Claire?"

"Not Captain St. Claire," Maudie put in, pausing to suck her teeth. "He hides away in his cottage, only coming out on the dark of the moon. No, Alex is a far better choice."

"I say, dear sister," Alex put in brightly, "was that trifle I saw you take down to the cellar to keep cool?"

Dear sister. Oh, but he was putting it on thick. Twitching ears or no, he didn't want to talk about sailing. Still, she could hardly deny the treat that was waiting.

"Yes, *dear brother.* Why don't you be a darling and fetch it for me?"

He leaned back on the bench. "Oh, I wouldn't dream of depriving you of the honor."

Maudie popped up. "I'll get it." She slid off the bench and hustled for the door that led down to the cellar.

Jess met her brother's gaze. He smiled. She wanted to

box his twitching ears.

Maudie returned and set the trifle on the table. Jess set about spooning it out, still fuming. At least Lark's eyes lit as he took a bite of the strawberries, cake, and cream mixture.

"Is that lavender I taste?" he asked after swallowing. "I thought most of it came from France."

Oh, don't let him take her for a smuggler now!

Maudie sighed. "Lovely stuff too, such a pretty purple. Perfect for luring in fairies."

"This came from the Inchleys," Jess told him. "Very likely they had it from a nearby farmer. France isn't the only place to find lavender."

"Or lace," her brother acknowledged. "Though the ladies seem to favor it."

And how would he know? She hadn't seen him around a lot of ladies.

Lark leaned toward him. "Hard to get French lace these days, unless you're a smuggler. A shame there are none around Grace-by-the-Sea."

Alex shrugged. "There are Free Traders all along the Dorset coast."

Her heart sank, but she could not give up so easily. "But not here."

"Maybe," he answered maddeningly. "But there might be one or two more in Upper Grace."

Jess opened her mouth, and she felt something press against her foot. Was that Lark's boot?

"Care to introduce me?" Lark asked her brother.

Alex leaned back. "If they're amendable."

She jerked her foot away from Lark's. "Alexander Chance, if you know something about smuggling, you report it, right now."

Alex scowled. "I'm no telltale."

"Your sister is right, sir," Lark informed him. "If there are smugglers in the area, you must report them. It's the only

way to keep the village safe."

"You're both wrong," Alex declared, slinging a leg off the bench. "There are many ways to keep the coast safe. Excuse me. I've lost my appetite." He rose.

"Alex," Jess protested, but he snagged his coat off the hook beside the door and slammed out. A moment later, he loped past the window.

"Forgive me," Lark said, rising. "I didn't mean to cause trouble between you."

Neither had she, but she'd been the one to press matters. Jess swung off the bench as well. "No, forgive us, Lark. We haven't been the best hosts. I suppose we're rusty."

"Even with feeding all those strays?" he teased.

"They made excellent stew," Maudie assured him.

Jess could not recapture the laughter of earlier. "Aunt, may I ask you to start clearing? I'll just walk Mr. Denby back to High Street."

Maudie didn't protest, though Lark looked at Jess askance. She went around the table to lead him to the door. She waited only until they had passed the cottage window before stopping him.

"I know how it sounded just now with my brother, but I can't make myself believe him to be in league with smugglers."

His smile was grim. "And yet he meets the criteria. He is from a genteel family, he has an easy manner that might draw other men to him, he seems strong and healthy, and he can sail."

Each fact pounded a nail in her heart. "But he must know the dangers. He must know it's wrong. No, there's something else at play."

His face tightened. "I wish I could believe that, but I fear your brother is hiding the truth from you. Alex could well be the Lord of the Smugglers."

Her eyes were wide, and he longed to slip into the expanse of blue like a tern diving for a fish. Then they narrowed, shutting him out.

"No," she said. "Alex can't be the Lord of the Smugglers. He may have an easy manner, but he's two steps out of the schoolroom. Can you see men flocking to follow?"

Men like Howland? Likely not. But that didn't mean her brother lacked supporters.

"There must be men his age," Lark said. "Henry Bascom's boy, for one."

"Boy," she echoed. "Exactly. Boys out for a bit of fun, not criminals bent on avoiding capture."

"Sometimes," Lark said, "they are one and the same."

"Not with Alex," she insisted.

He wanted to believe her, but loyalty might have made her blind. It had his father. Looking back, Lark could see that every bit of evidence his father had gathered had suggested the smugglers were among their neighbors, their friends. Like Mrs. Bascom, the ladies of his village always had lace, the public houses brandy. Tea canisters never seemed to run out, and even the poorest families could find gloves for their children in the winter, despite the high import duty on the things.

But his father had ignored the warning signs, certain that no one he knew could be so greedy, so lawless. Lark had never known in the end which hand had plunged the dagger into his father's gut. He'd seen guilt and hostility on every face at the funeral. It was just as well his mother had moved them all to Upper Grace. She and his sisters had tried hard to forget. He still remembered.

"I understand your need to protect your brother," he said, feeling his way. "We set out to learn the truth about

smuggling in the area. If it turns out he's involved…"

"He won't be," she said.

He inclined his head. "Perhaps not. I hope we can agree that whoever is involved must be stopped."

She nodded. "Yes. I have no argument with you there."

"Good. Then we have two more opportunities to pursue: questioning Jack Hornswag and Captain St. Claire. I'll request a meeting with the latter. We can beard Hornswag in his den in the morning."

She drew in a breath. "Very well. I'll see you at the spa, then."

That was his cue to leave her. He couldn't make his feet move. Indeed, emotion swept over him, stronger than the waves on the cove beside them. She had been bequeathed nothing but burdens—the management of the spa, the care of her brother and aunt. She was carrying them all well, yet he longed to come along beside her, help her when she faltered, encourage her when she soared. He wanted to soar with her.

Her eyes widened again, as if she could see the thoughts tumbling through his mind.

"You want to kiss me," she said.

He did. The realization only made the urge stronger. But he had no more right to kiss her than Vincent had had to pursue her. He wasn't ready to take a wife.

Even if Jess would make the perfect wife.

She knew that look. A groom's face held the same tender wonder right before he kissed his bride at the altar. Why would Lark look at her that way now?

She had watched him walk away before, but she'd been a green girl then, unsure of herself and her place in the

world. Now she understood the give and take in a courtship, had watched it play out dozens of times over the last few years as she was called upon to play matchmaker. Several ladies in the village owed their weddings to her efforts. Other guests had left betrothed and written her of happy marriages afterward. She knew what to look for in a gentleman's behavior to suggest he was interested in a lady. Lark's actions held a spark of interest.

He blinked at her question, and pink rushed to his cheeks. "I suppose I do want to kiss you."

She didn't suppose. She didn't think. She simply stepped forward and pressed her lips to his.

And she was flying, like a cutter shooting through the waves, fearless, boundless. His arms came around her, cradled her against him. It was magnificent, thrilling.

Terrifying.

She drew back, trying to find breath. He seemed to be having equal trouble locating equilibrium.

"Thank you," he said.

It was such a simple thing to say after such a kiss that she had to laugh.

He joined her. "Sorry. You took me by surprise. And here I was, trying to convince myself I should not think of you as a bride."

Her heart slammed into her chest, as if it too wanted to go flying. "And what did you conclude?"

"That you are impossibly precious to me."

Why did he sound saddened by the fact? "And this troubles you?"

"It does, for there is only one outcome I know for such feelings, and I have never been in a position to marry."

His eyes dipped down at the corners. So did his lips. Lips that had felt so wondrous against hers. Lips she had heard speak of devotion.

"Never is a very long time," she allowed. She crossed her

arms over her chest and looked him up and down. "You are healthy, established in your profession. You can make some claim to good character."

That won a smile from him. "Some."

"Then why can't you marry?"

He was quiet a moment, and she heard him draw in a breath. "I'm not sure you understand what it's like to be a wife of a Riding Officer, never knowing when her husband will return, *if* he will return. Being shunned by friends and family who believe him a traitor to their way of life. I saw what my mother and sisters endured. I will not allow my wife and children to suffer."

Oh! Stubborn! She knew that look as well. He'd left her once, despite the feelings she'd had for him. It seemed he thought he might have feelings now, but not deep enough, not true enough, to matter against his determination. Would she have to bury her feelings yet again?

Something pushed up inside her, like water rising on the incoming tide, demanding that she take a risk, show him what he was missing. Attempt to capture his heart and keep him at her side.

Dangerous thought. She had little evidence to hope for success. Yet he had kissed her back. He had run with her. He had confided in her. He obviously enjoyed working beside her on a common goal.

"I can see that your mind is made up," she said. "So is mine. We finish this investigation together, sir, but I propose a change in plans."

He raised his brows. "Oh? Someone else we must interview?"

She could feel her courage building. "No. You wanted to see the caves under Castle How. I've thought of someone who might take you into the Dragon's Maw. Be on the shore at midnight tonight. Your captain will be waiting."

Even if she was shaking in her half-boots.

CHAPTER SIXTEEN

L ARK HAD NO IDEA WHO Jess had in mind to take him into the caves, but he wasn't about to question her proposal. Getting a look under Castle How might provide any number of insights. Some smugglers had especially equipped hiding holes, complete with shelving to store supplies and goods, sleeping quarters, and even personal belongings. He might be able to discover the identity of the Lord of the Smugglers before morning.

"I'll be there," he promised Jess. "And thank you." The urge to kiss her was building again, so he made himself turn and head for the Mermaid.

But thoughts of her followed him, and he knew why.

For the first time, he questioned his beliefs. He had determined never to marry until he could assure the safety of his wife and family. He'd thought perhaps when the war ended, things would be different. Taxes could be low-ered. The smugglers would have less incentive to ply their trade, and those selling secrets would find fewer buyers. But England had been at war for decades. Would there ever come a time he could convince himself it was safe enough to wed?

The matter remained on his mind as he prepared for the night's adventure. He might dress as a gentleman to inter-act with the denizens of Grace-by-the-Sea, but he knew

how to blend in with the night as well as any smuggler did. His success and his life often depended on it. With his black wool sweater, black fitted jacket, black trousers tucked into his boots, and a dark cap pulled low over his forehead, he resembled nothing so much as a shadow. The few remaining patrons of the inn's public room didn't even remark when he slipped out before midnight.

Moonlight made the cove a place of light and shadow. The waves brushed the shore quietly. Directly ahead, a small boat was beached, its end bobbing.

Another shadow detached itself from the fishermen's sheds. Lark stiffened, but the moonlight etched the silver hair and aristocratic features he had come to know.

"Ready to embark, Mr. Denby?" Lord Featherstone asked.

Lark shook his head. "So, you're the one willing to sail into the Dragon's Maw."

A ripple went through the fellow. A shudder? "You mistake me, sir. I am merely Charon, here to ferry you across the River Styx." He gestured toward the boat. "Shall we?"

The allusion to the passage to Hades held no comfort. Bemused, Lark held the stern steady as the baron climbed aboard. Then Lark shoved the boat off the beach and jumped in. Featherstone made no move to take up the oars, so Lark applied himself. The water splashed as he rowed out into the cove.

"That's our ketch, there," the baron murmured.

Lark angled his strokes to head in that direction. His lordship grasped the hull as they came alongside, and Lark helped him snug the boat against the wooden side.

"Up you go, now," Lord Featherstone said. "Your captain is waiting."

Lark stood and grasped the edge that lay almost even with the row boat's. "How will you get back?"

His lordship shifted to take up the oars, patrician nose

in the air. "Just remember, my boy. We do mad things for love."

Love? Who was waiting for him on the ship? Lark swung himself aboard and leaned over to help the baron shove off.

He straightened to eye the boat. The ketch was long and sleek, and likely had a shallow bottom and short keel to allow it to glide into the cove. That meant it was all too easy to keel over. Whoever sailed it must be skilled.

He cocked his head to see around the mast, but his captain might as well have been a wraith for all he could see of the fellow. He was here, there, here again, checking ropes, tackle, the sails. He pointed to a thick rope stretching taut from the bow. Right. Best not to speak as little as possible, as Lord Featherstone had done. Voices carried over water. No need to wake the village.

Lark went to the rope and tugged. The boat had moved enough on the tide that the anchor came free. He hauled it in and stowed it in the bow. Turning from the task, he found that his guide had unlashed the mainsail and had pulled it up and into place. He pointed toward the jib, and Lark went to draw the triangular front sail into place as well. As the captain passed him for the tiller, he caught a whiff of lavender.

No! It couldn't be.

Before he could confirm his fears, the wind filled the sails, and the ketch shot forward. He clutched the mast to keep his footing. The breeze and tide pushing them, they darted across the cove and whipped through the opening between the headlands and out onto the open sea. The horizon disappeared in the moonlight, until there was nothing ahead but sea and stars.

The captain adjusted the tiller, and the ketch tilted as it swung to the east. They skimmed along the shore, the cliffs ghostly white against the night sky. Lark made his way to the stern.

"I thought you didn't sail anymore," he said.

Jess tipped back her head, and moonlight picked out her features. "Who else could I trust to take you?"

"Turn back," he said. "It's dangerous."

She cocked her head, and he could just make out the fluttering lashes. "Why, Mr. Denby, whoever said it wasn't?" She straightened to nod toward the bow. "Man the sails, if you please. As soon as the tide turns, we'll make a run for the Dragon's Maw. We'll need the sails as we approach to push us, but they must be down before we reach the opening, or we'll come in too fast and wreck against the cliff."

She was so calm, so sure, that he could not doubt her. Amazement courted awe and birthed an emotion he wasn't ready to name. He went to do as she bid.

She had to tack past the cliff face twice before he felt it. The hull shifted; the cant of the boat swung. The tide had turned. She leaned on the tiller.

"On my command," she called.

He had only served on a cutter twice, but he knew the expected response. "Aye, Captain," Lark acknowledged.

The ketch veered in toward the cliff, closer, closer, until he could hear the roar of the surf against the rocks. Boulders stuck up ahead, the way between impossibly narrow. Lark caught his breath. She wouldn't, she couldn't...

"Now!" she shouted, and he released the rope to let it whip through his fingers. Down came the sail, creaking in protest.

The boulders surged on either side, then darkness wrapped them.

"There's a lantern at my feet," Jess said. "Come light it. Quickly."

He felt his way back, stumbling as he reached her. The darkness pressed in on him like a blanket, covering his eyes, his face. Relief surged as his fingers touched the tinderbox.

A few moments later, the wick caught, and light flowed

around them. She took a deep breath.

"And here we are, sir. The caves under Castle How."

He turned and lifted the lantern high, higher. The light still didn't reach the walls on either side or the roof above them. They were gliding through black water, each movement, every creak magnified in the vast stillness.

"The incoming tide will carry us the rest of the way," she told him. "But we'll have to wait until the tide turns again before we can leave."

Lark glanced at her. "How long?"

"About five hours in this tide cycle. We should reach the cove just as dawn breaks."

He stiffened. "You could be seen."

"I brought a gown with me. If anyone notices us coming in, I can claim to have been a passenger with you for a night sail. Everyone will assume my brother captained the ketch."

He wasn't so sure of that. "You risked a great deal to do this for me—your reputation, your position."

She raised her chin. "I did it for the good of the village. We must know who implicates us."

That he could not argue.

Ahead came a whisper, made more rhythmic by the echo.

"We're near the shore," she said. "Prepare to drop anchor."

"Aye." Lark hooked the lantern to the mast and went forward. Out of the darkness, walls loomed, craggy and dark. Water glistened silver in the lamplight. Ahead, he made out a rocky beach.

"Lower anchor," she ordered.

"Lower anchor, aye." He picked up the chunk of iron and flung it out, heard it splash in the water. A moment more, and the ship swung to a halt.

They had reached the fabled caves. Would discovering their secrets warrant the danger to Jess?

Jess released the tiller, fingers stiff from her grip. She rose and went to join Lark in the bow. She'd forgotten how odd it felt to wear trousers. The striped pair she'd found among her brother's belongings were looser around her legs than those she'd worn as a girl but tighter in the seat. At least his jacket closed over her chest, which also felt odd without its usual corset. But she would never have been able to sail into the caves in her fashionable gowns and the stiff underpinnings they required.

Lark had fetched the lantern and now held it high again. By its light, she made out the beach, dotted with rocks that had fallen from the cave's roof. Walls enclosed the back of the main cave, with a darker arch recessed into one side.

She pointed to it. "That's the entrance to the stairs up to Castle How." Her voice echoed.

He appeared to be studying the beach. "No permanent structures."

He sounded disappointed. She could only be glad. "Just that ring of rocks, there. That's where we used to light a fire."

Even as she said the word, a shiver went through her.

"You're cold," Lark said. He started to shrug out of his coat, and she caught his hand.

"No need. I brought blankets and the last of the rolls from dinner."

His chuckle was multiplied against the rocks. "You thought of everything."

She'd thought too much. After he'd left her at the shore, she'd asked Maudie to take a note to Lord Featherstone's lodgings. She could only be grateful the baron had agreed with her plan, even though it raised his silvery brows. She'd have far preferred to convince Alex to sail the ketch, but he

had not returned before the appointed hour. She'd tried to nap, but her thoughts chased her, and it wasn't just concern for Alex that kept her awake. She was actively considering how to attract Lark. Wonder vied with worry. She was known for her matchmaking, but she'd acknowledged she lacked the skill when it came to her own heart. What made her think she could be any more successful this time?

Even if she had sailed into the Dragon's Maw for him.

He returned now with the blankets and draped one about her shoulders. "Your mantel, Your Majesty. I'll have your feast ready shortly."

"When was I coronated?" she teased, snuggling into the wool's warmth as he set out for the stern once more.

"Oh, years ago," he assured her, bringing her back a roll from the pack she'd carried aboard. "You are the undisputed queen of Grace-by-the-Sea."

She snorted. "That's Mrs. Greer. I am merely a lowly handmaid."

"You are nothing of the sort."

The warmth in his voice made her suddenly toasty indeed. She bit into the roll, then nodded to the beach as she swallowed.

"I thought you'd want to go ashore."

He crouched beside her, roll in one hand and gaze on the rocky beach. "So did I, but it's clear no one uses this regularly. There'd be some sign—disturbance of the rocks where a boat had landed, the smell of smoke in the air from a fire." He drew in the chill air and blew it out. "I've risked your life for nothing."

She shifted, her shoulder brushing his. "At least you've ruled this out as a landing spot."

"Which pleases you no end, I'm sure. One less possible tie to Grace-by-the-Sea."

His frustration echoed with his words. "*If* there are smugglers in the area, we will find them," she promised him.

"Since you do not intend to investigate the caves further, perhaps we should get some sleep. Otherwise, tomorrow will be a very long day."

"Good thinking. The change in the tide should wake us. I'll put out the light to save the oil."

She wrapped the blanket more securely around her and leaned against the side of the hull. The incoming tide rocked the ketch gently. The darkness was complete. She heard Lark settle near her.

Once again, she knew sleep was the prudent choice, but she couldn't seem to relax. The darkness pulsed against her eyes. She closed them, made herself take several calming breaths. Nothing helped. She had so many questions she wanted to ask him. Or perhaps merely one.

"Why didn't you come back to the spa before now?" she murmured.

The boat shifted as he did. "There seemed to be no need. It was enough to visit my mother and sisters, ensure to their wellbeing. The spa was another world, one I felt I had left behind."

She swallowed. He couldn't see her, didn't know how each word troubled her. Why was it so hard to hear this?

"And now?" she asked. "What do you think of Grace-by-the-Sea now?"

"It is like a peaceful garden," he allowed. "And I can see why you and the Spa Corporation wish to keep it so. The war, these smugglers, seem far away most days."

"Is that so bad?" she protested.

"No," he said. "At times, I find myself tempted to stay."

"Then stay." Though she couldn't see him, she opened her eyes and twisted to gaze in his direction. "Your mother and sisters would be so happy to have you near."

"And you?" he murmured. "Would you like me near, Jess?"

"Yes," she whispered. "Oh, yes."

Something brushed her hand. She grasped his fingers, clung to them.

"I'll see what can be done," he murmured. "I serve at the whim of the Excise Office. I had assumed I'd be reassigned to Kent when the Lord of the Smugglers was found. Would you ever consider leaving Grace-by-the-Sea?"

The gaping hole in her heart was her answer. But if she truly wanted a future with him, shouldn't she be willing to give as much as she asked of him?

"I'll see what can be done," she answered.

CHAPTER SEVENTEEN

DAWN WAS STILL ASLEEP WHEN they sailed back into the cove. So were most of the villagers. Jess brought the ketch as close to the shore as she could, and Lark splashed through the shallows to fetch the small boat. After she'd anchored, he rowed out to fetch her back.

"Are you sure you want to interview Jack Hornswag and Quillan St. Claire today?" he asked as he helped her ashore.

She nodded, hiding a yawn. She had managed a few hours of sleep in the cave, but likely not enough. "I'll be fine. See you at the spa at eight."

He brought her hand to his lips, pressed a kiss against her knuckles. Her legs felt wobbly as he released her. But she managed to reach the cottage and slide into bed with Maudie for a couple more hours of sleep. And still, Alex hadn't come home.

It was harder than ever to climb the hill that morning and perform her duties. Still, she had her Regulars all sorted and was instructing Miss Barlow in the fine-tuning of the fountain when Lark strolled in.

"I'll be back this afternoon," she told the lady and Maudie.

"We'll perform admirably," Miss Barlow assured her. "I'm delighted to assist. Being the hostess of such a prestigious spa is quite a calling."

It was indeed. But now, she had another.

She donned her bonnet and walked with Lark down the hill.

"No one the wiser, I trust?" he asked.

"Only Lord Featherstone. He has yet to arrive this morning."

He chuckled. "Last night was more of an exertion than he generally has in a week, I warrant."

They reached the Mermaid shortly after, and Lark insisted on calling Jack Hornswag out onto the side of the building to talk. He was protecting Jess's reputation. Ladies did not generally dally in the public rooms of an inn, after all, even if they were concerned about their village and smugglers. The innkeeper nodded to both of them, planted his feet in the chalky soil, and put his hands on his massive hips.

"Well? How can I help the hostess of the spa this morning?"

Jess smiled at him. "By answering a few simple questions. We are assisting Magistrate Howland in compiling the returns for the lord-lieutenant."

He spit toward the sea. "That for the lord-lieutenant. He's all for protecting his own, never mind those who have need of their things."

Lark's mouth tightened, but Jess kept her look pleasant. "It is rather daunting to think of transporting every person, animal, and crop inland to prevent the French from harming them. You must have a large cellar and many goods to protect."

"Large enough," he acknowledged. "But I told all that to the constable."

"And have you a boat or barge to help ferry things away?" Lark asked.

Mr. Hornswag narrowed his eyes at him. "I don't go out at sea. Hurt my leg in the war, and it's never been the same

since."

"You bear it bravely," Jess assured him. "What a shame a man of your skills must be confined to land."

He turned to her, and a smile broadened his face. "Ah, but all the pretty lasses are on land, Miss Chance." He nodded to Lark. "You might remember that next time you start asking about boats, Mr. Denby. Young Alex was saying how much you wanted to sail through the Dragon's Maw."

Jess started. "You've seen my brother?"

He nodded his massive head. "He was in my public room last night. And I'll tell you the same thing I told him." He loomed over Lark. "I don't trust those currents. Never have. Never will." He straightened with a nod, as if satisfied that was that.

Lark thanked him for his time and took Jess's elbow to lead her back up the hill.

"Not much help," she managed.

"No," Lark agreed. "And I take it your brother still doesn't know of our trip."

"He never came home last night," Jess admitted. "It's not the first time. I wish I knew what he was doing, besides loitering in the public room."

His hand slipped to hers, and he gave it a squeeze. "We'll find out."

Hope bubbled up inside her, like water rising in the fountain. He was holding her hand, offering comfort. How extraordinary. Maudie was always there for her, if in her aunt's own world, and Abigail could be counted upon for advice and counsel, but no one else since her father had died had made it sound as if they were in this together. As if she didn't have to rely only on herself.

If only Lark could be persuaded to take a risk and marry.

Lark ought to return Jess to the spa. Her guests would be looking for her. Crabapple would have questions on courting. Lord Featherstone would be looking for his daily dose of the spa waters. But he was loath to let her go. Perhaps that was why he suggested they take a walk along the shore path, just to tarry in her company.

"I'd like your opinion on some of the other boats," he explained. "It shouldn't take long."

"Very well," she said, as if she had nothing more important to do than to spend time with him. He tucked her hand in his arm, and they were off.

The shore path cupped the cove in either direction, running past cottages crowded up against the headland. Most were neat and trim, but, here and there, chipping paint and crumbling rock gave testimony of too many storms weathered. The waves ate away at the ground in front at high tide, their movement compelling. A gull soared overhead with a mournful cry.

Jess gazed out over the waters. "Did you disappear at odd times like Alex does when you were coming into your own?"

Lark barked a laugh. "Too often for my mother's nerves, I'm sure. And, I'm ashamed to say, I always had a ready story for my absence. I think she suspected I was up to no good, but mostly I was just exploring."

Her brows rose. "Exploring? Exploring what, exactly?"

He shrugged. "Everything, anything. I was convinced there was more to the world than the everyday life of Upper Grace."

She sighed. "We weren't enough for you."

He took her hand and brought it to his lips. "You would be enough for any man, Jess."

He was getting carried away again, but before he could think better of it, she stiffened. Jerking her hand out of his,

she grabbed his arm and tugged him into the shadow of the nearest cottage.

He looked at her askance, but she put a finger to her lips and nodded toward the path. A moment more and the vicar hurried past, glancing forward and back as if he feared someone had let the hounds out after him.

"Is there a reason you don't want the vicar to see us?" Lark whispered.

Jess craned her neck, gaze following the minister as he headed for High Street. "Odd that he would be down on the shore this morning. Monday is generally the day he takes some time to himself. What purpose did he have on this side of the cove?"

Lark glanced after the minister, who was still moving faster than most errands would warrant. "It seems he doesn't want anyone to notice he's been down this way. Interesting."

She did not look pleased. "More interesting that I see my own minster and my first thought is to hide. Perhaps my conscience is the one that requires examining."

"Why, Miss Chance," he teased, "what terrible thing have you done?"

She didn't answer, smile prim. "Perhaps you should tell me which of these boats troubles you, sir."

Lark eyed the cove. Most of the fishermen were out, now. Besides her family ketch, only one looked like it could fly through the water. The vessel was likely large enough to make it to France and fast enough to evade capture by a revenue cutter.

"Whose boat is that?" he asked Jess.

She followed his gaze. "Henry Bascom's."

He should have known. Yet why was it at anchor and not on its way to France?

"Lark?" she asked. "You're frowning. What is it?"

He nodded toward the ship. "The other fishermen are

out plying their trade. Why hasn't Henry Bascom joined them?"

Now she looked troubled. "I don't know. We could try his home once more, but we likely won't get far questioning his wife again if he isn't home or refuses to come to the door. Do you want to watch the harbor and see if he appears?"

That could take hours, and he felt the moments ticking away. "No," he said, turning for High Street. "I'll leave my card at Dove Cottage, see if Captain St. Claire is amenable to a visit."

Jess fell into step beside him. "He may refuse to speak to you too. After all, he is supposed to be an invalid."

"An invalid or too busy having adventures," Lark said.

She cast a glance in his direction, quick, but thoughtful. "Did you ever find the adventure you sought?"

"A bit," he allowed. "I never know what I'll discover on my riding circuit. Some days it's nothing more than hours in the saddle." He grinned at her. "And some days, I get to chase smugglers for miles across fen and ford."

"It sounds as if you like those days best," she said.

They started up past the shops. The barber came out, razor in hand, and waved it at Lark. Lark rubbed his chin with one hand but felt nothing catch against his glove. As they passed the baker's, something hit his top hat, knocking it partway off his head.

Jess stopped and glanced around. "What was that?"

Lark righted his hat, then bent to pick up a roll from the ground. It was clearly old—grey speckled one side, and it was hard as a rock. He glanced back in time to see someone duck into the doorway of the bakery.

"I think Mr. Ellison lobbed this at me."

She looked to the roll in his hand. "Don't be silly. Someone must have dropped that there on their way home with a dozen." She started forward.

He was surprised how much he didn't want the animosity starting up again, not here at Grace-by-the-Sea. But then, no one but Jess and the magistrate knew his true profession. Lark sent the bakery a frown and caught up with her. But as they passed Mr. Carroll's Curiosities, the dapper shopkeeper came out onto his stoop and crossed his arms over his chest, gaze on Lark.

Miss Archer went so far as to hurry out to intercept them. "Jess! My dear! Do we have you to thank, Mr. Denby, for prying her out of the spa again?"

"Mr. Denby and I are helping Magistrate Howland," Jess said before he could answer. "He must confirm the returns before sending them to the lord-lieutenant."

Miss Archer's green gaze was bright, but something simmered behind it. "Interesting. Is that why you tarried so long on the Downs on Saturday? I would suspect you were counting sheep, but there were none where we travelled. If Mr. Denby is only interested in confirming the returns, he must wish to speak to every shopkeeper and farmer in the area. Perhaps we should hold a meeting in the assembly rooms so you can ask us all at once. That way, Mr. Denby has no more need to monopolize your time."

A sensible suggestion, if confirming the returns was truly their aim. "Once again, you are too kind, Miss Archer," he said.

Jess merely smiled. "There is no need, Abigail. I enjoy spending time with *Lark*. And we are almost finished, in any event."

Miss Archer blinked, glancing between the two of them. As if she saw something, her smile widened. "Oh, well, then. Carry on. I wish you two only the best." Humming to herself, she trotted back toward her shop.

Lark watched her a moment. It seemed his profession remained a mystery after all. Howland was right. They were all concerned about how he was treating Jess. And

her use of his first name had told her friend they were indeed courting. He ought to correct the impression, but he didn't. Some part of him insisted on entertaining the notion.

Jess started forward as if nothing had happened. Indeed, if her topic of conversation was any indication, she was attempting to pretend they were two friends on a promenade through the village. "I hope I have a chance to renew my acquaintance with your mother and sisters while you're here. I always enjoyed talking with your family, Hester especially."

His oldest sister was a couple years older than Jess, but her life had been considerably harder, having married young and lost her husband at sea four years ago. Now she was raising her daughter alone.

"I'll mention that to her when I see her," he said.

They had reached the door of the spa. He held open the door for her, escorted her inside. She smiled at him. But as her gaze went to the Grand Pump Room, she froze and turned white.

He had no idea what had discomposed her, but he knew something was wrong.

Jess stared at the Grand Pump Room, stomach plummeting like a rock thrown from the headland. This was not her spa. Gone were the sparkling glasses by the fountain, waiting to dispense the shimmering brew. Gone was the chess set, the table looking oddly bereft. Gone were most of her guests, including Miss Barlow. Only the Admiral remained, huddled in one of the chairs overlooking the cove, countenance bleak. And the pamphlets! Not a one in sight. Well, she could not entirely regret the loss of those.

A woman in black bombazine trotted up to her, round face wreathed in smiles, grey curls half hidden by a huge white hat adorned with ostrich plumes that had been dyed a jaunty blue, and it was a moment before she realized she was looking at her aunt.

"We made a few changes," Maudie announced, as if she had noticed the dismay on Jess's face.

"So I see," Jess said. "Where did you get that hat?"

"Miss Barlow said I needed to look cheerier. Can you imagine? She found this on special at Beautiful Bonnets."

Mrs. Rinehart had probably been glad to be rid of it. "Where is the Welcome Book?" Jess asked, gaze scanning the room.

"Miss Barlow thought we should put it away," Maudie explained. "Strangers might use it to determine which of us to prey on."

And who had put that thought in the woman's head?

Lark lay a hand on her arm. "I'm sure it will only take a moment to put right."

She wasn't nearly so sure. Jess looked to her aunt. "And what have you done with Lord Featherstone's chess set?"

Maudie sniffed, chin coming up and setting her ostrich plumes to swaying. "Miss Barlow said it made the gentlemen disinclined to interact with the ladies."

She thought Lark swallowed a chuckle.

"Miss Barlow has some strong opinions," Jess said.

"Isn't it a blessing?" Maudie agreed.

Jess turned to Lark, her hands going to untie the strings of her bonnet. "Go leave your card for Captain St. Claire. I'll settle things here."

He hesitated. "Are you certain?"

She nodded, but her steps were already taking her to the welcome desk.

She found the Welcome Book underneath. Several of the pages had been rumpled, but she smoothed them out

and set the book back in its place. There was no sign of Mrs. Greer's precious pamphlets.

She went to the Admiral next. He surged up from his chair at the sight of her, and she almost expected him to envelope her in a hug, so eager was his countenance.

As if he realized his emotions were showing as well, he effected a sterner look.

"See here, Miss Chance," he blustered. "What is the meaning of all these changes? I'll have you know I've spent many a happy hour over that chessboard."

"As have Lord Featherstone and Mr. Crabapple," she assured him. "Never fear, Admiral Walsey. I will return the board and pieces to their rightful place soon."

"Yes, well." He humphed and tugged down on his waist-coat. "It's good to have you back. Carry on."

Jess moved around the room again, mentally cataloging the remaining tasks to set the spa to rights. She discovered the glasses from the previous day piled in her father's examining room at the back of the spa. A shame she couldn't tell which had been used.

"I must wash them all," Jess told Maudie, who had followed her.

"Miss Barlow says gentlewomen do not wash," Maudie informed her with a sniff.

"Gentlewomen who wish to remain employed do," Jess replied. Glancing around, she found that the Admiral had left them as well. At least that meant it was safe to be out of sight of the Grand Pump Room. "Why don't you go play something to cheer us?"

As her aunt hurried for the harpsichord, Jess returned to her father's examining room. Hot mineral water could be pumped there as well. The sound of a sonata drifted through the door as she drew some water into the examining room sink and rolled up her sleeves. Lark returned just as she immersed her hands in the water. He took one

look at her and began to shuck off his coat.

Jess caught a glass before it slipped from her grip. "What are you doing?"

"Preparing to help," he said, rolling up one sleeve to reveal a firm arm. "You wash, I'll dry."

Jess stared at him. "You're really going to dry glasses?"

He frowned. "Of course. Didn't I just say as much?"

She laughed. "You did indeed. The towel is over there."

Again, he surprised her. Her father had been focused on his patients. He'd never pitched in on the day-to-day operation of the spa. Her mother had served as hostess until her passing. Her father had worked with Maudie until Jess was old enough to assist him. And Alex had long ago disdained the minutia of the spa. Lark dove in as if it was nothing.

And she couldn't remember when work had been so pleasant. He told her stories of odd items he'd discovered during his duties, from a model of the Sphinx made of spun sugar to an eight-foot Burmese python. She shared about some of her more colorful guests, such as the lady equestrian from Astley's Amphitheatre and the American heiress whose funds came from oysters.

"And here I thought the spa was so ordinary," he said, toweling off the last glass.

"It is now," Jess said, wiping her hands on another towel. "We had far more guests when my father was alive. The Spa Corporation is right that a physician is needed, but I don't relish handing over the reins to someone else."

"A Newcomer," he said. "That's what you call people who come here temporarily."

"He'll only be a Newcomer for a short time," she allowed. "Like you. I have hopes you will earn the rank of Regular."

He wiggled his brows. "Because I know how to ingratiate myself with the right people."

She chuckled. "You have never ingratiated yourself in

your life. Put on your coat. I'll wheel these out by the fountain."

Once through the door, she found most of her guests had returned. Perhaps the Admiral had told them that it was safe. Mrs. Harding was consoling Mr. Crabapple over the loss of the chess set. Lord Featherstone was attempting to elicit a smile from Miss Cole, while her mother watched as if suspecting him of nefarious purposes. And Miss Barlow stood across the Welcome Book from Maudie, noses nearly touching and hands braced on the wood.

Lark joined her before she could intercede and nodded toward the door. "If you take on Miss Barlow, I can deal with her. I could practice my ingratiating manner."

She followed his gaze to find that Mrs. Greer had entered the spa as well. Frown evident, the lady glanced around the room before focusing on Jess and raising her chin.

"No," Jess said. "I'll deal with her. Just see if you can find the chess set." She hurried for the door.

"You have been absent," Mrs. Greer complained, long nose pointing at Jess as she came up to the lady.

"I believe Mr. Howland explained the reason to your husband," Jess reminded her.

She gave a long-suffering sigh. "He did. But why must it be you? Surely there are others better equipped to confirm the returns."

"Regardless," Jess said, "we have only one more person to interview. I should be back at my position tomorrow afternoon."

Mrs. Greer clucked her tongue. "Totally inadequate. The woman acting in your stead was far more accommodating."

Very likely. Miss Barlow was hurrying up to them now. "Artemis! How lovely to see you." She offered Mrs. Greer her outstretched hands. "And Miss Chance as well. How might I be of assistance?"

She made it sound as if Jess were the guest and a Newcomer at that!

"Susan, dear," Mrs. Greer greeted her. "You have been a breath of fresh air. I do hope you've considered my suggestion that you extend your stay in our fair town."

She released Mrs. Greer's hands and dropped her gaze. "You are too kind, but I fear the cost of room and board will require my mother and me to leave shortly."

"Nonsense," Mrs. Greet insisted. "Why, I'm certain Miss Chance and Mrs. Tully could make room for you. The Spa Corporation owns their cottage, after all."

Jess gritted her teeth. "Alas, we have but one bed." Out of the corner of her eyes she saw Ike Bascom slip through the door and dart to Maudie at the Welcome Book. Whatever he said made her aunt clutch her chest and rush toward them, hat slipping back on her head to hang from its ribbons behind her.

"And I believe you have a pallet in the loft," Mrs. Greer reminded her. "You and your aunt can sleep there."

"No, we can't," Maudie said, puffing up to them. "We'll be far too busy tending to Alex."

Jess frowned at her, but Mrs. Greer drew herself up.

"Your nephew is a perfectly healthy young man who should have long since found gainful employment. The Corporation cannot be expected to foot the bill for his living."

Anger shot through Jess, pushing the words from her mouth. "How I choose to spend my salary is none of the Corporation's business."

Mrs. Greer blinked. "It most certainly is. As the hostess, you are the face of the Spa. Your reputation must be spotless, your habits wholesome, and your finances frugal."

"Oh, the frugal part is easy," Jess said. "Your miserly salary sees to that."

"That's planted her a facer," Maudie cheered as Mrs.

Greer sputtered. "A shame we must go, but Alex needs us. Terrible doings at the cove."

"What are you going on about now?" Mrs. Greer demanded. "Fairies? Mermaids? Spies?"

"My nephew," Maudie shouted, as if she thought the lady was hard of hearing. "Young Mr. Bascom just brought word. Alex has been beaten and left on our doorstep. So, I do think we will be too busy to continue arguing with you, alas."

CHAPTER EIGHTEEN

L ARK HAD LOCATED THE CHESSBOARD behind
the fountain and was setting it in its rightful place
when he glanced up to see Jess sway on her feet. He was at
her side in a moment.

"What's happened?" he asked, hand on her elbow to
steady her.

Her eyes were wide and deep. "Alex," she said. "He's
been hurt. I must go."

"Oh, really," Mrs. Greer said, "how can you believe a
word your aunt says? She's spouted nothing but dribble
for years."

"Takes one to know one," Mrs. Tully retorted.

Lark put his other hand on Mrs. Tully's back. "It's a matter easily sorted. Excuse us." He ushered her and Jess to the
door, ignoring Mrs. Greer's imperious frown.

"What could have happened?" Jess worried as they
headed down the hill for the cove. "Did he fall off the
headland in the dark?"

"Came across a gathering of trolls?" her aunt suggested.
"They tend to congregate near the castle this time of year."

Lark had other ideas but stating them in the face of Jess's
concerns would have been cruel indeed, so he kept quiet.

Jess's brother lay curled up in front of the cottage's
hearth, as if seeking the warmth of the banked fire. She

went down in a pool of blue cambric beside him.

"Alex? Can you hear me?" She reached out a hand, then drew back as if afraid to touch him.

A groan fluttered up, weak and pained. "Thin' I bro' a rib," he slurred.

Lark crouched beside her. "Give me the direction of the physician, Jess, and I'll fetch him."

"There isn't one." For the first time, her calm, soothing voice caught. "We haven't been able to attract another since Father died."

"There's that fellow in Upper Grace," Mrs. Tully put in, a dark shadow behind them. "More of a sawbones than a physician, and you likely won't get him to come down the hill, not for our family. He'll want gold, and plenty of it."

Jess reached out a hand again, more surely this time. "We'll have to treat Alex ourselves. Aunt, get the blanket from the bed. We'll roll him onto it and use it to lift him."

Mrs. Tully hurried to comply.

He only wanted to hold Jess, give her whatever strength she needed. "I've never done more than bandage a skinned knee," he admitted. "But tell me what to do, and I'll do it."

She nodded.

Mrs. Tully returned with the blanket, and Jess spread it on the floor next to her brother. Lark took Alex's shoulders, Jess the hips, and they gently turned him. She gasped as his face came into view. His right eye was swelling and purple, his lips split. Blood trickled out of his mouth.

"Someone didn't want him to talk," her aunt said.

Lark could not contest her story this time.

They managed to transfer Alex to the bed, where Jess set about opening his waistcoat and pulling up his shirt. Lark was no expert, but even he could see that one side of the youth's ribs was thicker than the other, swelling and red.

"How do we know if a rib is broken?" he asked.

Jess seemed to have gathered her usual composure. "Bro-

ken or bruised, Father would have prescribed the same cure. His head and shoulders should be elevated. That will help keep his lungs clear. Maudie, get more pillows."

Her aunt bustled out of the room. Something thunked as she started up the ladder for the loft.

Jess stepped back from the bed, drawing in a deep breath. "He's blessed to be alive."

"I don't think whoever did this wanted him dead," Lark said, crossing his arms over his chest. "Your aunt was right. This was a warning."

She shot him a look. "You think smugglers did this."

Lark shrugged. "I doubt there'd be many other reasons."

Mrs. Tully hurried back in, arms piled high with pillows. One tumbled out as if trying to flee. She dumped the remaining ones on the bed. "I can ask about more in the village, if you like."

"This should be sufficient," Jess promised her, moving to tuck one under her brother's head.

Mrs. Tully's eyes glittered. "Perhaps we should bandage him, like an Egyptian mummy. I've always wanted to unwrap one of those."

"Warm water and a washcloth would be more helpful," Jess suggested.

With a sigh, her aunt left again.

Lark helped Jess pile pillows under the youth's head and shoulders, until Alex was reclining on the bed. His eyes were as open as he could make them with the bruising, but he uttered no more than a grunt as they settled him into place. Still, he watched them with his good eye as they finished and his aunt returned with a wash basin, cloth, and towel.

Lark bent closer before Jess could start on her brother's face. "Who did this to you?"

"Strangers," he managed, wincing as his lips moved. "No one here."

Lark wished he could believe him. Alex could be trying to protect his sister and aunt. Surely the less they knew about the men who had struck him, the better.

"Where?" Lark pressed as Jess wrung the cloth out in the basin.

"On way home," Alex said.

"Smugglers?" Lark asked.

He shrugged, then winced.

Jess frowned at Lark before turning to Mrs. Tully. "Aunt, will you continue the ministrations? I'll just be a moment. Lark?" She tilted her head toward the main room of the cottage. He followed her out.

Once in the main room, she fisted her hands and turned to face him. Though she was still pale, her eyes snapped fire. He wanted to gather her close, promise her all would be well, but there was still too much he didn't know.

"I understand the need to determine how this happened," she said, "but surely you could wait to interrogate him."

He grimaced. "Forgive me. I only want to protect him, and you. He claims strangers beat him. I'm finding that difficult to believe. Surely a pack of unknown men would be noticed in Grace-by-the-Sea unless they came into the area under cover of night. Standard practice for smugglers."

"What will you do?" Jess asked.

Excellent question. More and more, he felt as if his hands were tied behind his back.

"For now, nothing," he answered, "though it pains me to say so. I can only hope your brother will have more to tell us when he's had time to rest."

Who could have done this? Jess couldn't imagine any-

one near Grace-by-the-Sea willing to harm her brother, or anyone else for that matter. But now was not the time to ponder. Now she needed to make sure Alex was all right.

"Maudie and I will stay with him until he's out of danger," she told Lark. "I hate to ask it of you, but would you do me two favors?"

"Anything."

He could not know how that vow buoyed her. "Bring Alex back some mineral water from the spa."

He did not question her belief in the healing waters. "Of course. And?"

"Watch over the spa?"

His smile inched into view, like the sun coming out from a dark sky. "Afraid I might get into trouble otherwise?"

"Afraid *they* might get into trouble," she qualified. "Miss Barlow seems determined to prove herself the superior hostess. And I'm already on questionable ground with the Spa Corporation. Perhaps the charming Mr. Denby can convince everyone that all is well."

He swept her a bow. "I'll do my utmost." He sobered as he straightened. "And I'll watch the village for strangers and the headland for a light in the castle window."

Jess caught his hand. "Just be careful."

"I will, Jess," he murmured. "I promise."

She released him to fetch the key to the spa door. "You'll need this to lock up and open." The iron felt heavier than usual as she transferred it to his hand. It hadn't been out of her possession in more than a year.

He flipped it up and caught it to hold it in one fist. "I will do the spa proud."

That she could not doubt.

Still, she could not shake her misgivings as she and Maudie nursed Alex that afternoon and evening. Abby stopped by with extra blankets, a sweater from Mrs. Mance to protect Alex from a chill, and a book from Mr. Carroll,

adventure stories to cheer her brother. The Inchleys sent their son down with a kettle of stew along with a loaf of bread from Mr. Ellison. Mr. Wingate brought a word of comfort. Lark came with mineral water for Alex and let her know everything at the spa was back to normal. She only wished she could say the same for the rest of her life. She was no longer sure what normal meant.

She yearned to ask her brother more questions, but the way he kept shifting on the pillows and the occasional grimace told her he was in pain and in no position to answer. She was also not about to send him up the ladder to bed; she and Maudie would have to sleep somewhere else so he could stay where he was. She didn't much like the thought of Maudie navigating the ladder more than once either. So, Jess went up and stuffed the pallet through the opening to let it fall to the floor below. Then she and Maudie made up the pallet on the bedroom rug, so they could be near Alex should he need them.

Sleep was difficult, and not just because she kept rising to check on her brother. The thoughts she'd held at a distance all afternoon crashed over her like waves. Like it or not, she must face the fact that Lark was right. Smugglers may have come to Grace-by-the-Sea. But who were they and why had they suddenly appeared? How could she and Lark stop them before someone else was hurt?

Her brother woke just as the sun brightened the curtains on the window the next morning. His groan as he attempted to sit roused Maudie as well. With a yawn, her aunt went to start breakfast, the hem of her nightgown swishing across the floor. Jess moved to Alex's side. Cupping his face in her hands, she turned it gently this way and

that. How odd to feel the prick of stubble on his cheeks. She must remember he was becoming a man.

"The swelling's gone down some," she told him as she released him. "Though I imagine you still hurt."

"A bit," he said bravely, words surer now.

Jess perched on the bed beside him. "What happened, Alex?"

"I'm not really sure," he confessed, dropping his gaze. "I'd gone to the Mermaid with Ike. When I left for home, they were waiting for me."

"They," Jess said. "Who? How many? Why?"

"I didn't recognize them," he admitted. "There were four or five of them. And as to why, they said I was to take a message: Questions aren't welcome."

Jess scrunched up her face. "Did you even ask them any questions?"

"I didn't have a chance. It wasn't my questions that concerned them. It's the ones you and Mr. Denby are asking."

Jess recoiled. "What? But we've only talked with the vicar, Mr. Hornswag at the Mermaid, and Mrs. Bascom. Nothing we said could be taken as threatening. They were perfectly legitimate questions any law-abiding citizen has the right to ask."

Alex caught one of her hands. "I don't think these are particularly law-abiding citizens, Jess. You're messing in matters beyond your ken. Leave be."

If only it was that easy. She could return to the spa, pretend nothing had happened, pretend she didn't see the darkness creeping closer. Wasn't that what she'd done when Lark left the first time and when she'd learned Mr. Vincent was a dastard? Ignore the pain, control her sphere of influence, pretend things were fine. But problems didn't go away by ignoring them, worse luck.

"I might have let things be, once," she told Alex. "But these men invaded our village. They hurt you. If Ike

Bascom hadn't helped you home, I don't know what would have happened to you. I'm more Larkin Denby's ally than ever now. We will find the men who did this to you, and we will stop them."

"You know," her brother said, eyeing her. "I begin to feel afraid."

Jess clutched his hand. "Lark will protect you, Alex."

"Oh, I'm not afraid for myself," he told her. "I'm afraid for those men. I wouldn't want to be them facing you with that look in your eyes."

Lark had spent the better part of Monday afternoon not far from Jess's cottage, tucked between the bank and the shore path. For one, he had wanted to be close enough should she need anything. For another, he wanted to make sure those who had injured Alex did not return to finish the job. But all was quiet at the cove, and he was about ready to walk up to the spa when he spotted the vicar approaching along the shore. Lark put himself in his path.

"Good day, Vicar. I'm surprised to see you down this way."

The vicar frowned at him. "Miss Archer let me know young Alex was injured. How does he fare?"

He was all solicitation, but Lark could not forget how he'd hurried away from the shore the other day, as if he feared someone might notice him. "He's in some pain, I believe. He may even have a broken rib."

The minister made a sad face. "A shame. I cannot condone such violence." He glanced across the cove in the direction of the Bascom cottage.

"Yet you approve of men who bring such violence," Lark said.

He stiffened, gaze returning to Lark. "I do no such thing, sir. I have ever worked to protect those caught in the middle."

Lark eyed him. "The middle of what?"

"Suffice it to say," the minister replied, raising his chin, "that a wife is not always at liberty to leave a husband, even if he raises his hand to her and their children. Or their friends."

Was he saying that Bascom took his ire out on his wife and children? Any respect Lark might have found for the fellow evaporated. "You think Henry Bascom beat Alex?"

Now his gaze darted away. "I did not say as much. I offer sympathy and comfort, discreetly, when needed."

Which might explain his purpose at the Bascom cottage that day. If Henry Bascom had known his wife had spoken of his treatment of her, he might only retaliate.

Lark stepped aside to allow the minister to continue to the cottage. "I'm sure Miss Chance will welcome your help, Vicar."

Mr. Wingate nodded as he passed. And Lark had turned to go up to the spa for Jess. At least he might set her mind at ease about that.

Jess told him about the conversation with her brother the moment he checked in on them after opening the spa the next morning.

"I wish I had more to add," he said when she'd finished. "Unfortunately, when I took Quillan St. Claire my card the other day, his manservant made sure I understood that the captain was not at home to visitors."

"So it will not be easy to pursue that avenue either." Her face sagged, as if all her worries had caught up to her at last.

He took her in his arms. "We'll find who did this, Jess. It's only a matter of time."

He felt her sigh against him. "I'm not sure how much help I can be, what with nursing Alex."

He released her and winked. "Then I guess I'll just have to besiege Dove Cottage."

Her smile brushed him softly, made the moment brighter. "And how are things going at the spa?"

"Everything shipshape," he told her. "Even Mrs. Greer was impressed."

Jess looked impressed as well, and he felt himself preening.

Alex moved out of the bedchamber just then, their aunt right behind. Jess and Mrs. Tully must have managed to help him change, for he wore a linen shirt open at the neck and the breeches of a gentleman. He nodded to Lark.

"Mr. Denby. Thank you for assisting us."

Lark nodded. "Anything for you and your sister. Jesslyn told me about your beating being a warning. I'm sorry you had to take what was meant for me."

Jess went immediately to his defense. "Lark, this wasn't your fault."

Her brother raised his head, his battered face dark with bruises. "No, but all I can say is better me than Jess."

Cold doused him. "No one would dare accost your sister."

Jess's eyes widened, but Alex shook his head. "I wish I could believe that, but you didn't see these men. Hard. Fearless. I don't think much gets in the way of what they want."

"The very kind I hope to stop," Lark assured him. Determination straightened his spine. He glanced at Jess. His intentions must have been written on his face, for she nodded as if agreeing.

He turned to meet her brother's gaze again. "It's best if

you know the truth, Alex. I'm a Riding Officer, on assignment from the commissioner at Weymouth. I'm here to stop the smuggling."

He waited for the protest of innocence, the denial of wrongdoing.

"Good," Alex said. "We don't need that sort here."

He looked so sure, face settling into a scowl made more menacing by his injuries. Lark took a step back and glanced at Jess again. She was studying her brother, and, if he wasn't mistaken, she was watching his right ear.

"So, you've never had a hand in smuggling," she said.

What had her aunt said the other day, that the youth's ears twitched when he was lying? Lark focused on Alex's ears as well. They remained still as he said, "No. But that doesn't mean I don't know a few who have dabbled. No one you need arrest," he hurried to assure Lark. "Just friends out for a bit of fun."

Fun, he said, as if England's secrets weren't going out as illicit goods came in.

Jess did not appear mollified either. "And that gold coin you offered me?" she demanded.

"Gold coin?" Lark echoed, glancing between them.

Alex dropped his gaze and shuffled his feet. "It didn't come from smuggling. That's all I'm at liberty to say."

Mrs. Tully had been watching the interplay as avidly as Lark. Now she nodded. "Mermaid treasure. I thought so. Just don't let anyone else know you've found it, my lad."

Alex smiled at her. "I won't, Aunt."

A shame that was another story Lark could not believe. But if Alex, who had no profession, no employment that anyone could see, could earn a gold coin, chances were his methods weren't legal.

His aunt nodded, then turned to Jess. "I'll watch the boy tomorrow so you can return to the spa. You didn't like Miss Barlow's changes, I could tell. Go make things right

again, Jesslyn."

Jess turned to Lark, face still wary. "It seems I'll be resuming my duties in the morning, Lark. Perhaps you could collect me at eight and we could walk to the spa together? There's much we should discuss."

Her brother, for one. If he had to guess, he'd say she didn't believe Alex either. But, lacking any proof, Lark could hardly request a warrant. And what would he do if he had to arrest Jess's brother?

Was this why his father had hesitated to believe their friends and neighbors might be involved in smuggling?

The question poked at him as he took his leave of Jess and her family. He'd thought his father too kind-hearted for the job he had undertaken. It had been easier for Lark, stationed in a portion of Kent to which he had no ties. He could suspect anyone, investigate anyone, without meeting friend or family. He'd thought it would be the same in Grace-by-the-Sea.

But Grace-by-the-Sea was made up of friends and family. How could he look Mrs. Mance in the eye and arrest the vicar? What would Miss Archer have done if Mr. Carroll had turned out to be the Lord of the Smugglers?

And what would Jess do when he disrupted her beloved village to stop the fellow?

CHAPTER NINETEEN

L ARK COLLECTED JESS AT EIGHT the next morning, as he had promised. By then, she'd been able to determine what she would say to him.

"Much as it pains me to admit," she confided as they walked the shore path, "I must agree with your assessment. There are smugglers in Grace-by-the-Sea."

He had earned the right to gloat, but he merely nodded. "I'm sorry it proved true, Jess. Did Alex confess his part, then?"

She blew out a breath as they started up High Street. At least the shops hadn't opened yet, so she did not have to talk to anyone but Lark. "No. But who else but smugglers would have treated him so shabbily to send us a warning?"

"The vicar thought he might have crossed Henry Bascom," Lark offered.

Jess shook her head. "Alex said there were four or five of them, and no one he knew."

"Could he be protecting a friend?" Lark asked.

Jess snorted. "Any friend who would stand by and watch another take a beating is not much of a friend, in my book. No, if Alex had known his assailants, he would have told me." Immediately her confidence faltered. "At least, I hope he would. I've never seen him so closed-mouth, Lark. I don't know what to make of it."

They were nearly at the spa, but he stopped to take her hand. "You have every right for concern. His silence serves no one."

How warm his grip, even through her gloves. But his words gave her pause.

"Perhaps it does, Lark," she said. "I'm convinced he would not protect his attackers, but what of a friend who might be implicated in smuggling too?"

"Ike Bascom, perhaps?" Lark suggested. "We'll talk to Alex later, Jess. See if we can convince him to tell us more."

Jess nodded. Hand in hand, they continued to the spa.

Lark bowed as he offered her the key to the door. "This weighed heavily in my pocket the last two days, as if it knew it belonged to you."

Now, if she could just say the same for his heart.

"There you are!" Mrs. Cole cried before Jess had even hung up her bonnet. The lady Londoner was the first to come through the door and rushed up to Jess, hands worrying in front of her frilly muslin gown. "There was talk of canceling the assembly this evening. Please say it isn't so."

"No, indeed," Jess assured her, going to hang her bonnet on a hook. "The assembly will go on as planned."

Mrs. Cole followed her. "Oh, good." She drew in a breath, then seemed to recall herself. "Forgive me. I meant to ask after your brother. I understand he has been unwell."

"He is recovering," Jess told her, hanging her bonnet from its usual hook.

"No doubt another dose of your excellent mineral water is called for," Mrs. Cole said. She glanced toward where Miss Barlow and Mrs. Harding were entering. "I must say, it simply hasn't been the same without you, Miss Chance.

Why, Penelope almost refused to come with me to the spa this morning, claiming all the eligible bachelors would stay away with you gone. I had to use my most stringent tone to convince her otherwise."

As if her daughter still remembered, she was huddled beside a potted palm, head down and one hand wrapped around the middle of her fine muslin gown.

"I'll assure Miss Cole as well," Jess said. Mrs. Cole had just departed when the Admiral stumped up.

"Mr. Denby," he declared, "is a hero."

"Is he?" Jess glanced to where Lark was helping one of the older ladies into a seat near the windows.

"Indeed." The Admiral rocked from the heels of his boots to the toes and back. "He rescued the chess set from obscurity and restored it to its rightful place. And he has helped defend it from a certain encroaching female." He frowned at Miss Barlow, who was removing her bonnet.

"I'm sure she was only trying to help you acclimate to good society," Jess told him.

"You do that," he protested. "And you don't make me feel like a doddering fool in the process."

"Never," Jess said. "Why, where would the spa be without its commanding officer?"

His round cheeks reddened. "Very kind of you to say, my dear, but it has become clear to me who has the ability to order full sail here at the spa at Grace-by-the-Sea." He patted her arm. "Good to have you back."

He made way for Lord Featherstone, who put his hands on his hips. "And how is a gentleman to press his case when the lady disappears for days at a time?"

"You, sir, have no case to press," Jess reminded him with a smile. "And if you did, I am convinced nothing would keep the lady from your side."

He dropped his arms. "See how well you know me?" He took a step closer and lowered his voice. "How is young

Alex? Denby confided the reason for your absence."

At least one of the reasons. She doubted Lark had told her Regular about the smugglers. "Healing," she told the baron, "but it will likely be a few weeks until he is himself again."

Lord Featherstone nodded thoughtfully. "Please give him my regards. I'll stop by this afternoon and visit him."

"I'm sure he would enjoy that."

He must have seen his friend approaching, for he excused himself as Mr. Crabapple minced up.

"Is everything all right, Miss Chance?" he asked, blinking his rheumy eyes. "I have greatly missed your advice these last few days. Mrs. Harding has yet to give me permission to use her first name."

"How odd," Jess commiserated. "Have you given her leave to use yours?"

He trembled. "Oh, I would never be so bold."

"You could try," Jess encouraged him. "Her name is Eugennia. Perhaps if you told her yours and used hers, she might follow suit."

He straightened. "I shall attempt it at the assembly tonight." His face puckered. "There will be an assembly tonight, will there not?"

"Most assuredly," Jess said, gaze going to Miss Barlow, who was now fiddling with the controls on the fountain. "Excuse me while I make preparations."

She joined the woman. Miss Barlow's dark hair was coming loose of its pins, as if she had worked overly hard already today even though she had only just arrived.

"You'll find a small turn to the left to be sufficient," Jess said.

Miss Barlow spared her a glance. A moment more, and the fountain began its contented bubbling.

"I'm still learning," she said with a tight smile.

And had no need to continue, as far as Jess was con-

cerned. "I should be able to give my duties full attention the next few days," she told the woman. "Thank you for your help in the meantime."

She sniffed as if holding back tears. "I understand you did not appreciate my improvements."

Not in the slightest, but she tried to soften the blow. "It was kind of you to try, but there are so many traditions at a place such as this. No one can possibly know them all."

She sniffed again, chin coming up, and she began to remind Jess of Mrs. Greer. "And not everything should be considered a sacred tradition. One must be open to change."

Jess leaned closer. "And one must know when change is not advisable."

She nodded, but she stalked off before Jess could say more.

Indeed, the rest of the day passed in a blur. Lark continued to hover, helping her keep her guests entertained by swapping stories and teasing Miss Cole out of her doldrums. Still, she barely had time to rush home, check on Alex and Maudie, and change into her evening gown before opening the assembly rooms.

The crowd was larger than usual—besides the Spa Corporation councilmembers and their families, other prominent villagers, and guests from the spa, several young men had come in uniform, the gold braid on their shoulders glittering against the red on their chests.

"Officers of the militia of West Creech," she heard Mrs. Greer enthuse. "From very fine families."

"So long as they don't steal a dance," Lark said, threading Jess's hand through his arm.

Jess allowed herself the luxury of basking in his smile for a moment. Perhaps that's why she didn't notice the three women approaching until they stood right next to them.

"Larkin?" the oldest asked. Her hair, parted in the mid-

dle, crimped around her face, and piled up in the back, was grey now, but Jess remembered it a golden brown. Wrinkles fanned eyes as dark as her son's. She clutched her fringed shawl to her generous chest.

"What are you doing here?" the youngest lady demanded, gloved hands on the hips of her white muslin gown. Her hair was as golden brown as Lark's, but her eyes were clear blue and narrowed in suspicion. "You're supposed to be in Kent."

"I'm sure there's an explanation," the third lady said. The golden glint of her hair matched the bright tone of her voice.

Other guests were glancing their way, some with raised brows. Lark recovered himself in time to remove Jess's hand from his arm so he could sweep them all a bow.

"Mother, Hester, Rosemary," he said as he straightened. "I'm delighted to see you."

"That's all you have to say?" Rosemary, his youngest sister, asked.

Hester stepped forward. She looked much as Jess remembered her, but instead of the lighter shades of a young lady on her first Season she wore an aubergine-colored gown befitting a matron. Odd to think of her as a married woman and mother when she was only a couple years older than Jess.

"Miss Chance," she said in her gentle voice, "thank you for sending us invitations every season. We decided to show up this week, and look what a pleasant surprise you offer us." She smiled at her brother.

She was the only one. Lark's mother appeared to be on the verge of tears, and Rosemary looked as if she could impale him on the lorgnette that hung from a satin ribbon on her chest.

But before either Lark or Jess could speak, a murmur ran through the crowd, and people scampered away from the

door as if driven by a strong wind. Mrs. Denby and her daughters turned to look that way as well.

A man stood in the doorway. He was tall and well-built, raven locks brushing the collar of his black naval coat with its gold-braid trim. One look, and he commanded the room.

"Who is that?" Rosemary asked, suddenly breathless.

"That," Jess said as the apparition strode toward her, "is Captain Quillan St. Claire."

The fellow was perhaps an inch or two taller than Lark and possibly outweighed him by a stone or two, but Lark couldn't see what the fuss was all about. Men inclined their heads to him. Ladies fluttered their fans and their lashes. His mother drew herself up and positioned her shawl to advantage. Hester shrank in on herself. Rosemary twirled her lorgnette by the ribbon as if to draw his attention. And Mrs. Greer scurried to intercept him.

He reached Lark and Jess first. He took Jess's hand, bowed over it.

"Miss Chance." If ever a voice had dripped honey, his was it. "Thank you for your kind invitation."

"I am delighted you chose to accept at least one of them, Captain St. Claire," she said, that sunrise pink beginning to cover her cheeks as she removed her hand from his. "And here are others who would also like to make your acquaintance." She nodded toward Lark and his sisters. "Mrs. Denby, Mrs. Todd, and Miss Denby, of Upper Grace, and Mr. Denby, who has left you his card."

All this, and she never forgot their purpose. Lark shot her a grateful look as his mother and sisters curtsied. He stuck out his hand. "Captain St. Claire. An honor."

"Mr. Denby." His grip was firm but swift to disengage.

"Captain St. Claire!" Mrs. Greer heralded him, reaching their sides at last. She paused to gather her breath, hand pressed against the cream silk on her bosom.

"Madam," he said, inclining his head.

"To what do we owe this honor?" she trilled.

An insufferably proud smile hovered on the fellow's lips, as if he'd fully expected the adulation. "I came for one purpose only. To claim a dance with Miss Chance."

Jess might have squeaked. Rosemary certainly did, lorgnette falling. Lark took a step closer.

"Miss Chance?" Mrs. Greer glanced between the former naval officer and Jess as if much perplexed. "But why?"

Lark could have given her a dozen reasons why a man might want to partner Jesslyn Chance. St. Claire only needed one.

"Oh, we are old friends," he assured the wife of the Spa Corporation president. "I only remain in Dove Cottage because of her."

What was this? Jess had never mentioned a close connection. He had to be posturing. But why?

As the couples began lining up for the first dance, St. Claire offered Jess his arm. "Shall we, my dear?"

Even though he had sought to meet the naval officer, Lark wanted to shove the bumptious fellow back into hibernation, run him out of Grace-by-the-Sea.

Jess's head came up, and she placed her hand firmly on Lark's arm. Her voice, however, was its usual sweetness. "I regret, Captain, that this dance is spoken for. Perhaps the next."

Mrs. Greer stared at her as if she'd suddenly sprouted feathers. "Nonsense. You cannot refuse one of the heroes of the Battle of the Nile."

"I certainly wouldn't," Rosemary declared.

"I'm sure Captain St. Claire would be delighted to part-

ner you instead, Mrs. Greer," Jess said smoothly.

Lark wasn't sure how it happened, but suddenly Hester stumbled forward, bumping into the captain. He caught her by the shoulders to steady her, but she broke away, face flaming. Her gaze speared Rosemary, who was once more twirling her lorgnette.

Mrs. Greer stepped between the captain and them. "Delighted to accompany you, Captain, I'm sure." She shot his sisters a pointed look. Hester dropped her gaze. Rosemary tossed her head. His mother heaved a sigh.

St. Claire took Mrs. Greer's arm. "I will remember this, Miss Chance," he murmured as he passed them to lead the lady out.

"I must open the dancing," Jess told his sisters and mother. "I do hope you'll find partners. I can introduce you after this initial set."

"I'm sure we'll be too busy catching up with my brother," Rosemary said, eyes once more narrowing.

He owed them that, but he could not forego the opportunity to question St. Claire. "I'll return when I can."

"Yes, so you've said," Rosemary returned. "Frequently."

"Rosemary," their mother chided. "Larkin has important work to do."

Rosemary looked Jess up and down, to the point that the pink returned to Jess's cheeks. "So it seems."

Hester stepped in front of her sister. "Thank you, Miss Chance. We'll look forward to talking with both of you as soon as you are free."

Lark led Jess out onto the floor.

"You do not need to tell me I should have called on them before now," he said. "I let my work take precedence."

"A nearly fatal flaw, it seems," she remarked, as if he wasn't beginning to think as much. "But at least you will have an opportunity to question the captain."

"An old friend, he claims," Lark said.

"Father was his physician," Jess explained as they took their place at the head of the growing line. "But I haven't spoken to him more than twice in the eighteen months he's inhabited Dove Cottage. I have no idea what possessed him to claim closer acquaintance now."

Neither did Lark, and he didn't like it.

CHAPTER TWENTY

JESS THOUGHT SHE HAD THOROUGHLY discour-
aged the naval captain, but she had no sooner finished
a dance with Lark than Quillan St. Claire showed up at
her side again. Most of the ladies in the room were watching her, waiting. More than one wanted to have that dark
gazed fixed on her face, as if she were the trifle at the end
of a meal. Jess could not understand his purpose.

She was willing to acknowledge he was a handsome
man, with that black hair and heavy-lidded eyes. And he
certainly tried to exude a certain charm. But there was
something hard, unyielding about him, that would have
kept her at a distance even if she were not becoming
enamored with Lark again.

"Perhaps in lieu of a dance, we might walk," he said,
offering her his arm. The set of his face said he refused to
accept defeat. Perhaps that was why she felt compelled to
thwart him.

"How kind, Captain, but I should attend to my duties as
hostess. I'm sure Mr. Denby would enjoy your company. I
believe he has some questions for you."

Lark moved closer to the naval officer. "It will only take
a few moments."

Captain St. Claire offered him the briefest of glances.
"Surely we should not deprive the ladies of your company,

sir, even for a few moments."

"I am convinced they will survive," he said.

Captain St. Claire leaned around him to eye Jess, smile as sharp as a razor. "Would you really prefer that I speak with Mr. Denby, my dear? I would not want to disrupt your plans for the assembly. I know how much you value an orderly event."

Jess had a sudden image of the two facing off across the hall, swords drawn and faces resolute. No, no! There hadn't been a duel in Grace-by-the-Sea in, well, ever! And she certainly didn't want to be the cause of the first.

"Perhaps I can spare some time," she said with a look to Lark. "Excuse me, Lark."

The use of his first name was a calculated gambit, but it had the effect she'd hoped. Lark offered her a smug little half smile as she accepted the captain's arm.

"So, he's stolen a march on me," Captain St. Claire remarked as they started around the room on the periphery. Another set was forming, Mrs. Greer among the dancers. She cast Jess and the captain a curious look. Lark's sister Rosemary was also in the line, partnering one of the young militia officers. Hester and Mrs. Denby were holding up one wall. She would have to see what could be done there.

But first she had to give this fellow a set down and see what she might learn.

"You and I have never had an understanding, Captain," Jess reminded him. "So, you can cease posturing."

He pressed his free hand to his chest. "Alas, dear Jesslyn, you wound me."

Jess stopped, forcing him to stop as well. "And I never gave you leave to use my first name, sir."

"Did you not?" His black brows arched. "Why, it must have been another beautiful lady in the village."

Jess raised a brow as well. "If you cannot remember who,

sir, I can only question your devotion."

"My besetting fault," he agreed with a sigh. "And here I came tonight with the express purpose of proving my devotion to you."

"Rubbish," Jess said.

He tutted. "Such language, Miss Chance."

Jess puffed out a sigh. "Captain St. Claire, I wish we could just speak plainly."

His mouth quirked. "Ladies first."

"Very well," Jess said, continuing around the hall with him at her side. "There are smugglers in Grace-by-the-Sea, and you are suspected of leading them."

He laughed. "Oh, but your aunt has an imagination."

"It is not my aunt who should concern you. Really, sir, have you nothing to say for yourself?"

"Only this." He leaned closer and lowered his voice. "Have a care, Miss Chance. You are rushing in where angels fear to tread."

Jess frowned at him. "What are you talking about?"

"Something of greater consequence than the gossip flying at the moment." He tipped his chin toward the rest of the hall, and Jess became aware of the number of fans plying, the gazes following them. She looked to Lark across the room, and he nodded his encouragement.

"Careful, now," Captain St. Claire murmured before she could question him further. "We would not want to give Mrs. Greer reason to think we've quarreled. Think of your position at the spa."

She refused to allow him to intimidate her. "My position has no bearing on this discussion, sir."

They passed the door to the supper room. Adding a platter of steamed shrimp in cream sauce to the table, Mrs. Inchley glanced up and gasped. Jess hurried him past.

"I disagree," he said. "How do you think the Corporation councilmembers would react if they thought you

were stirring up trouble with these inquiries of yours?"

They were already concerned, if Mrs. Greer's reaction to her absence was any indication. "They will come to see the wisdom of my actions when the truth is revealed," she told him.

He shook his head. "Ah, the truth. A slippery fellow, to be sure. Which truth will they embrace, do you think? The capture of poor fishermen hoping to eke out a little more for their families, or the damage to the village's reputation as the unsavory home of smugglers?"

"Neither," Jess said. "These so-called smugglers are dangerous. They beat my brother Sunday night to ensure his silence. They must be stopped."

She felt the sudden tension in his arm, as if she'd pulled a thread taut while sewing.

"Your brother was hurt? When? Where?"

Gone was the cloak of charm, the veneer of sophistication. His dark eyes were fixed on her face as if he would see the facts written there.

"Three nights ago, along the shore," she confessed. "He did not recognize his attackers."

He nodded slowly. "But he will recover."

It was not a question. "Yes," Jess allowed. "Though I would have liked another opinion on the condition of his ribs."

"Please give him my regards," he said. "And assure him I will be glad to receive him again when he is healed. Now, I have monopolized your time far enough."

Jess blinked. They had made a full circuit of the room. Lark was standing directly ahead, arms crossed over his chest. Hester and his mother stood just a bit farther on, as if making sure they would not interrupt the conversation. Captain St. Claire released her arm and took her hand to bow over it.

"Have a care, Miss Chance," he said as he straightened.

"Dark forces are afoot. We don't need another Chance injured." He stepped back and strode away.

Lark took his place at her side. "Are you all right? What did he tell you?"

Jess took his hand, needing to anchor herself in his strength for a moment. "He appeared to be trying to warn us to cease our questioning."

"Why?" Lark asked, gaze following the captain as he moved about the room, stopping to speak to this person, that couple. "Did he confess to some involvement in the smuggling?"

"No. He said nothing tangible, but he changed when I mentioned Alex's injuries. He didn't know, Lark. I'm sure of it. If he were leading the smugglers, surely he'd have heard."

"If he's this Lord of the Smugglers," Lark said, "he could well have ordered the beating."

"No," Jess said. "The news of the attack shook him. And he went so far as to request that my brother call on him. Again. As if Alex had made a habit of visiting him."

"I take it that surprises you," Lark said.

"A great deal. Maudie and I have both despaired of Alex since Father's death. He seemed to have lost his way. We'd all expected him to become a physician, you see, but without a mentor under whom to apprentice, that dream died with Father. He'd certainly never attempt a call on someone of Captain St. Claire's stature."

"Easy prey for smugglers," Lark murmured. "Quick money, few skills required."

Jess shuddered. "Oh, Lark, I don't want it to be so."

"It's not too late," he assured her. "Your brother is young. If he has helped these miscreants, we may be able to convince the magistrate to be lenient, if Alex testifies against them."

Jess swallowed, mouth dry. "How lenient?"

His face looked as bleak as she felt. "Transportation instead of hanging."

The walls seemed to be folding in around her. "So, Quillan St. Claire was right. By helping you, I've not only endangered my position, but my brother's life."

On the far side of the assembly rooms, James Howland nodded politely to Quill. Having finished a dance with Mrs. Greer and promenading with Miss Chance, his old friend had finally deigned to come within conversation distance. James had not been about to single him out. It would only have fueled the gossip that was hurling itself around the columned space.

"What are you doing here?" he asked now.

"Good evening, Magistrate," Quill responded with a nod to the two ladies who were passing. They giggled. Quill smiled. As soon as they were out of earshot, he moved closer.

"I thought perhaps a word of warning might suffice to quiet speculations," he said, putting his back to the wall.

James snorted. "You've only fanned the flames. Every gaze in the room is on you."

"Well, perhaps not every," Quill said with that infuriating smile.

"Do you take nothing seriously?" James demanded.

He eyed him. "The same matters you do. And smile. This is an assembly. We are enjoying ourselves."

James pasted on a smile that the muscles of his face protested. "You've wasted your time in any regard. I doubt Larkin Denby takes well to warnings."

"The very reason I warned Jesslyn Chance instead."

"Did that help?" James asked.

"Likely not," Quill admitted, shoulders braced against the pale walls and hands going to the pockets of his breeches. "But I learned something. Did you know Alex Chance was beaten?"

James stiffened. "No. When? Why?"

Quill's face hardened, but at the dark deed or James's questions, he wasn't sure. "Sunday night. And his sister believes the smugglers sailing out of Grace Cove to be responsible."

James thumped back against the wall. "That can't be right."

"I promise you it isn't right," Quill said. "This is the first I've heard of it. And losing Alex makes me a man down."

"Then it seems we must allow Miss Chance and Mr. Denby to continue their investigation," James said.

"And hope they bring us answers," Quill agreed. "Too much is at stake to do otherwise."

Lark's mother and Hester were waiting just down the wall for him; Rosemary was finishing a dance and would likely reappear at his side to demand explanations. Yet Lark could not move without attempting to erase the pain that radiated out of Jess.

"I would not endanger you or your family for the world," he told her, holding her hand in his. Even through the gloves, her fingers felt cold, stiff. "If you want to leave the investigating to me, I will understand."

"The risk is greater than I knew," she acknowledged. "But how can I step away? These smugglers harm the people I love."

"And you are a staunch defender of all three. I see that. May I not have the honor of defending you?"

Her lips trembled. "No one has ever offered that before."

He glanced at his mother. Rosemary had indeed rejoined her and Hester. His mother and Hester were trying to appear as if they didn't notice him. Rosemary's hem rose and fell with her tapping foot.

He returned his gaze to Jess and stroked his thumb across the back of her hand. "I might have, had I realized what the future held. I came to Grace-by-the-Sea determined to make a difference in this war by safeguarding our shores. I found something more. I found camaraderie." He met her gaze. "I found you again."

The blue deepened, softened, and it would have been all too easy to bend his head and kiss her. But that would make a declaration he couldn't make. Yet.

"I am coming to care for you, Jess," he murmured. "Give me time to see this all settled, and we'll talk."

She nodded, then she tipped her head toward his waiting family. "You promised to talk to them as well."

He released her. "And that, alas, I can delay no longer. Do you need any help tonight?"

She smiled. "No. I'll be fine. But I will hope for your escort home."

He bowed over her hand. "Count on it."

She slipped away to return to her duties. He turned for the wall.

"So, marriage, is it?" Rosemary greeted him.

"Pay no attention to her," Hester said, stepping forward to enfold him in a hug. "It's so good to see you again, Brother."

Guilt poked him in the back as he disengaged. "And you all as well. I'm sorry I didn't let you know I would be in the area. It was a sudden assignment."

His mother sent Rosemary a look. "So, you are here on behalf of the Excise Office."

Lark took a step closer and lowered his voice. "Yes, but

the fewer who know of that, the better."

His mother paled. "You still blame your father's profession for his death?"

"And so do I," Rosemary put in. She turned to Lark. "That's why I wish you'd found some other work that interested you."

"Serving England is nothing to be ashamed of," Hester said quietly, and he thought she must be remembering her late husband.

"Indeed, it isn't," Lark replied. "But it's easier to catch smugglers if they don't know you're after them."

His mother sucked in a breath. "Smugglers, in Grace-by-the-Sea?"

"Why not?" Rosemary asked. "They're everywhere along the coast."

For once, he could not argue with his pessimistic sister. "Very likely, these days. But there are those working to oppose them." He looked from face to face, each more worn than he remembered, and guilt dug in its claws again.

"I shouldn't have stayed away so long. As soon as this assignment ends, I'll make time to come see you. I promise."

His mother's smile was fleeting, but hopeful. "I will look forward to that."

Rosemary edged closer, gaze darting about the assembly hall. "So, who do you suspect?"

Lark chuckled. "I should probably ask you that question. You always were better at reconnaissance than I was."

"And is that something to praise?" Hester asked primly.

Rosemary didn't so much as spare her older sister a glance. "I suspect Captain St. Claire, of course."

"Of course," Lark agreed.

"And that chap he was talking with, the magistrate."

Lark's brows went up. "James Howland? Why?"

Rosemary cocked her head in obvious thought. "A

magistrate is in a position to know about, and hide, any number of things."

"Rosemary," their mother scolded. "What an unkind thing to say. Why, I've only heard the best things about Mr. Howland."

"Fair, kind, considerate," Hester agreed. "And terribly conscientious."

"Perfect way to cover his crimes," Rosemary insisted.

Lark held up a hand. "Peace. My thoughts match Rosemary's."

His youngest sister raised her chin.

"But I have no proof and nothing specific on which to base my theory," he continued. "And there are others who might be involved. Miss Chance is assisting me in looking deeper into the matter."

"Oh," Rosemary said knowingly, "is that all."

"Rosemary." His mother sighed in exasperation before turning to him. "Larkin, I recall your friendship with Miss Chance when we visited the spa years ago. She was a sweet-natured, bright young lady then. That hasn't changed."

"And she's been so kind to keep up the acquaintance all these years," Hester added. "She sends us invitations to the assembly every summer."

"She always remembers my birthday with a note," his mother said with a fond smile.

"Mine too," Rosemary admitted. "You obviously made an impression on her."

"One she has not forgotten," Hester agreed.

Lark looked to where Jess was speaking with Mr. Crabapple. By the way his head was bobbing, she was giving him more advice on winning his dear love. Mrs. Harding was out on the floor, dancing with one of the young militia officers.

"In truth," he said, "I haven't forgotten her either. But

things are more complicated now. I go where I'm needed. She is loyal to the village and her spa."

"That could change," Hester predicted. "A wife goes where her husband takes her."

"Only if she can't convince him otherwise," Rosemary said.

Lark nodded, but he could not shake the idea. Could he make Grace-by-the-Sea his home? He'd be close to his family. And he could court Jess in earnest, win her heart, put down roots in the Dorset chalk.

But would he be putting them all in danger?

CHAPTER TWENTY-ONE

W HAT AN EVENING! FIRST LARK'S mother and sisters had appeared and then Captain St. Claire had issued his dire warning. And Jess had thought assembly nights challenging as they were!

She made sure to bid farewell to the Denby ladies as they left for the evening.

"Again, our thanks for including us," Hester said.

"You are very welcome," Jess assured her. "I hope you'll come again this summer."

Rosemary looked to Lark, who was standing at Jess's side. "So long as we have a reason."

His mother leaned forward and pressed a kiss to his cheek. "Be careful," she murmured as she leaned back, gaze tearing again.

Lark clasped her hand. "I will, Mother. And I'll come see you soon."

With a nod, she led her daughters from the hall. There would be a convoy to Upper Grace tonight, escorted by the officers from West Creech.

Lark kept his promise to Jess and walked her home. Voices called goodnight here and there as other members of Grace-by-the-Sea reached their own homes. Mr. Drummond, the lamplighter, was carrying his lantern for Mrs. Harding and Mr. Crabapple as they strolled for Shell

Cottage. The golden light brightened the street toward the cove, allowing her to see the number of times Lark checked the headland and the castle.

"All dark tonight," Jess noted.

He chuckled. "Caught me looking, did you? You're right. There's no light tonight. Perhaps the smugglers have moved on."

She wished she could believe that.

Mr. Drummond's lantern faded as they reached the cove. The moon had flashed in and out among wispy clouds, peppering the waves with light and shadow. A cool breeze blew away the rest of her fatigue. She was walking in the moonlight with a man she admired. She let herself simply enjoy the moment.

Lark stopped at the shore path, head turned as if he listened for the waves. "I've been thinking about the future."

"Me too," she admitted.

"If we catch these smugglers," he started.

"When we catch them," she corrected him.

He lay his hand over hers on his arm. "When we catch them, I may return to Kent. Or I could be reassigned somewhere else. So, I'm not sure of my situation."

She'd known that, but hearing it stated so clearly was hard. "Must be difficult," she murmured. "Being always ready to leave."

He shrugged. "It hasn't bothered me in the past. Now…"

"Now?" Jess encouraged him.

In the darkness, she could just make out his face as he watched her. "Now I am sure of only one thing. I don't want to lose you, Jess."

Warmth pushed up inside her. "I don't want to lose you either, Lark."

He leaned toward her, and she met him halfway. His lips caressed hers, gently, sweetly, and she wanted to float in the feeling, let it carry her where concerns were forgotten.

He straightened far too soon for her. "I'll see you in the morning, then. We can determine our next steps together."

"Together," she promised. She didn't feel the path as she wandered to the cottage.

Alex and Maudie were seated at the table, playing cards, as she entered. The pile of pasteboard in front of her aunt told her who was winning.

"Alex, I'm glad to see you up," Jess said, the issues of the day settling back onto her shoulders like snow fallen off the roof.

"Can't keep a Chance down," he joked with his usual spirit. He laid out a card, then swept in the trick. Maudie pouted.

Her aunt turned to her as Alex dealt the next hand. "At least tell me something interesting happened at the assembly," she begged. "Trolls cavorting on the supper table? Gentlemen dueling over dances?"

Lark and Quillan St. Claire came immediately to mind. "Alas," Jess said, moving to join them, "nothing so dramatic. However, Captain St. Claire made an appearance."

She was watching for it, otherwise she might have missed the way her brother dropped his gaze and wiggled on the bench as if it had grown harder.

Maudie's eyes lit. "Oh, ho! Is he still as handsome as midnight? Did his injury cause him to limp? Did he dance with every lady in attendance?"

"He was handsome enough," Jess allowed. "I noticed no limp. And he only danced with Mrs. Greer, that I noticed. But he asked to be remembered to you, Alex, and to tell you to call on him. Again."

Maudie's gaze flew to her nephew. "*Again!* Do you mean to tell me you're on speaking terms with Quillan St. Claire, the pirate king, and you never invited me along?"

Alex grimaced, laying down his cards, backs up. "All I did was renew an old acquaintance of Father's, Aunt. I'm

sure you would have found the conversation boring."

His ears twitched.

Maudie humphed and clutched her cards closer.

Jess kept her tone calm with an effort. "I doubt any conversation with Captain St. Claire would be boring," she said. "In any event, he seemed surprised to hear you had been hurt and rather concerned about the matter."

Alex ducked his head. "I'll call on him as soon as I feel up to it. Please excuse me now. I must have overexerted myself." He swung his legs off the bench and climbed unsteadily to his feet. Jess had to hold herself still to keep from going to him.

"Is Quillan St. Claire involved in smuggling?" she asked.

His gaze leaped to hers, eyes wide. "No! I swear it! But that's all I'll say about the matter." He turned and stumped for the bedchamber, shutting the door soundly behind him.

"Another story," Maudie complained. Then she reached across the table and peeked at Alex's forgotten cards.

Would that it were so easy to dismiss her brother's words. But she couldn't *make* him tell her what was going on. Yet how could she protect him when she felt utterly in the dark?

The morning brought Jess little respite from her concerns. But Alex was doing well enough she felt comfortable bringing Maudie with her to the spa. Once more her spirits dipped when she didn't find Lark at the door before her. She had barely started the fountain and arranged the glasses when Abigail came in. Her friend tended to do things quickly, to speak in a rush, but this time she flew to Jess's side, her blue skirts belling.

"Jess! You must come. Everyone's talking about it."

Of her guests, only Lord Featherstone and Mrs. Cole and her daughter were in attendance. They wandered closer.

"What is it, Abigail?" Jess asked. "What's happened?"

Abby paused as if surprised to find herself the center of attention, then she squared her shoulders resolutely.

"It's that recruiting agent. He's posted a list on the very door of the church, naming every man who he intends to conscript."

Mrs. Cole pressed a hand to her chest. "Conscript?"

"Into the army," Abby confirmed. "They'll have to leave Grace-by-the-Sea, march away to some foreign shore."

"Well, perhaps not march," Lord Featherstone put in with a kind look to Jess.

Her stomach felt hollow. "Have you seen whose names are on it?"

Abby shook her head. "I couldn't get close enough, everyone was crowding so. But Mrs. Bascom said Ike her oldest was on it, and Mr. Carroll too."

"Mr. Carroll?" Jess's mind balked trying to imagine the dapper shop owner with a musket in his arms.

Maudie reached for her black bonnet. "We must go see."

"Indeed, perhaps we should all go," Lord Featherstone said.

Jess glanced at him to find that he had paled. But surely the king would not demand service from an aristocrat or a man approaching sixty.

She found out a short time later. The piece of parchment had been nailed to the wood of the church door and fluttered in the breeze like a dove caught in a trap. Mr. Howland stood on one side, but she was surprised to see Lark on the other as, one by one, the villagers approached to look at the list. Others gathered in groups among the headstones, like mourners arrived too late for the burial. Jess got in line behind Mrs. Greer.

"No one would dare conscript my husband," she said, loud enough to carry. "But I thought I should look in case I must replace one of the servants."

Jess's body was so tight she could barely shamble closer.

Out of the corner of her eyes, she spotted Maudie moving from group to group, patting shoulders and murmuring support.

Mrs. Greer reached the top step and nodded to Mr. Howland. "Magistrate. I take it you had a hand in compiling this list."

A dozen gazes swung his way.

He stood taller. "I did not, madam. I have steadfastly maintained that the men of Grace-by-the-Sea protect the coast by their very presence here. But there is no denying the king's order. I'm simply thankful Mr. Denby agreed to keep me company on this sad responsibility."

Now the gazes veered to Lark. Jess offered him a smile she could barely muster.

Mrs. Greer squinted at the list, then reared back so fast she nearly collided with Jess. "My Geoffrey is on this list. What is the meaning of this?"

Mr. Howland raised his voice. "All able-bodied men between the ages of fifteen and fifty-five must report within the next fortnight to West Creech to be enlisted in the army. It may be they will patrol the coast, but they may also be sent to reinforce regiments on the Continent."

"But not Geoffrey," Mrs. Greer protested over the murmur the magistrate's words raised. "He's not equipped for such things. Why, he can't remember where he puts his pipe tobacco most days."

"I'm sorry," Mr. Howland said, voice kind. "There's nothing I can do. If you've seen what you need, please move along."

She turned, stumbled on the step, and Jess caught her arm to steady her. She wasn't sure Mrs. Greer even saw her before she continued down the steps, glassy-eyed.

"Miss Chance?" Magistrate Howland prompted gently.

Jess rallied and lifted her skirts to climb the last step. Mr. Howland helped hold down the parchment, but he needn't

have bothered. The list was in alphabetical order, and the name Alex Chance was near the top.

Lark tensed, ready to leap forward and catch Jess if she collapsed, as so many of the other women had done. He could understand their fears. Some lads trained from childhood to join the military. Wealthy men bragged when they joined a prestigious unit, spent hundreds of pounds to buy a commission. The men of Grace-by-the-Sea wouldn't be joining as officers, and they'd never trained to serve. They'd be enlisted men, the infantry, the ones expected to charge at the enemy, bayonets flashing.

The ones who died in droves on the battlefield.

Small wonder the women in their families despaired to find their names on that list.

Jess stepped back, face white but head high. "Thank you, Magistrate. Two weeks, you said?"

"Yes, Miss Chance. If Alex needs anything, please let me know."

"Thank you." She turned to allow the next woman to take her place.

Lark darted after her. "Jess, wait." He caught up with her at the bottom of the steps.

She met his gaze, her own bleak. "If we could walk a little ways, Mr. Denby?"

Howland had requested his aid to keep the peace, but surely the magistrate could manage a few moments without him. He offered Jess his arm and led her away from the church.

She did not head toward the spa or down into the village. Instead, she wandered toward the path up the headland. At the first turn, she sank onto the little stone bench over-

looking the cove and made room for him beside her. The granite was warm beneath him. He still felt cold.

"I saw the list after the recruiting officer nailed it in place," he told her. "There was no time to warn you."

Her fingers knit together in her lap. "Alex, Mr. Carroll."

"Even Captain St. Claire," he acknowledged. "Everyone but James Howland."

She glanced up at him. "Because he's a magistrate?"

"And Mr. Carroll has a shop to run, and Mr. Greer is needed as an apothecary. They were not exempt."

She pressed a hand to her brow. "I'm not at my best at the moment, Lark. What are you saying about James Howland?"

Lark ticked the familiar reasons off on his fingers. "He is strong. He knows how to lead. He comes from an aristocratic family. And he knows the area better than anyone."

She met his gaze. "Do you suspect him of leading the smugglers, then?"

"Perhaps," Lark allowed. "But I can only wonder how his name came to be excluded. Smugglers generally have the funds to bribe those willing to look the other way."

When she remained silent, he swiveled to face her fully and take her hands in his.

"I may have a solution to all this," he told her. "It came to me this morning, after I saw the list. I can ride to Weymouth, speak to the commissioner. I'll tell him Alex is working with me. Excise men are exempt from impressment or balloting."

Tears sparkled in her eyes. "You would do that?"

"Yes, anything," he said, bringing her fingers to his lips and pressing a kiss against them. "Alex would be safe. And perhaps I can discover who ordered Howland safe as well. I can make my report to the commissioner, request aid. I should be back in a few days."

She pulled away her hand, eyes widening. "So long?"

Every fiber of his being protested, ordered him to stay here, at her side. He hardened his heart. "It's the only way."

She nodded, chin coming up. "I understand. Just come back to me, Lark. Promise?"

"Promise," he said. "If I have to fight off Napoleon himself."

Jess told her brother about his conscription later that morning. Relaying the bad news was easier knowing that Lark was riding for Weymouth. She had taken the extreme step of closing the spa for the rest of the day, sending those guests who were so inclined into the village to shop. She and Maudie found a few of the doors closed there too as they headed down the hill for the cove. Nearly every family in the area would be dealing with the impending loss of husband, father, son, or brother.

"Two weeks, eh?" Alex asked when she explained. He had been sitting at the table, blank parchment in front of him, quill and ink in hand, when they had entered.

Jess nodded. "Enough time to make you uniforms, gather supplies. But it may not come to that."

"I'll pack us bags," Maudie said. "We'll escape to the Highlands and live with the Scots. They'll ask no questions."

Alex stuck the quill in the stand. "I won't run, Aunt. If the king needs me that badly, I'll go."

"You may not have to," Jess insisted. "Lark has a plan. Give him a few days, and all may be well."

Maudie patted Alex's arm. "I'll have a chat with Mr. Josephs about a fast horse, just in case." She trotted out the cottage door.

Jess nodded to the paper. "What were you going to

write, Alex?"

He folded the note, even though it held no words as yet. "Nothing important now." He glanced up at her. "I never wanted to be a soldier, Jess, but I'll do my part. We must keep Napoleon from invading, whatever the cost."

She put her hand on his shoulder. "But if the cost is your life, that seems too dear."

He rose, taller now, shoulders broader than she remembered, and face more set. "I know what Father would say. One life in exchange for many is a fair deal."

He was right. Her father had been wont to say such things. But he'd never had to leave the Dorset chalk for a foreign shore.

Would Alex?

CHAPTER TWENTY-TWO

THE SHOPS WERE OPENING WHEN Jess and Maudie came through the village the next morning. Mr. Carroll was sweeping his stoop, head high. He nodded to Jess as she passed. She wanted to run to him and hug him close, but he went inside before she could act on the impulse. Mr. Lawrence's son was being ushered into the haberdashery by Mr. Treacle. The tailor nodded to Jess as well.

"I've put in an order for more red wool," he called to her. "Send Alex my way when he's ready to be measured."

Though his work would increase for a time, he did not seem pleased about it.

Abby was unlocking her door as Jess passed and darted out to hug her and Maudie. "I'm so very sorry," she murmured as she disengaged, eyes tearing. "Alex is so young!"

"But not the youngest," Jess said.

Abby glanced toward her shop. "I wonder whether I should paint battle scenes." She shuddered. "Sorry. It just seems so dismal. Why must they all go away? Why can't Mr. Howland lead a militia right here?"

Jess glanced up the headland toward the castle. "I don't know."

"It's the trolls," Maudie put in. "He's too busy protecting the area from them."

"That must be it," Abby said with a fond smile. She gave Jess's hand another squeeze before letting her go her way.

Lark would help Alex. How many others would have no such assurance?

Though none of her guests had been directly affected by the conscription, they must have sensed the mood in the village, for they spoke quietly among themselves and made few demands of her. Lord Featherstone came and lay a hand on her shoulder.

"If you need anything, you have only to ask," he said.

"That's what I'm supposed to say to you," Jess reminded him with a smile.

Miss Cole wandered closer, face puckered and peaked. "Mr. Denby's name was not included on that odious list, was it?" she asked Jess. "Mother wouldn't let me look."

"No," Jess admitted. "Neither Mr. Denby nor any gentleman guest of the spa would be included. This is not his home."

Would it ever be?

She could not focus on that now. She had work to do. A presentable gentleman and a young lady and her father had arrived, and Jess made introductions, settled them into conversation. Was that interest in the fellow's face when he spoke with Miss Cole? The young lady certainly looked pleased, cheeks pinking. Perhaps Jess could further the acquaintance at the Midsummer Masquerade. Yet, would any of her friends in the village find the will to attend when so many would be gone by then?

Somehow, she made it through the morning, but that afternoon brought a note from Mr. Greer.

"What does he want now?" Maudie asked, neck craned as she tried to read over Jess's arm.

"There's to be a council meeting this evening, and I'm expected to attend," Jess said. She refolded the note. "At least I was invited this time."

"The sacrificial lamb," Maudie intoned, straightening.

Jess could not deny the tremor that shook her. Nor could she question the chill when she walked into the council's meeting that night.

The Spa Corporation board members met regularly in the private parlor at the Swan. The paneled room boasted a large fireplace of stones from the cliffs, pale and rough, a brass chandelier, and a long plank table that could seat twenty on its flanking benches. A high-backed chair stood at either end. Mr. Greer sat at the head as president. The apothecary had changed since she'd last seen him. His carriage seemed slumped now, and his long face seemed grey, as if his conscription had taken its toll already. He motioned Jess to the foot of the table before lowering himself onto his seat.

Abigail chose to sit as close to Jess as possible, her smile supportive. The others took their places around the table: Mr. Lawrence, the jeweler, one of his stick pins glinting gold and red in the lapel of his tailored coat. Mrs. Kirby, the leasing agent, with her Titian hair piled up high. Mr. Bent, who coordinated servant employment for the rental properties and great houses, with his pointed nose and trim mustache. Mr. Ellison, as round and plump as the rolls he baked.

"Thank you for coming," Mr. Greer said with a nod down the lines. "Especially after the blow we all received. But I can assure you the Spa at Grace-by-the-Sea will carry on." He picked up a closely written note and held it high. "I have here the response from Doctor Bennett. He has accepted our offer and will arrive in Grace-by-the-Sea within the fortnight to take up his work at the spa."

Was it possible to cheer and cry at the same time? The village needed a physician so badly. Alex wasn't the only one who could have used his services. Yet his arrival meant the end of her father's legacy.

The councilmembers were not nearly so ambivalent. They applauded the statement, beaming at each other.

Mr. Greer lay down the paper. "Yes, the spa is in for a number of changes. That's why I asked you here, Miss Chance."

Every gaze swung her way. Only Abigail looked contrite.

"Doctor Bennett indicates he has no need for a hostess."

Though she had feared as much, she still felt as if she were going numb. "That surprises me," she said politely. "A physician must tend to important matters, his patient's wellbeing, developing and testing the various treatments to be offered. Who will see to the mundane matters that keep the guests happy? The pouring of the waters, the tours of the village?"

"The position of spa hostess is very exacting," Abby agreed, glancing around at the others. "It requires focused attention. Surely a physician will not wish to serve as host and healer too."

Mr. Lawrence squirmed on the bench. "Perhaps not, but there have been distressing rumors that you have not been as attentive as you should be of late, Miss Chance."

Mr. Ellison nodded. "Leaving the spa unattended. Closing it even." He shook his head as if the idea was heresy.

"Because the magistrate, Mr. Howland, requested her assistance," Abigail reminded them. "He petitioned this very body. We agreed to allow it."

"But why did he ask for her help to begin with?" Mrs. Kirby asked with a frown. "Surely a gentleman would be better suited to accompany Mr. Denby to confirm the returns."

Jess could not tell them that Lark could not accept the help from a gentleman when every gentleman in Grace-by-the-Sea was suspect. Only think how they would react when it became clear smugglers prowled their shores!

"We should allow Miss Chance a defense," Abby put in.

Mr. Greer nodded, but he leaned back in his chair as if distancing himself from whatever Jess would say.

She spread her hands, thankful that they did not shake. "Esteemed councilmembers, I have ever given faithful service, first as a volunteer, then in assistance to my father, and now as your hostess. My motto and guiding principle have been to make the guests happy, whether at the spa itself, in their interactions with the village, or at the assembly and events. If I have failed in that duty, I sincerely apologize and will work tirelessly to remedy any shortcomings."

Mr. Lawrence glanced to their president. "She has given exemplary service in the past."

Mr. Bent cocked his head. "Have we ever had an actual complaint about her?"

Surely not, but Mr. Greer leaned forward. "I'm sorry to relate that we have. Miss Susan Barlow has confessed that Miss Chance went out of her way to belittle and demean her in the eyes of the guests."

They were all looking at her again. Abby was shaking her head, plainly disbelieving the complaint. Mrs. Kirby and Mr. Bent looked shocked.

"What have you to say about this, Miss Chance?" Mr. Ellison asked, clearly confused. "Do you know this person?"

"Miss Barlow agreed to perform some of my duties while I was helping the magistrate," Jess explained. "She attempted to institute a number of changes without my input or yours."

"Yet I understand these were beneficial changes," Mr. Greer said.

His wife thought so, in any event. "Changes some of the guests resented," Jess told him. "In some cases, changes my father would have refused to allow."

Mr. Greer sighed. "And there we come to the crux of the matter. Your loyalty to your father's memory is commend-

able, Miss Chance, but you continue to allow it to interfere with the efficient running of the spa. With the arrival of Doctor Bennett, we enter a new era, with new ideas and bold directions. I must agree with him that your services will no longer be needed."

Abby stood. "And I disagree. You cannot make this decision without us. I demand a vote."

Mr. Ellison nodded. The others looked to Mr. Greer.

His mouth worked a moment, then he nodded. "Very well. All in favor of allowing Miss Chance to remain as hostess of the spa, despite her recent poor performance?"

"All in favor of allowing Miss Chance to continue her exemplary service to the spa?" Abby corrected him. She thrust up her hand.

Mr. Lawrence joined her more hesitantly.

Mr. Greer nodded. "Opposed?" He and the other three members raised their hands. At least Mrs. Kirby and Mr. Bent looked sorry about the matter.

"Motion carries," Mr. Greer said as Abigail sank onto her seat, face falling. "You may have the next fortnight to put things to rights at the spa and the cottage, Miss Chance, with the idea of turning over both to Doctor Bennett when he arrives. You are excused for the rest of the meeting."

Jess stood, head high and heart quaking. Abigail bit her lip as if to keep from crying. Mr. Lawrence hung his head. She moved to the door, leaving them behind. She must think of her future.

Whatever that might be.

Lark's ride to Weymouth seemed longer than he remembered, for all he arrived as the sun was setting on Thursday.

Perhaps it was the fact that he'd left Jess behind, though she had accompanied him in his thoughts as surely as if she had sat on the saddle with him. He'd ridden past a flock of sheep grazing on the Downs and remembered the day they'd run together along the headland. The blue sky reminded him of the blue depths of her gaze. The very air smelled of the lavender sachet she favored. He was lost and never happier.

Except for the matter of her brother and the smugglers.

"A difficult situation, to be sure," Commissioner Franklin had acknowledged when Lark met with him Friday morning in his offices overlooking Weymouth Harbour and explained what he had surmised in Grace-by-the-Sea. "I see your point about Howland, but we can't go accusing someone of his station without proof."

"And what proof would you want?" Lark asked. "To catch him at the tiller of a sloop filled with brandy?"

The commissioner eyed him. "That would certainly help."

It would, but he doubted Howland would be so obvious. He would be the leader. Other men were fetching and unloading the cargo.

"Then send me back with a squad of dragoons," Lark begged. "Someone who can stand with me against these smugglers."

Franklin grimaced. "I'd like to, but we're spread thin as it is. We had a run in with a sloop last night, I understand. They were trying to land just east of Grace Cove. Cutter chased them to farther to the east and lost them." He shifted on his padded chair. "Probably dispersed up some creek by now, the goods halfway to London."

"Just east of Grace Cove, you say?" Lark leaned forward. "That could be the group we've been seeking. I never have found any evidence they sail from the cove proper, despite the information we were given, though I did spot an older

landing place along that stretch of cliff."

The commissioner nodded. "If you can discover when a cargo is coming in, I will have men stationed to help you catch the criminals in the act."

"I'll do my best, sir," Lark promised. "But there's another matter I wanted to bring to your attention. I could use an assistant on this assignment, and I have the very man. Alexander Chance, son of the previous physician. His insights into the area could be invaluable."

"But can the boy be trusted?" The commissioner's face tightened. "We've had more than one officer turn traitor for profit."

"Not Alexander Chance," Lark vowed. "He comes from a good family, and he's a respected member of the community."

That last bit might have been an overstatement, but the Chance family had built the village. There were still those who remembered.

"Very well," the commissioner agreed. "At half your salary, of course, and only until you finish this assignment."

Now came the tricky part. "And when the assignment is finished," Lark said cautiously, "I have a proposal about what I might do next."

"Oh?" Commissioner Franklin leaned back in his chair. "Fancy returning to Kent, do you?"

"No," Lark said. "I was wondering about the stretch from the Durdle Door to Brandy Bay recently. Do you have a Riding Officer there?"

"Not at the moment," the commissioner replied. "It's a difficult assignment. Rugged headlands, secluded coves. Hard for one man to keep an eye on that four miles of coast."

"One very determined man could do it," Lark countered, "if he was based in Grace-by-the-Sea."

Franklin chuckled. "It seems you enjoyed the spa more

than you'd thought."

"It's a charming village," Lark said, "and my mother and sisters live in Upper Grace. It has become clear they would prefer my company more than once a year or so."

"Ah." The commissioner swung his gaze out the window. In the harbor below, dozens of ships rode at anchor, masts pointing at the grey sky. He seemed to study them a moment before turning to meet Lark's gaze. "You have distinguished yourself in the service, Mr. Denby. I'm not sure a Riding Officer post still suits you."

Lark's heart sank. "I'm pleased you find my work useful, sir. I can assure you I would continue to serve you well along the Dorset coast."

"I'm sure you would," Commissioner Franklin said. "That's why I'd like to make you Riding Surveyor for the area from Weymouth to Poole."

Lark stared at him. A Riding Surveyor made nearly twice as much as a Riding Officer. He could afford a house. He could support a wife! And if he could catch these smugglers, Grace-by-the-Sea might be one of the only villages where he wouldn't have to worry about his wife being ashamed, shunned, or harmed because of his profession.

"I'd put five men under you, each managing a four-mile stretch," the commissioner continued, as if he thought Lark's stunned silence meant he required more persuasion. "Four are already in place and good men. The fellow at Osmington Mills was the one who gave us the intelligence on this Lord of the Smugglers. You could suggest someone to take the post through Grace-by-the-Sea. Perhaps this Alexander Chance, if he proves worthy."

Lark stood. "Sir, I would be honored to accept the position."

The commissioner allowed himself a smile. "Good. Now, just see that you catch these smugglers."

"I will," Lark said. "I'll send word as soon as I know

more. Thank you, sir."

The commissioner waved a hand. "Off you go, now. Do us proud."

He would. And he'd do one better.

He'd propose marriage to Jess.

CHAPTER TWENTY-THREE

JESS TRUDGED HOME FROM THE council meeting, shoulders tight and skirts sagging. Her position, her home, gone. Her family's place in Grace-by-the-Sea, all but obliterated. What was she to do now?

She had reached the door of the cottage when she heard it, the splash of wood through water. She turned to eye the cove. In the darkness, she could just make out a small boat heading for the shore. Who was coming in so late?

The door opened behind her, shoving light past on either side, and a hand grasped her shoulder.

"Get inside, quickly," Maudie whispered. "King Neptune is rallying his forces to attack."

"The Lord of the Smugglers, more likely," Jess said, turning and pushing into the cottage. "Where's Alex?"

"Out," Maudie said.

Of course he was.

Whatever he was doing, she had to stop him. She might not be able to manage her own future at the moment, but she could protect his.

Jess strode to the wall to fetch her winter cloak. She'd considered wearing it once to follow her brother but had dismissed the idea because she was determined to be a lady, the revered hostess of the spa.

What had that achieved?

Her father had taught her to stand up for herself, to help those who could not. He'd taught her to sail, as if she was every bit the equal of the young men in the village. She'd been the one to choose the path of gracious lady, to attempt to hem in every part of her life with the idea that that would somehow make her better, more attractive, more suitable. Less likely to attract the attention of scoundrels like Walter Vincent.

Less likely to lose someone dear to her like Lark.

Somehow, in dealing with the pain of his leaving, she'd lost her way. His return had only made that obvious. What was most important was protecting those she loved: her family, her guests, her village. She slung the cloak about her shoulders and pulled up the hood.

"Stay here," she told Maudie, heading to the door.

Maudie caught her arm, eyes wild. "Don't go! It's dangerous!"

"More dangerous for Alex than me," Jess promised her. "But I'll be careful."

Maudie must have seen something on her face or heard it in her voice, for she released her hold. Jess slipped out the door and shut it behind her. Wrapping her cloak closer, she crept down the shore path, her back to the sheds. The small boat was nearly ashore. She could see a figure at the oars. She was angling to meet the boat when a hand seized her arm and pulled her close.

"What are you doing?" Alex demanded, voice low and sharp. "He'll see you."

"Who?" Jess asked, but she hunkered down with him in the shadow of the shed.

"Mr. Bascom, unless I miss my guess," Alex whispered.

Though her curiosity burned, Jess kept her mouth shut as the little craft crunched onto the shore. The man jumped out, hauled it farther up the beach, away from the rising waters. As he turned, the moon popped out from behind a

cloud to outline his heavy, bearded face.

Alex was right. It was Mr. Bascom. Was he trying to steal a march on his competitors again? But surely with such a fitful moon, he would catch few fish tonight. Why, he wouldn't even be able to haul nets on his own.

Which meant he hadn't been fishing at all.

Jess sucked in a breath as the realization hit. "I knew it," she whispered to Alex. "He's the Lord of the Smugglers."

"Right," Alex said, but his tone did not sound certain. She'd have given anything to see his ears.

Mr. Bascom reached into his coat and pulled out something. Moonlight glinted on metal as he lifted his hand to point a pistol in their direction. "You can come out. I know you're there."

Alex's grip on Jess's arm tightened. She didn't move, didn't speak.

Bascom scowled at them. "Think, boy. I could as easily shoot your sister as you."

Alex groaned, but he released Jess. Before she knew what he was about, he'd stepped away from the shed into a patch of moonlight and held up his hands. "It's just me."

Oh, the brave, dear boy! Jess glanced around, looking for something, anything, she might use to shield him.

"No, it isn't just you," the fisherman said. "Or you wouldn't have come out bold as brass. But you better hope your sister is listening, or there will be no one to come save you."

What was this? Jess froze, staring at the tableau before her.

"I don't need saving," Alex said, head high. "I fight my own battles."

"That you do," Bascom allowed. "I'm sorry you found your way into this. You've been a good friend to my Ike. But you'll be coming with me, now."

Jess swallowed.

"Why?" Alex asked.

"As a sort of protection," he answered. "You see, some friends of mine plan on coming through Grace-by-the-Sea tomorrow night. A revenue cutter stopped us from landing where we'd intended, and I haven't found another place just yet. Preventers are patrolling too much of the coast these days. But we have orders to fill, so we'll be coming right through the village when the tide's at its lowest."

What would that be, after midnight tomorrow? Most villagers would be asleep then, never knowing the dark cargo passing their homes.

Alex must not have realized the time, for he shook his head. "No one in Grace-by-the-Sea will stand for that."

Not if they knew it was happening.

"They will," Bascom predicted. "They must. Because if anyone tries to stop us, you'll be heading into the sea with an anchor around your neck. Did you hear that, Miss Chance?"

Jess drew in a breath and stepped out of the shadows, holding herself tall and proud. "I heard that, Mr. Bascom. But this is your village too. How could you betray it?"

He snorted. "My village? You spa people think you're the only ones that matter." His voice took on a mincing tone. "Must have the best fish for the guests, never mind hungry families. Your boy needs new shoes? A shame. I'm too busy making slippers for some delicate miss who already has a dozen pairs." He spit toward the water, then held the gun higher.

"Not this time. This time, I get what's coming to me. You're the spa hostess. Everyone in the village will listen to you. That nosy fellow you've been keeping company with will listen to you. If you want to see your brother alive again, you tell them all to stand down, look the other way, tomorrow night."

"I'll tell them," Jess vowed. But she wasn't about to tell

him what else she would do. "Watch out for yourself, Alex."

"You too," her brother said before Henry Bascom reached out his free hand and marched him away from the cove. Jess watched long enough to know the fisherman didn't head for his cottage but straight up High Street, as if he had friends waiting on the Downs.

Friends, or other smugglers. Perhaps the same ones who had left those wagon tracks down the coast. Neither they nor their customers likely cared that a young man's life hung in the balance.

Drawing another deep breath, she turned for the cottage, mind working.

Maudie was waiting just inside the door, hat pin in her fingers. "What's the word to pass?" she asked, needle-sharp point poised.

"Never surrender," Jess said, stepping inside and shutting the door.

Maudie lowered the pin. "Close enough. Where's Alex?"

"Taken," Jess said, removing her cloak with cold fingers. "By Henry Bascom."

Maudie nodded. "To feed to the mermaids in exchange for good fishing. Never worry, Jesslyn. They take good care of lads like Alex. Why, they've been holding my Francis for thirty years."

Something caught in Jess's throat, and she returned to her aunt's side to give her a hug. Maudie's body felt frail, precious.

"Oh, Aunt," Jess murmured. "I'm so sorry."

"It's all right," Maudie answered. "You needn't worry about me. I know there are no mermaids, no fairies, though I did think I saw a troll once."

She pulled back to eye Jess with a smile. "But wouldn't life be interesting if they were all around us?"

Jess had to smile as well. "Yes, Aunt, it certainly would." She sobered. "But I don't think they would be kind to

Henry Bascom. He's a smuggler. And he plans to bring the rest of his crew and his cargo through Grace-by-the-Sea tomorrow night."

Maudie put her hands on her hips. "I won't stand for it. This is a law-abiding village. Ask the trolls. Besides, no smuggler ever felt the need to come through the village before."

"I know," Jess said. She should probably sit at the table, but concern for Alex kept her on her feet. "Lark thought they might be using the caves under Castle How."

"Not them, the cowards," Maudie scoffed. "The last ones to sail in besides you and Lark were Alex and Ike Bascom. They wanted to prove they could make it through the Dragon's Maw."

Jess frowned at her. "How do you know?"

Maudie pointed to her right ear. "His ears, girl, his ears."

"And the light in the castle window?" Jess challenged.

"Fairies," Maudie said knowingly.

"It makes as much sense as the rest of this," Jess allowed. She eyed her aunt. "What if we alerted Magistrate Howland?"

Maudie sighed. "What can he do by himself? Grace-by-the-Sea has no local militia. That's why so many of our lads will be marching away shortly."

And even those had no training in fighting. Why, the only two people who might know what to do about this were Captain St. Claire and Lark.

One she could not trust. The other held her heart.

Might as well admit it, if only to herself. She had fallen in love with Larkin Denby all over again, only this time was deeper, stronger. She wasn't an infatuated girl on her first Season. He wasn't a boy bent on adventure. It didn't matter that his work might take her far from these familiar shores. It didn't matter that she'd have only herself, no dowry, no family name, to contribute to the marriage. All that mat-

tered was that they were together, her family safe.

Henry Bascom had threatened the wrong village, the wrong people. She would do what she must, and hope Lark arrived in time to help.

If anyone had been watching Jess as she went about her work on Saturday, they would have noticed nothing out of the ordinary. She stopped by Mrs. Rinehart's shop and came out with a flowered bonnet. She spent a few moments chatting with her good friend Abigail. She greeted Mr. Carroll as he was sweeping his stoop and exchanged pleasantries. She ventured into the grocer's as if to inquire about biscuits for tea. She opened the door of the spa exactly on time, started the fountain, and arranged the glasses.

And plotted a revolution.

Lord Featherstone was the first to arrive. He listened intently to her, as if she was advising him on which wealthy lady might welcome his advances. Mr. Crabapple came next, followed by Mrs. Harding. They too spoke with the spa hostess for some time, but that was nothing new. Mrs. Cole and her daughter and the Admiral also received attention.

Miss Barlow and her mother arrived last. Susan Barlow settled her mother by the fountain before repairing for Jess's side.

"I was so sorry to hear about the result of last night's meeting," she said, dark eyes sagging. "I had no idea what the council was planning. I thought they wanted a hostess."

What, had Mrs. Greer called on her immediately following the meeting? "They are responsible for the wellbeing of the spa," Jess told her with her usual smile. "If my presence interferes with that, they are right to discharge me."

"How brave you are," Miss Barlow enthused.

She had no idea.

Her Regulars and Newcomers settled, Jess busied herself with correspondence. Mr. Inchley's son arrived at precisely ten, as she had requested, and took her notes to deliver. She found herself watching the door, not just because of those notes. If only Lark would return!

Mr. Howland graced the spa with his presence at half past ten and caused a bit of a flurry among the unmarried ladies. Jess rescued him from Miss Barlow, stationed him in a quiet corner, and brought him a glass from the fountain.

"I'm sorry to hear you are under the weather, Magistrate," she said for the benefit of her Newcomers. "But you've come to the right place."

He accepted the glass from her. "I received a note to come quietly, without anyone seeing me," he murmured. "But must I drink this?"

"If you wish to keep up pretenses, yes," Jess whispered back.

He bravely slugged back a gulp. By the twitch of his cheek, he was trying not to react.

"There," Jess said aloud. "You'll be feeling better any moment."

He leaned toward her. "Why the secrecy? If you wished to speak to me privately, you could have come by the office."

Jess batted her lashes, as if he'd said something charming. "The smuggler who kidnapped my brother last night might disagree. Henry Bascom promised nasty consequences should anyone stop him and his henchmen from bringing their cargo through Grace-by-the-Sea tonight."

The glass slipped from the magistrate's hand. Jess caught it before it fell.

"Your brother was in the caves last night?" he asked, leaning toward her.

Jess kept her smile pleasant. "You are misinformed, Magistrate. I believe Alex and his friend have been sailing into the caves for fun. These smugglers have a more nefarious bent, and Henry Bascom appears to be leading them." She couldn't help a roll of her eyes. "Some Lord of the Smugglers."

"Indeed," Mr. Howland said darkly. "And you say he plans to return tonight?"

She nodded. "At lowest tide."

"Just after midnight, then," he murmured. "Not enough time to ride to Weymouth for help."

"No," she said. "We are on our own."

He eyed her. "Something tells me you have a strategy in mind, Miss Chance."

"I live for strategy, Mr. Howland. At least, I did." Despite her best efforts, her smile slipped. "You may have heard the other news from last night. The Council has hired a physician. He will be here within the fortnight, and I and my family are to vacate the spa and the cottage for him."

He raised his brows. "Now, *that* is a tactical error. I doubt this spa will function without someone of your talents, Miss Chance."

"You will shortly have an opportunity to find out," Jess said. "But not before I have my brother back and our village safe. If you play your part, all will be well."

He snapped a nod. "What would you have me do?"

Jess glanced up as the door of the spa opened. Mrs. Cole began fussing with her hair, and her daughter darted away from Mrs. Harding to put herself in the path of their latest guest.

Captain St. Claire bowed over her hand and held it sufficiently long that Miss Cole blushed, and her mother descended upon them to clear her throat. He released her with another bow and made for Jess's side.

"I believe you wished a moment of my time, Miss

Chance," he said with a frown of puzzlement to the magistrate.

"Captain St. Claire," Jess said. "A true pleasure. I'm sorry to have kept you from your appointment with the magistrate. If you'll give me just a moment, I'll explain to you both exactly what you can do for the spa, the village, and our nation."

Lark made better time returning to Grace-by-the-Sea than leaving it. He wasn't surprised. Every inch of him was eager to tell Jess what had happened, to reassure her that Alex was safe from conscription or impressment. And to tell her how much she had come to mean to him. Surely if she knew he planned to stay in Grace-by-the-Sea she would be willing to consider a true courtship.

He had his horse stabled at the Mermaid and was climbing the hill to the spa by half past two. Mr. Inchley, the grocer, nodded at him from the window of his shop and tapped a heavy finger to his nose, as if sharing a secret. Interesting. Mr. Carroll peered out of his door and offered him a salute. Lark nodded, interest changing to concern. Had his true profession become known? Then why the respect?

Miss Archer came out of her shop to intercept him, smile bright. "Mr. Denby! I'm so delighted you could make it."

Lark calculated in his head. No, he hadn't missed an assembly. It could only be Saturday. Was there some event planned at the spa today? Jess had mentioned a midsummer masquerade, but surely that was later in June.

"Were you expecting me, Miss Archer?" he asked.

She took his shoulders and turned him up the hill. "No, but Jesslyn is. Now, hurry! You mustn't let her down."

"Wouldn't dream of it," Lark said, bemused.

He strode up the hill for the spa. He half expected to find things in shambles again. Had Miss Barlow countermanded Jess's orders? Had Mr. Crabapple fallen into apoplexy over some slight from Mrs. Harding? Was Miss Cole inconsolable about the lack of eligible bachelors? It wasn't as if he could be particularly helpful in any of those cases, but he would stand by Jess's side, come what may.

But everything looked as pleasant as usual when he entered the spa. Mrs. Tully was playing the harpsichord—a military march of all things. Lord Featherstone and the Admiral were engaged in a battle on the chessboard. Jess was at the welcome desk. She looked up as he came fully into the room and broke into a smile. He went straight to her side.

"I returned as quickly as I could," he told her. "Miss Archer seemed to think you needed me."

"Desperately," Jess assured him, laying a hand on his arm and peering up at him with her big blue eyes. A fellow could lose himself in that look. Or find himself again.

"Anything," Lark said. Funny how that word was so easy with her.

Her smile turned tremulous. "You may change your mind when you hear what I have to say. Mr. Howland questioned my plan. He said it verged on anarchy."

Lark raised his brows. "Anarchy? You're the spa hostess. What did you suggest? Dispensing melted chocolate instead of mineral water?"

"Worse," she said. "I have it on good authority that the smugglers you've been seeking will bring their cargo through Grace-by-the-Sea tonight. They're holding my brother hostage against my silence and your good behavior. I propose to confront them at the shore, take my brother back, and stop them from ever returning to our village."

Lark stared at her. This was the peaceful, gentle, ladylike

hostess of the spa, calm, cordial, composed. This was the woman he loved.

"Well," he allowed with a grin, "it should be an interesting evening."

CHAPTER TWENTY-FOUR

"**Y**OU NEEDN'T HAVE WARNED HER that strongly," Quillan St. Claire said, leaning against the mantel in James' office that afternoon.

They had parted after leaving the spa, but Quill had found his way to the office now. Neither had spoken about Miss Chance's audacious plan until they were safely behind closed doors.

James eyed him from his place at the desk. "You know my position. Between my family and you, I'm hemmed in nicely. I cannot disobey the earl without risking my mother's future, and I cannot betray your activities and still call myself an Englishman."

Quill pushed away from the hearth. "My activities have nothing to do with this. And I'll be hard-pressed to find another man more willing and able than Alexander Chance." His face hardened. "He's a good lad, James. He doesn't deserve this. You know it."

"I know it," James allowed, feeling his gut tighten. "And I don't like what's happened any more than you do. But Denby already suspects me of being part of this band of smugglers."

He shrugged. "The light beckoning sailors is in your home."

"Castle How," he said, "has never been my home. And

you might have considered that before putting up that ridiculous light."

Quill frowned. "I thought it was you putting up the light."

James stared at him. "It wasn't you?"

Quill shook his head. "No. I swear to you."

James closed his eyes. "Then someone else has been using the castle." He sighed and opened his eyes. "I'll have to discover the culprit and soon."

"After we route the smugglers, old man," Quill suggested. "You needn't feel compelled to fall in line with Miss Chance's mad urgings. Summon the men of the village, charter a militia. They'll follow you. And, by chartering a militia, you save us all from conscription."

James leaned back in his chair. "I wish I could. But the earl refused to consider it. I've written to him twice with various arguments. I event went up to see him, but he left me to cool my heels."

His frustration must have been showing, for Quill raised a brow. "And he cares nothing about the village being overrun by criminals?"

James snorted. "The earl couldn't care less what happens in Grace-by-the-Sea, so long as he profits. It wouldn't surprise me if he and Lord Peverell weren't two of this bands customers."

"Then they can rot." Quill started for the door. "Your hands may be tied, but I plan to help Miss Chance all I can." He paused and glanced back at James, gaze merry. "And good luck locking me up for it."

He was out the door before James could call him back. But his words seemed to echo in the prison of a room his august family had so tastefully decorated for him.

One by one, the spa guests left for the day, until only Lark remained. Miss Barlow and her mother had made their farewells, and Jess could not be sorry that they were leaving in the morning. She straightened the Grand Pump Room, collected Maudie, and secured the door. As Lark escorted her and Maudie home through the village, shops were shuttered, and their neighbors hurried inside. The cottage felt empty without Alex waiting to greet them.

"Cutlasses, daggers, pistols, and quarterstaffs," Maudie muttered, sliding into the seat of her rocking chair. "They'll be well-armed tonight. Smugglers always are."

"So I would imagine," Jess said. Though it was still hours to midnight, she could not sit. She paced from the hearth to the door and back. Lark met Jess at the foot of the table and put his arms about her, holding her gently.

"Everyone I met agreed with our plan," he reminded her.

"Except Magistrate Howland," she said. "And I cannot fully understand why."

"Howlands look after themselves," Maudie said, setting her chair to rocking. The quiet creak would once have soothed Jess. Now it played on her nerves as if they were the keys of a harpsichord.

"I'd be fine with that," Lark told her, "so long as he stayed out of our way."

"He made sure I knew I could be prosecuted if we caused a disturbance," Jess informed him. "What does he call an invasion? These smugglers are the criminals, not us. If anything happens to Alex..."

"We will save him," Lark promised.

They must. Anything else was unthinkable.

Dark seemed a long time coming. The tide took forever to recede. Lark seated himself at the table, beckoned Jess to join him. The bench had never felt harder.

"It ends tonight," he told her, slipping an arm about her shoulders.

She allowed her head to rest against his shoulder. "I never thought it would come to this. Smugglers, in Grace-by-the-Sea?"

His shoulder rubbed against her hair as he shrugged. "There's a reason people don't look out their windows after dark in some villages."

"No one wants to indict a neighbor, a friend," she realized. "Or a brother."

He shifted, and she raised her head to meet his gaze. "Sorry, Lark. I didn't want to remind you of your father."

"A smuggler too, was he?" Maudie asked, pausing in her rocking.

"No," Lark assured her. "A Riding Officer, like me. But he couldn't look the other way, and I won't either."

"Good for you," Maudie said, setting her chair to moving at an even faster clip. "Whatever your position, do it to the best of your ability. My father and brother always said that."

He gave Jess a squeeze. "And that's one of the reasons they cannot do without Jess at the spa."

In all the trouble, she'd forgotten to tell Maudie. "They can do without me," she said, glancing at her aunt. "I've been excused from my position."

"I knew they'd want an older woman," her aunt said, hitching up her shawl. "Never fear. I'll make you my assistant."

She smiled for Maudie's sake. "They have no need for anyone from our family, Aunt. The new physician accepted their offer. He wants to run the spa. And, as he will need somewhere to live, we are to vacate the cottage for him as well."

Lark's arm tightened protectively about her. "They had the temerity to throw you out?"

"I won't go," her aunt said.

"Yes, Aunt, you will," Jess said. "Where, I don't know yet."

Someone knocked at the door. Jess stiffened, but Lark rose to answer it. He let in Captain St. Claire. Gone was the gold-braided dress uniform of a naval officer. He wore a loose black coat and trousers and had pulled a black felt hat low over his dark hair. A bandolier of pistols was slung about his chest, a cutlass sat in the sheath on his belt, and the hilt of a dagger stuck out of one of his tall boots. She could almost believe him the pirate her aunt had named him.

"Mrs. Tully, Miss Chance," he greeted them with a nod. "No reason for concern. We'll have young Alex back in no time."

So Jess could only hope.

They extinguished all light, banked the fire to a glow, and took turns watching out the window for movement on the water. Jess's fingers wrapped around Lark's, held tight. He slipped his free arm about her shoulders, his smile encouraging.

"Hst!" Maudie jerked her head toward the darkness outside. "Someone's there, and I don't think it's a mermaid."

The captain stood. "It's time. Stay behind me while I speak to them."

Lark stepped forward. "Not tonight, St. Claire."

The naval officer eyed him. "You think you can handle this, a Newcomer to Grace-by-the-Sea?"

"He's not a Newcomer," Maudie said. "He's family."

Jess's heart swelled. "Yes, yes, he is."

Lark bowed to Maudie. "Thank you, Aunt." Then he looked to St. Claire. "And to answer your question, I have no expectation of leading us tonight. I yield to the superior authority of all things in Grace-by-the-Sea, Jesslyn Chance."

The cove was dark as the smugglers rowed in. The village was dark as well, the only light shining from the upper windows of the Mermaid where a few hardy souls must have been preparing for bed. Even the moon had gone into hiding. A breeze blew fitfully out to sea. The waves whispered against the shore.

The longboats cut through the water, ground onto the shore. Wagons creaked as they rolled down High Street, driven by men who would take the cargo inland. Still nothing else moved on the shore. The rowers began unloading casks, boxes, piling them at the foot of High Street to be divided by destination.

Henry Bascom pushed Alex forward, until they both stood on the shore path.

"Funny," he said, glancing around. "I thought that sister of yours would be waiting for us, wringing her hands."

"I make it a practice never to wring my hands, Mr. Bascom," Jess said, stepping out of the shadow of a shed. She had the satisfaction of seeing the fisherman start.

"I've fulfilled my part of the bargain," she continued. "Give me my brother."

She thought he might argue, but he let go of Alex and shoved him toward her. "Take him, then. I suppose there's no point keeping him. We're just about done here."

They were indeed, far faster than she'd expected. If she could just get Alex away... She held out her hand, and her brother stumbled toward her.

"Just you remember," Bascom warned. "This lot means business. Best not to cross them."

"You will find, sir, that I mean business too." She grabbed Alex's hand and yanked him out of reach. Maudie caught

them both close as they ducked into the shadows.

And chaos ensued.

Mr. Carroll darted up to where the crates lay stacked, snatched up one, and disappeared behind the Mermaid.

"Hey!" a smuggler shouted, breaking away to give chase.

Lord Featherstone walked up and seized another, only to vanish behind a shed. Before another smuggler could take off after him, Abigail, clad in breeches and long coat, swooped in from the other side and made off with a third. When one of the smugglers attempted to follow, he ran smack into the Admiral and landed on his rump on the street.

"Impolite, sir!" Admiral Walsey thundered, brandishing his walking stick.

The other smugglers attempted to rally, but like gulls, Mrs. Harding, Mr. Crabapple, Mr. Lawrence, and her other neighbors dived and dipped, plucking treasure from the pile, sometimes from the very arms of the smugglers. Their unwanted visitors bumped into each other trying to stop them. Shouts rang out, a pistol flared.

Henry Bascom ran into the fray. "Don't shoot! Dead bodies bring the Preventers!"

"So do live smugglers," Lark declared, bearing down on them with Captain St. Claire at his side.

Fists flew. Cargo fell and broke open. Champagne bottles rolled for the water. The smugglers bunched together, backs to each other and gazes darting about.

"Now can I shoot?" one of them begged.

"Enough!" A musket roared before the command had finished echoing. Gazes shot up High Street, and everyone froze. The moon came out from the clouds to shine on muskets and cutlasses. Then a lantern brightened the night, held high on the pole of Mr. Drummond. Next to him, Mr. Howland sat on his horse, men on either side.

"I told you there was something about a red coat," Mau-

die reminded Jess.

The Grace-by-the-Sea militia, formed that very night it seemed, had only a single red coat among them, and Mr. Greer was wearing it. But they marched smartly down the street. Shutters opened, flooding the way with light. Voices called encouragement, shouted in the name of honor, of decency.

Three of the smugglers broke for the water. The rest held up their hands in surrender. Lark and Captain St. Claire went after the runaways.

Jess sagged against her brother and aunt. "We did it."

"And without a single troll," Maudie marveled.

Jess freed herself from them to see what Mr. Howland intended.

"I'm a Sea Fencible," Henry Bascom was saying as the militia surrounded them. "I led them here for you to capture. I was only playing at being a smuggler."

"Then you are a much better actor than I would have given you credit for," the magistrate said. "Henry Bascom, you and your cohorts are hereby under arrest for avoiding the king's taxes, kidnapping, and attempted murder. You will come peaceably, or there will be repercussions."

"Huzzah!" Alex shouted.

Lark and the captain hauled the remaining smugglers into the group. The militia marched them away from the shore. More huzzahs sounded as they moved through the village. The men of Grace-by-the-Sea raised their chins and lifted their knees higher.

The magistrate remained at the shore, but he had turned in the saddle to eye the shadow of the shed, as if he could see her, Alex, and Maudie there. He inclined his head in a bow, then looked to Lark and the captain.

"Thank you for your help, Mr. Denby, Captain," he said. "Tell your accomplices I expect every last item in that shipment to be accounted for."

Maudie heaved a sigh.

"You have my word, Magistrate," Lark said.

"Have someone secure the boats," he said. Then he turned his horse and rode after the militia.

Jess, Maudie, and Alex went to join Lark. From the lanes around the cove, Mr. Carroll, Abby, Lord Featherstone, and the others came out of hiding.

"Well done," Lark told them all.

"That stopped them," Alex crowed.

"And since the magistrate formed a militia, I expect we will have no more concern about conscription," Mr. Carroll put in, beaming. "The recruiters at West Creech will have to get on without us."

"A veritable triumph all told," Lord Featherstone agreed.

"I expected to attend a rout or two at Grace-by-the-Sea this summer," Mrs. Harding said, smile wry, "but this was not what came to mind."

"Miss Chance has ever devised entertainment for the delight of the village and our guests," Captain St. Claire said. "If you will excuse me, I'll see to the boats. Mr. Chance, if I could have your assistance?"

"I'd be delighted." With a smile to Jess, Alex followed the naval captain.

"The usual time tomorrow at the spa?" Mrs. Harding asked.

"Of course," Jess told them all.

Lord Featherstone patted her shoulder before going to escort Mrs. Harding and Mr. Crabapple to their lodgings. The widow was hanging on her swain's arm and declaring him a hero. Jess could imagine his blush.

Mr. Lawrence stepped closer. "You will ever have my admiration for this, Miss Chance. And I will remind Mr. Greer when next the council meets." With a nod, he headed for home.

"Quite the adventure," Mr. Carroll said, stars reflected in

his spectacles. "Please keep me in mind if you have more planned."

"Me too," Abigail said, swirling her cloak about her. She leaned closer. "Particularly if Captain St. Claire is involved."

One by one, they thanked Jess and took their leave, until only she, Lark, and Maudie remained.

"Well?" Maudie demanded, glancing between the two of them. "Get on with it."

"Aunt," Jess said, "would you stoke the fire, so the cottage is warm for Alex?"

"You don't fool me," Maudie said. "You want time alone with your sweetheart." She shook a finger at Lark. "Don't disappoint me, young man."

Lark bowed. "Never, my dear aunt."

Jess's heart started beating faster as Maudie trotted off.

Lark turned to Jess. "In the morning, I must interrogate the smugglers, then ride to Weymouth to report."

Her mouth felt dry. "Your work in Grace-by-the-Sea is done."

"For the moment." He glanced up the street, now empty and darkening as shutters closed once more. "Odd that Henry Bascom ended up being the Lord of the Smugglers."

Jess sucked in a breath. "You think there's another?"

Lark straightened. "No. I must believe the pieces of this puzzle have finally aligned themselves. Bascom was in league with smugglers who sailed along the coast here."

"So, not Grace Cove," Jess felt compelled to point out.

"No." She could hear the smile in his voice. "We were wrong there. But I wouldn't have been surprised if the lander has come through the village on occasion. I expect we'll find that he and his men were the ones who beat Alex. A revenue cutter nearly caught them the other night as they were coming in, so they had to find another spot to offload their goods. Regardless, I have been granted a

new assignment."

This was what she'd been waiting for. She swallowed. "Where?"

"Riding Surveyor from Weymouth to Poole."

Jess started. "Then you could live in Grace-by-the-Sea."

He nodded, closing the distance between them and taking her hand in his. "I could make this my home. Take a wife."

She licked her lips. "You know a lady who would marry a rogue like you?"

"I can only hope." He went down on one knee on the path. "Jesslyn Chance, esteemed hostess of the spa, queen of Grace-by-the-Sea, will you do me the honor of marrying me?"

Once she had dreamed of an offer from him. Now it felt sweeter, surer, more lasting. "Yes, oh, yes."

He rose and took her in his arms, holding her tenderly. His lips brushed hers once, twice. The third time she leaned into him and felt his arms tighten. Cradled close, she knew she had truly found her place, at his side, in his heart. Whatever the future brought, they would face it, together.

"So, my sister is marrying Larkin Denby," Alex said to Ike as the two of them kindled the fire in the caves beneath Castle How the next evening. "I'll have a Riding Officer in the family."

Ike grimaced. "At least you have a family. My mum gave up her work cleaning the castle for Mr. Bent and is heading inland with my brother and sisters to find another position. She's had a hard lot with my da, but I never thought he would throw in with smugglers."

"I never thought anyone around here would throw in with smugglers," Alex admitted. "And I'm sorry about your father. What will you do now?"

Ike shrugged. "Hire on with another fisherman, if one will have me. As it is, I'm damaged goods."

A noise echoed through the cave, rhythmic. Tap, tap, tap.

Alex rose, Ike right beside him.

"What's that?" his friend asked, peering around the cave.

Alex stiffened. "Someone's coming down the stairs from the castle."

Ike pulled a knife out of his boot. The thin, short slice of silver looked far too fragile to protect themselves. Alex put up his fists.

Captain St. Claire stepped down onto the rocks of the cave floor. "Chance," he said with a nod to Alex. "Mr. Bascom."

The knife wavered in Ike's grip. "What's he doing here?"

Alex cuffed him on the shoulder. "Put that down. Is that any way to greet the Lord of the Smugglers?"

Ike glanced from him to the captain, who was moving toward them. "But I thought you said you don't work for smugglers."

"He doesn't," Captain St. Claire told him. "The title is merely a term to scare off the curious. What we do is far more important to England than porting trinkets and grog. You were concerned for your future, Mr. Bascom. The entire future of England is at stake. And I have enough gold coins for you both, if you can keep quiet about the matter."

DEAR READER
    Thank you for choosing Jesslyn and Lark's story. This is the first in a series about the Spa at Grace-by-the-Sea on the Dorset coast of England, where romance and adventure come home. I hope you'll want to become a Regular.

If you enjoyed this book, there are several things you could do now:

Sign up for a free e-mail alert on my website at *www.reginascott.com* so you'll be the first to know when a new book is out or on sale. I offer exclusive free short stories to my subscribers from time to time. Don't miss out.

Post a review on a bookseller site or Goodreads to help others find the book.

Discover my many other books on my website.

Turn the page for a peek of the second book in the Grace-by-the-Sea series, *The Heiress' Convenient Husband.* Going to investigate a light in the family castle, James Howland discovers a woman hiding there who claims to be a prisoner of his master, the earl. An heiress, Eva Faraday, has been banished to Dorset for refusing to marry the man the earl picked for her. But perhaps the perfect husband for her is the man the earl least expects of mutiny.

Blessings!

Regina Scott

SNEAK PEEK:

The Heiress' Convenient Husband,

BOOK 2 IN THE GRACE-BY-THE-SEA SERIES
by Regina Scott

CHAPTER ONE

Grace-by-the-Sea,
Dorset, England, June 1804

WHOEVER WAS USING HIS CASTLE was in for it. James Howland grimaced as he rode up onto the headland. He might serve as magistrate for the village of Grace-by-the-Sea and local steward for the mighty Earl of Howland, but the castle he approached now was hardly his. Everything he had, everything he'd accomplished, was a result of his distant illustrious connection to the Howland family. Well, almost everything.

He glanced down the slope beside him to the village. As the sun neared the horizon on the warm June evening, lamps were beginning to glow. A few couples strolled arm in arm, heading home from some event at the spa that nourished the local economy with the hundreds of visitors it attracted each year. Among those thatched-roofed cottages lived the men he had recently organized into the local militia to save them from conscription. His smile tilted up. Odd how good it felt to defy his lordship for once.

It wouldn't last, of course. Once the earl heard James had refused his direct order to stay out of the king's preparations to defend the coast from Napoleon's impending invasion, James would have to pay the cost. Perhaps it

would come as a tithe on his income. Perhaps a refusal to be summoned to London for some event. He could only hope it wouldn't take the form of a slight to his mother, who served as companion to the earl's wife. At least his lordship likely wouldn't remove him as magistrate. It came in too handy that the man enforcing the law was in the pay of the Howland family.

In the end, he would have to accept whatever punishment amused the earl. It was a small price to pay for ensuring the safety of his neighbors, his friends, and his village.

And there he went again claiming ownership he could never have.

He clucked to the roan, and his gelding, Majestic, obligingly broke into a canter up the graveled drive. Majestic was becoming accustomed to the trip. James usually checked the castle that served as the earl's hunting lodge quarterly, but a strange light had appeared in the window twice recently. Ghosts, Mrs. Tully in the village claimed. Rubbish. Someone was sneaking inside.

He'd thought it might be his old friend, Quillan St. Claire, who was using the caves beneath the castle proper, but the formal naval captain had disclaimed all knowledge. Quill had his own battles to fight. James did what he could to help. It was the least to be expected of any Englishman with Napoleon massing his troops just across the Channel. So, to determine who might be lighting that beacon, James had been stopping by at various hours every day for the last week. He'd never spotted anything out of the ordinary.

Until tonight.

He reined in to stare at the turreted stone castle as it came fully into view among the trees that circled it. Light blazed from a dozen windows. Even the stables to the east were lit up. What affrontery! Blood roaring, he put heels to Majestic and galloped to the entry.

He leaped to the ground and tied the gelding to the balustrade that edged the stone steps. Pulling out the pistol he'd brought with him as a precaution, he cocked it and took the steps two at a time to the terrace and the front door. His free hand was on the latch when it was yanked from under him.

The manservant in the doorway blinked as if just as surprised to find someone on the other side of the portal. He was tall and thin, with a thatch of black hair threaded with grey and a long nose pointed enough to skewer apples. He didn't seem to notice James's weapon as he drew himself up.

"May I help you, sir?"

James pushed past him into the house, setting the fellow to sputtering like a wet tea kettle on the hob. "Who are you, and why are you in my castle?"

The servant's bushy black brows came down. "*Your* castle? This moldering establishment belongs to the Earl of Howland. I have met his lordship, and you are not he."

"No, indeed." The warm voice came from above and danced with merriment. James glanced up the wide stairs that ran up one side of the grand entry hall to the landing across the back. A lady moved along the wood rail to start down the stairs. Her dark-brown hair was piled up at the top of her head in a loose pile of curls. Her ears dripped diamonds that caught the light as she moved. The purple gown showed off a slender figure.

She could not be called beautiful with that long nose and unruly hair. But as she reached the flagstone floor and started toward him, he felt the ridiculous urge to take a step back.

He held his ground. "Why are you here?"

She tsked, eyes the color of a perfect summer sky twinkling at him. "I was banished here, sir. No need to introduce yourself. You must be James Howland, the earl's watchdog.

I recognize that chin. I'm Eva Faraday, his prisoner."

He didn't respond. How every dissatisfying. But then, Eva could not say she had ever had a satisfying response from any of the Howlands.

He certainly seemed typical of the breed. The same golden-blond hair waving about a firm-jawed face. The same cold blue eyes that could spear her in place. As good a physique as the earl's heir, Viscount Thorgood—tall, broad-shouldered, many-caped great-coat swirling about long legs. But she'd refused to do the viscount's bidding, and the earl's, and she had no intention of doing his.

"I wasn't notified his lordship intended to house a prisoner in the castle," he said, watching her. Then he glanced at Yeager, her manservant. "Complete with jailer, it seems."

Yeager sniffed. "I've had the honor of serving Miss Eva and her late father since she was a girl."

"Thank you, Yeager," she said with a smile. "If you could see how Patsy is doing with the unpacking, then ask Cook what's to be had for victuals."

"Aye, miss." He cast Mr. Howland a narrow-eyed look before heading for the stairs.

Mr. Howland's jaw looked even harder. Did he eat rocks for breakfast? "Exactly how many people do you intend to house?"

"Six," she allowed. "I have a coachman and groom in the stables. We'd hoped we could hire additional help once we settled in."

Was that noise his teeth grinding? "I have received nothing to indicate any of you are allowed here."

"So you said," she replied. "But it's only to be expected, really, when you go off in a fit of pique. The earl, that is.

Not you personally. I don't imagine you have the luxury."

Oh, but those eyes snapped fire. "Tell your maid not to bother unpacking. You'll all be staying at the Swan until I can confirm matters with his lordship."

Eva shook her head. "I'm afraid that's impossible. I have no money to pay for an inn."

He waved a hand. "You're paying them."

"My father's will left funds for their wages," she informed him. "My portion is held in trust until I reach the age of five and twenty." Or she married, but she refused to dangle that carrot. The earl liked to use it far more than necessary already.

He crossed his arms over his impressive chest. "Nevertheless, I must insist that you leave."

Was every Howland this pig-headed? If only she could wash her hands of the lot of them! But the earl was trustee over her funds, and he would give her nothing unless she bent to his will. This man might be willing to live like that. She wasn't.

"And I must insist that we stay," she said. "I promise to disturb as little as possible. I'll need a bedchamber, a withdrawing room, the dining room and kitchen, and quarters for the staff. From what I can tell, that's less than a quarter of the space in this pile."

She thought she caught a sigh. "The castle hasn't been used as a habitation in years. You'll need coal, candles, food. How do you intend to pay for them?"

She smiled. "I intend to put them on the earl's credit. He sent me here. He can pay for the privilege."

"No," he said, tone as solid as his chin. "The budget here doesn't allow for such expenses."

She waved a hand. "Then send the bill directly to the earl."

He caught her hand mid-air and held it, gaze fastened on hers. "Have a care, Miss Faraday. I'm only trying to protect

you. This castle is more dangerous than you can know. It isn't safe for you here."

If he was trying to frighten her off, he was doing a good job. She could almost believe the concern in his voice.

But the earl could sound concerned too, even as he tried to steal her future.

She yanked from his grip. "Then make it safe. Tell me what dangers to avoid. This is apparently to be my home until I earn my inheritance in ten months. Help me survive my imprisonment."

He eyed her a moment, and she steeled herself to keep fighting. Truly, what else was she to do? If her father had guessed the depths to which the Earl of Howland would sink to get his hands on her inheritance, he would never have made the man trustee and expected him to care for her. She was used to fighting for what was best for her and her servants. James Howland would simply have to accustom himself to the fact.

"Very well, Miss Faraday," he said. "I'll help you. You may stay in the castle until I hear from the earl."

Best not to let him see her relief. "How very sensible of you."

He inclined his head. "But you must allow me to do my duty as well. I am responsible for safeguarding the earl's interests in Dorset."

And she would try not to despise him for it. "Of course. Shall I send you a report each week of what furniture I've moved? Which dishes we used?"

That smile could have frozen the waves on the Channel. "No need. I'll be able to verify all that on my own. I'll be moving into the castle with you, Miss Faraday."

Learn more at
www.reginascott.com/heiressconvenienthusband.html.

OTHER BOOKS BY REGINA SCOTT

FORTUNE'S BRIDES SERIES
Never Doubt a Duke
Never Borrow a Baronet
Never Envy an Earl
Never Vie for a Viscount
Never Kneel to a Knight
Never Marry a Marquess

UNCOMMON COURTSHIPS SERIES
The Unflappable Miss Fairchild
The Incomparable Miss Compton
The Irredeemable Miss Renfield
The Unwilling Miss Watkin
An Uncommon Christmas

LADY EMILY CAPERS
Secrets and Sensibilities
Art and Artifice
Ballrooms and Blackmail
Eloquence and Espionage
Love and Larceny

MARVELOUS MUNROES SERIES
My True Love Gave to Me
Catch of the Season
The Marquis' Kiss
Sweeter Than Candy

ABOUT THE AUTHOR

REGINA SCOTT STARTED WRITING NOVELS in the third grade. Thankfully for literature as we know it, she didn't sell her first novel until she learned a bit more about writing. Since her first book was published, her stories have traveled the globe, with translations in many languages including Dutch, German, Italian, and Portuguese. She now has more than forty-five published works of warm, witty romance.

She loves everything about England, so it was only a matter of time before she started her own village. Where more perfect than the gorgeous Dorset Coast? She can imagine herself sailing along the chalk cliffs, racing her horse across the Downs, dancing at the assembly, and even drinking the spa waters. She drank the waters in Bath, after all!

Regina Scott and her husband of 30 years reside in the Puget Sound area of Washington State on the way to Mt. Rainier. She has dressed as a Regency dandy, learned to fence, driven four-in-hand, and sailed on a tall ship, all in the name of research, of course. Learn more about her at *www.reginascott.com*.